Sinners

Sinner's Gin

"This is a sexy, fast-paced, hurt/comfort, murder mystery with… scorching hot sexy times!"

—Gay Book Reviews

Whiskey and Wry

"It's one thing to write a great book. It's a whole other level of talent to write song lyrics, too, and Rhys delivers."

—Happy Ever After, *USA Today*

Tequila Mockingbird

"The author has done it again with a complex intriguing story line that explodes from the beginning and never slows down…"

—Guilty Indulgence Romance Reviews

Sloe Ride

"*Sloe Ride* is rife with mystery and intrigue. If you're looking for unconventional characters and action, Rhys Ford's books would be a perfect match for you."

—Fresh Fiction

Absinthe of Malice

"It made me laugh, it made me angry, it made me irritated and at times, I was gutted. But in the end… it made me smile and be grateful I got to go on this journey with the guys."

—The Novel Approach

Published by DREAMSPINNER PRESS
www.dreamspinnerpress.com

ABSINTHE
of MALICE

RHYS FORD

DREAMSPINNER
PRESS

Published by
DREAMSPINNER PRESS

5032 Capital Circle SW, Suite 2, PMB# 279,
Tallahassee, FL 32305-7886 USA
www.dreamspinnerpress.com

Absinthe of Malice
© 2016 Rhys Ford

Cover Art
© 2018 Reece Notley
reece@vitaenoir.com
Cover content is for illustrative purposes only and any person depicted
on the cover is a model.

Digital ISBN: 978-1-63477-326-3
Mass Market Paperback ISBN: 978-1-64108-198-6
Trade Paperback ISBN: 978-1-63477-325-6
Library of Congress Control Number: 2016902320
Mass Market Paperback published December 2019
v. 1.0

Printed in the United States of America
∞
This paper meets the requirements of
ANSI/NISO Z39.48-1992 (Permanence of Paper).

This book is dedicated to the bad-boy characters who've kept my heart racing and the men who've played them.

And to Mary Calmes who still owes me ARCs in exchange for chapters from this book. I am joking. Because I love Mary. And I'm waiting for Miro and Ian.

ACKNOWLEDGMENTS

To the Five who are my beloved sisters of writing: Penn, Lea, Tamm, and Jenn. And to my darling siblings in love and coffee: Lisa, Ren and Ree.

So many thanks and wow, love outpourings to Elizabeth North and the rest of the Dreamspinner Press staff who make me stand up, pull up my socks, and brush my hair so I look decent in public.

A special shoutout and heartfelt hugs to Grace and everyone she throws into my editing pool, because each and every one of them rocks so hardcore you can feel the bass in your teeth.

A rocking thank-you covered in chocolate and caramel to the Crewe, my beta readers, and the Dirty Ford Guinea Pigs. Oh, only the Gods in Heaven, Hell, and Starbucks Temples everywhere know how much you all endure my word spew and jerking you around with my plotting. Love you all. So damned much.

ONE

Devil by my side, devil that I know
Riding down the Crossroads, heading
*   to the next show*
Hearing my name on the crowd, never
*   thought I'd be back*
House lights going down, time to dance
*   in the deep-silk black*
—Breathing Again

THE ROAD wound around them, a blacktop
snake with metal guardrail markings and a dashed
yellow stripe down the middle of its back. It grew fat
and thin as the lanes increased, then dwindled down to
one, a single strip of ebony tar cutting into the Earth's
flesh.

They were somewhere outside of New York.
Or maybe it was Boston. Miki'd lost track of where

exactly they were heading since they'd all stumbled out of a cheap motel that morning. It didn't matter where they'd been. It was where they would end up that mattered. That single shining spot somewhere at the snake's head, a pearl embedded between the ki-rin's horns to guide them where they would begin.

Where Crossroads Gin would begin.

The gig they played at Dino's was the first kiss of a months-long fuck the band had fallen into. No amount of prep, compromise, or cajoling would prepare them for the orgy to follow. Miki dreaded the road. He hated the haul from one place to the next, but he loved the feel of the boards under his boots and the squeal-sing of a mic when he wrapped his hand around it for the first time. He'd been giving oral to microphones for so long he'd almost forgotten what to do with an actual dick when one appeared in front of him.

That wasn't a problem now. No, now Miki's big-gest worry was the echoing hollow inside him, be-cause Kane was nearly three thousand miles away, and he was stuck in an elongated metal box hurtling toward the unknown.

In the time and space between Sinner's and Crossroads, Miki'd discovered he really didn't like the unknown.

The road sang its own song under the van's heavy tires. A *clip-clip shush* punctuated every once in a while by a deeper thrum when they passed over a crease or snick in the asphalt. If Miki wasn't careful, he'd be lured into sleep, rocked by the gentle move-ment of the drive and the low humming Damien did in his throat as he worked out rhythms to the melodies Miki'd laid down for him a few weeks before.

Forest and Rafe were passed out across the two rows of seats behind them, propped up by pillows and thin, velvety blankets Brigid insisted on packing. Rafe snored, nothing delicate or gentle about the sounds barreling from his open mouth or the snorting gulps he took every few minutes. Their bassist was a loud thrum of bumps and noises, even in his sleep, and after a particularly long *cha-cha-cha* snuffle, Miki debated shoving a sock between Rafe's teeth.

A rare streetlight flashed yellow through the van's interior, sliding past the lightly tinted windows. The glow turned Rafe's hair wheaten and snagged just a little tuft of sunlight-shot gold peeking out from under an argyle-patterned blanket.

The lump of red, gray, and black fabric could have been a free-form sculpture for as much as Forest moved underneath it. A few hundred miles ago, their drummer pulled a blanket out from under the long seat and cocooned himself so tightly Miki wouldn't have been surprised if Forest emerged with bruise-hued wings. Only a little bit of his hair poked out of a fold, and one long, pale foot rested against the chair's arm, wedged in tight between the vinyl seat and a metal brace.

"Zoning out, Sinjun?" Damie's raspy growl tickled Miki's ear. "You're supposed to be keeping me company, remember?"

"Yeah, right. Like you don't love to hear the sound of your own voice. We going to pull over soon?" The clock on the dash said it was two in the morning, but he wasn't sure anymore about what time zone they were in. Across the horizon, a faint lightening of the sky showed between a copse of trees, but for all Miki knew, it was the sun coming to beat them into submission.

"Yeah, the motel's supposed to be another fifteen miles." The nearly pitch interior went pale and Cheshire, a curve of teeth lit up by the dashboard lights. "I'd ask if you wanted to drive—"

"Right, I can't back a goddamned car out of the garage, and you're going to put me behind the wheel of a Death Star." The van was huge, over twenty feet long, and just the thought of the driver's seat cushions hitting Miki's ass made him break out into a cold sweat. "I'll leave that shit to the three of you."

A yawn stretched itself up from his chest, wrapped around his uvula, and then clawed its way out of his lips. The roof of his mouth went thin, pulled in on itself, and Miki gagged on his own tongue. Wiping the spit off his chin with the back of his hand, he grumbled at the wet on his skin.

"Nothing worse than choking on yourself." Damien laughed at Miki's uplifted middle finger. "Not the way I'd want my obit to read."

"I read your obit. Made it sound like you were a cross between Hendrix and Jesus." The captain's chair was supposed to be comfortable, but Miki hadn't quite found the right slant to it. Adjusting it back another notch, he leaned into the curve, a knot unraveling from his lower back. "Edie had you walking on water and playing the national anthem in your sleep."

"Well, you know… it's me." The teasing was light, but the undercurrent between them darkened the already black shadows they'd gathered. Another mile marker flew by, a pale stone sentinel counting off the click while bringing them closer to Damien's crazy dream.

They'd been together for more than a decade, even if they took off the time Damien spent walled up in an institution after a semi tore through their limo, ending the lives of their band members and leaving Miki alone and broken. He'd folded in on himself, tangling his grief with barbed-wire words and songs sharp enough to cut his own heart out.

Damien—alive—had been a fucking godsend, a gift Miki never in a million years would have imagined he'd be given. Much like falling in love with a damned cop. A damned Irish cop named Kane Morgan.

"Talk to me, Miki," Damien urged gently. "Tell me what's going on in that busy head of yours. What's buzzing in there?"

"Just…." He didn't know how to say what he felt.

Words only came to him on slips of music and strings. His world had been pretty much black-and-white for so long, he didn't know what to do with the infusion of color. Of Kane's eyes, bright enough to mimic ice but so very warm when they raked over Miki's body, or the blush dew pink of his lover's mouth after kissing Miki senseless. He'd fallen for a man with the same coloring as his best friend, inky-black hair and blue eyes, but so very different in personality. The roll of Kane's slightly accented words, a strong Gaelic purr from long summers and holidays spent in his Irish parents' homeland.

He missed his cop. Missed waking up next to a thickly muscled man who teased him into smiling. And he missed his fucking dog. Miki huffed, frowning over the thought of Dude sprawled on the living room couch without him. The last thing he'd ever expected was that he'd miss the damned fucking *dog*.

"Every roll of the tires is taking me farther from… home, Damie." He scoffed, alarmed and shocked at the rawness welling up inside his soul. "I mean, before… it was okay. You're… family. And still are, but… it's like I'm leaving *home*. And I've never had a fucking home before. You… I mean, I'm always… we're… shit, I don't know what the hell I'm saying."

"You miss Kane." Damie nodded. "I miss Sionn. Yeah, I have you, but that other piece of me? It's not here. He's not here. I get that. But it won't be for long. We can do this. We kind of have to do this. If we're going to be a band, we need to get tangled in with each other. Know each other. Think I'd drag you guys across country to play in shit-hole clubs if I didn't think it was important?"

"Yeah, because you're a dick," Miki shot back.

"Not that much of a dick," he snorted. "I'm leaving home behind too, so I know what you're feeling, Sinjun. But you know, they're fucking waiting for us to come home. That's the awesome part about this shit. You know home's *right* where you left it."

"You think this is going to work?" Miki kept his whisper low, hoping the road noise would mask his words. "Us. Them. All of this shit. The band. Think we can pull this together? Between us?"

"Yeah," Damie replied smoothly.

Too smoothly for Miki's tastes. One glance over the cab, and Miki saw the glint in Damie's blue gaze. Reaching over, Damie squeezed Miki's thigh lightly.

"Trust me, Sinjun. It'll be—"

The deer came out of nowhere. Or at least Miki thought it was a deer. It could have been fucking Bigfoot for all he knew, because the blacktop world with its backlit trees was suddenly full of eyes and fur and scrambling slender legs. The van skidded a bit when Damie tapped the brakes, and Miki grabbed at the dashboard, his heart pounding hard and fast. The flutter of beige and glowing eyes was gone in a blink, swallowed up by the darkness on either side of the road.

"You okay, Sin?"

The question was soft, prodding and poking at the panic gripping the small of Miki's skull. Damie slowed the van down, banking into a curve.

"Do you want me to pull over? You look like you're going to chuck up your Cheetos."

His lungs hurt from working to suck in as much air as they could, and Miki couldn't get his heart to stop running laps around his panic. The moment flashed by so quickly, a tear of steel and screams—his own screams—but no one in the van heard anything, felt anything. Their bassist kept snoring, and their drummer was still tightly wrapped up in his crazy shroud. The road was open, clear sailing until morning for all intents and purposes, but Miki's tongue refused to crawl back up out of his throat.

"No, I'm good. I'm fucking great," Miki snarled back. "Let's just get to the damned motel so we can get some sleep. I'm kind of tired of the world trying to kill me."

THE ROCKING Oyster Bar was a dive. There'd been a halfhearted attempt to bolster it up, mask its furniture-store beginnings by painting the windows black and power washing its brick exterior, but when it was all said and done, no amount of lipstick was going to do the pig any good.

It still was a pig, and an ugly one at that.

"What a fucking dump." Rafe kicked at a chunk of gray something near one of the van's tires. It exploded into a flurry of dusty feathers and bones. Shaking the remains of the dead pigeon off his sneaker, Rafe cursed, spitting out a rapid-fire string of Portuguese.

"I don't know. It's kind of cool. Very eighties." Forest lifted one of his bass drums out of the back of the van to load up the flat foldable dolly Damien bought in San Francisco. "And our name's up. We've got that going for us."

"Yeah, that it is." Damie's grin was stupid, wide, and manic. "So fucking cool."

Miki gazed at the white message board with its mismatched letters. According to the red-and-black jumble, CROS5RO4DS GIN was headlining that night, right after a band called L'4NGE. The apostrophe was an upside-down comma, but the Rocking Oyster made it work as best they could.

They stood shoulder to shoulder, a patchwork cobble of a broken band resurrected by Damien's dream, a fallen bassist who'd lost everything and found himself again in his life's ashes, and a session drummer who'd never imagined he'd leave the safe confines of the recording studio he'd inherited from the old musician who'd taken him in. Miki stared at the ground, seeing their shadows cast from the sun behind them. The lineup was different, yes, and the vibe was oddly strange and comforting at the same time, but the whispers of the past remained, reminding him the shapes on the blacktop weren't the ones he was used to.

No, maybe not, he agreed with the self-doubt pawing at him, but they were going to fucking rock the place to the ground.

"Maybe they should buy some more *A*s," Miki commented. The band's name displayed in weather-beaten letters made everything so much more real, even with the sign's plastic sunglass-wearing oyster playing a pink Flying V above the board. "Looks like we're some tweaking hackers who play Rock Band on the weekend."

The air bit, scraping its cold fangs across his face. Miki'd stolen one of Kane's jackets for the trip, an ancient black leather biker piece Kane grew out of years ago. It'd been buried in Kane's closet, a cherished memento of younger days, but it still smelled of Miki's Irishman. It also fit Miki a hell of a lot better than anything Kane currently owned.

"You going to help unload or just stand there being a grammar Nazi?"

Damie shoved a guitar case at him. Miki snagged the handle, then held his hand out for another.

Damien stared at him for a second, then asked, "What?"

"Give me two. Or I'm going to be off-balance." His knee ached a bit from sitting in the van for hours, then trying to sleep on the rock-hard mattress at the motel. He'd gotten in three hours before someone began jackhammering a headboard against the wall they shared with the next room. It'd gone on for a good ten minutes. Then it was quiet long enough for him to breathe a sigh of relief.

Then it began again.

Damien had the worst poker face, and Miki could see the debate the guitarist was having with himself wash over his features in a tide of conflicting emotions.

"Just give me the fucking guitar, D." Miki waved his hand. "And make sure someone stays behind so we don't get our shit ripped off."

"You're such a bossy shit," Damien replied, but he handed Miki another case. "Don't drop them."

"You're fucking lucky I've got my hands full right now," Miki spat back. "Or I'd kick your ass for saying that."

Despite the creeping slither of pain digging up out of his kneecap, Miki's body fell into the rote pattern of setting up a stage. For all its humble beginnings, the Oyster was set up well. Whatever money they didn't spend on the outside was blown on the sound system and a dual band stage running along the short side of the rectangular building.

It stank. Most clubs did, but the familiar sour beer and sweat rankness was stronger than Miki'd remembered. A stale whiff of pot smoke lingered under the club's still air, probably carried through the air-conditioning vents from the back rooms. A few metal tables and chairs were scattered around the front half of the club, but half the space was devoted to an open floor in front of a wide wooden stage. The risers were about four feet tall, and from what Miki could see, the sound-and-light system seemed decent enough. A strip of white tape bisected the stage lengthwise, marking where the curtain would fall so their equipment wouldn't be tangled up with the opening act's gear.

Behind him, Forest whistled a low, long, sweeping note. Dragging the dolly behind him, he came to a stop, bumping into Miki when the weight of the dolly shoved him forward, but the look on their drummer's face was pure childlike wonder.

"What?" Miki turned his attention back to the stage, trying to see whatever it was that struck Forest dumb. "What are you looking at?"

"This place… the stage." Forest gave a throaty laugh. "Up until right fucking now, this wasn't… real. Now… I'm in a goddamned band."

"Dude, I fucking hope so, because I'd hate to think we've come all this way for the damned chicken wings," he replied. "Because I sure as hell ain't eating any seafood in this rathole. Not even the oysters."

"See, you're used to… this, Sinjun. All of this stuff. Me? This is… my first time. I kind of want to savor it. Studio shit and once in a while a gig just for backup, but… this? It's goddamned… amazing."

"Nah, you're never really used to it. Not if you're lucky."

It was the truth. No matter how many doors they went through, from backwater bar to arena, Miki'd never grown used to it. The nerves were still there. So was the pressure to put everything he had into shouting out lyrics at a faceless crowd. They'd gone from no one knowing the words to a mantra chant of thousands screaming his own thoughts back at him.

Catching a glimpse of the blond man coming through the door, Miki said, "The moment you get used to it, you end up like Rafe did."

"Thanks for that," Rafe grumbled at their backs, lugging in a rolling suitcase. "Asshole."

"No problem." Miki matched Rafe's rueful grin. "Dick."

"But yeah, kid, don't ever get bored." After leaving the suitcase in the middle of the open area, Rafe dusted off his hands. "You get bored, your brain starts to look for shit to do. To catch that high again. Then it all goes to crap, and you spend the next couple of years eating crow, if you don't end up dead from stupidity. So yeah, Fore, go ahead and fucking celebrate we're in a goddamned band. It doesn't get any better than this."

The frizzy-haired older woman who'd opened the door for them left the band alone to set up, returning to inventorying the alcohol behind one of the two bars. Her safety-orange caftan was subdued compared to the graffiti on the walls, enormous scrawls of robots, chickens, and the occasional *Alice in Wonderland* character, but it was the painting of the club's mascot that drew Miki in.

Nearly nine feet tall and a virulent purple, the oyster's partially open shell was lined in black-light friendly paint, and a pearl sat on its lewdly drawn tongue. Or at least Miki thought it was a tongue. It was hard to distinguish between its body and face, other than a pair of eyes and what looked like an ear.

"Do oysters have tongues?" He set the guitars down, moving aside when Damien edged into the backstage area set aside for them. "I mean, aren't they one giant tongue? Or… whatever?"

"I can't say I've spent a lot of time reflecting on an oyster, Sin." Damien nudged him in the ribs. "How about we get shit plugged in, work a quick sound check in, and then we can talk about oysters and their tongues?"

THE SOUND check was a disaster.

Rafe was a beat behind, and Forest skipped through a chorus, throwing them all off. A few songs in, Miki gritted his teeth when an amp blew, screeching its death in a wave of feedback. One of the strings on Damie's guitar snapped, catching Miki's arm and tearing him open. Slapping a hand on the oozing wound, Miki called time and stalked off stage.

Or tried to.

The stage ended before he thought it did, and he went over the edge, stepping off into nothing but air. He tumbled onto the painted, cracked cement floor. His relatively good knee hit something, probably a riser, but he wasn't sure. Either way, he landed badly, curling up over his legs with his elbow smarting and stinging as he lay on the floor.

Shoving out what little air he had left in his lungs, Miki swore, "*Fuck.*"

"Sinjun!" Damie was a step behind him, landing better but with a loud enough thump. His shoes squeaked on the floor. Dangling from his neck by an old strap, Damie's guitar swung wide and smacked Miki's chin as he pushed himself up from the floor.

Miki wasn't sure if the blood in his mouth was from his lip, chin, or where he'd bitten his tongue when the guitar struck him, but there was definitely blood. Shoving Damie's hand off his knee, he swallowed, trying to clear the spreading metallic taint from his tongue. It didn't help. If anything, swallowing only made things worse, and Damien was squeezing at his throbbing knee like it needed a defibrillator to survive.

"Get off of me," Miki growled. He must have sounded like he meant business, because Forest skidded to a stop a few feet away. "I need to get the fuck away from this right now. Just… give me some fucking space."

He didn't remember getting up off the floor, but Miki did feel the smack of the metal back door on his palm when he pushed past it. Hawking a mouthful of bloody spit, he touched lightly at his chin, feeling the welt forming there. His tongue swelled at the tip, a bubbling-up slit where his teeth had gouged into the meat. Sucking on the cut, he drew up blood again, then spat it out.

"Should have grabbed some water." A broken cinder block was enough to keep the heavy fire door wedged open, but Miki didn't relish shoving his way back in just to grab something to drink. Not after theatrically storming out like some damned diva. Rubbing at his face, he muttered, "Fuck, I'm going to have to spend, like, five minutes apologizing for that crap."

His jacket held half a pack of *kreteks*, so he shook one out, then fished the lighter out of the same pocket. Cupping his hand over the end of the clove, Miki coaxed the end to a bright red burn and sucked in a mouthful of fragrant smoke, thankful for the sear in his chest.

"God, I'm so fucking stupid." He blew out a stream of smoke, letting it billow around him. "And you know what D's gonna say. 'So things don't fucking go right. Who cares? Keep your shit together, dude. Make it right. Don't fucking just walk out.' I should have just stayed in there and—breathe, you shit. Finish this one clove, head back inside, and kiss some ass."

Sundown was still a few hours away, but it was getting cold, and Boston's heavy cloud cover dribbled gray over the surrounding buildings and darkened the Oyster's back alley. A garbage truck trundled by, leaving its sour kiss in the air and kicking up debris as it passed. A few feet away, the alley jogged, and the truck strained to make the turn, blowing back a storm of dirt. Miki ducked his head to avoid the dust in the air, and when he straightened back up, a young man stood a few feet away, buffeted by the truck's wake.

He was young, dressed in near-rags Miki knew cost more than some of Damien's guitars. Skinny to the point of being in danger of sliding into a heating grate if he crossed the sidewalk wrong, the teen listed to one side from the weight of the black backpack he'd slung over his shoulder. Thick black glasses hid the color of his eyes but did nothing to mask his heavy eyebrows. Lank brown hair hung on either side of his narrow face, and he pursed his lips when he saw Miki.

"Hey, you're Miki St. John." The Boston was strong in his reedy voice, cracking when he hit Miki's name. "Was that you guys inside? Playing?"

"Yeah." Miki stubbed out the clove against the wall, making sure it was dead, then tossing it into the open, now empty dumpster.

The kid didn't look too much like a threat, but the alley was a short one, and he didn't know if anyone else lurked around the corner. A quick flicking look reassured him the parking lot was a short sprint away, but he couldn't depend on his knee.

The cinder block remnant by his foot would have to be his first option if something funky happened. The kid took another step forward, and Miki raised his chin, straightening up to his full height. Up close, the teen was a pimpled, baby-faced kid with a patch of hair under his nose struggling to grow thick enough to be called a smudge.

"I got tickets for tonight," he said, taking another step closer.

Miki felt his belly coil up, and his fingers itched to grab the block. "We're on late. Maybe around eleven."

"Yeah, I probably won't go. 'Cause you guys sucked."

Smug derision spread over the kid's face. Miki cocked his head, and the kid's cheeks flushed pink.

"Probably going to see if they'll give me back my money."

He wasn't off. Not by a long shot. But Miki'd be damned if some kid with manicured fingers and a backpack with someone else's initials all over it was going to slag the guys he'd just driven cross-country with. Stepping into the kid's space, Miki pushed himself in close until he was nearly nose to nose with the teen. The young man's breath smelled of mint and tea, and he quivered when Miki smiled at him.

"You go do that, kid," Miki said softly, cutting in low so the kid had to strain to hear him. "You go and fucking do that if you want to. But just so you know, you do *that*, and you're going to miss the best fucking show of your goddamned short life."

TWO

Sinjun, inspire me.

You got a second chance at life, D. There's a guy who loves you, and you're out on the road with the only three guys who can stand being with you for hours in a van. What more fucking inspiration do you need?

See? That's why I keep you around. You put things in perspective for me.

Yeah, well, you'd see more if your head wasn't up your ass.

—Outside of Kentucky, 1 a.m.

IT WAS like old times. Better than old times, really. The voices behind him were different, deeper and richer and rough with experience and grit, but Miki—fucking Sinjun—brought the place to its knees.

Feral and growly, his best friend, his brother really, struggled to connect with people. Distrustful and skittish to the bone, Miki was an enigma to most people who met him. It was hard for anyone to connect the almost beautiful, lanky sprawl of bristle and sneer with the charismatic and compelling rock star prowling across the stage. Sinjun came to life with the boards under his feet. Not because of a preening ego—Damie had enough of that for both of them—no, Miki bloomed under the lights and noise because of its chaos and the energy driving it.

He became a god in the tsunami of sound, curving the storm around him and mastering its force to throw it back into the faceless black, washing them in his whiskey-rasped grace.

A count off from Forest's sticks on his skins, and Crossroads Gin was flying.

Sinjun prowled and coaxed, pulling out every filthy-mouthed angel note he had in him. Rafe fell into the beat, closing his eyes and plunging down into the depths of his strings, giving something for Miki to crawl on, ebony shards of glass for them to drag their souls over. Driving them forward, Forest lashed at the air, beating out the rhythm for their race to the darkness of the early morning, where the lights would go dim and the floor empty of the thrashing, sweaty sea in front of them.

Above it all, Damien soared.

At some point, he'd sliced open a finger or maybe the heel of his hand. It stung a bit, nothing to drag him out of the music, but the sweet kiss of pain was there, as well as the hot splash of his blood on the strings. It didn't matter. None of it. Not the blood on his Gibson "Phenix" or the sweat soaking his Hizoku Ink T-shirt, a rivulet running down his back and past the waistband of his jeans like a lover's damp stroke over his electrified skin.

"Thank you for having us along for the ride, Boston!" Miki stopped his feline prowl across the stage long enough to snag a sip of Rafe's beer. He licked the foam from his lips with an obscene swipe of his tongue, then grinned at their roar. "Are you ready for some rock and roll?"

The hitch in Miki's gait was gone, burned away by the adrenaline rush coming up from the pit. It'd happened before. Damien'd seen him in action at Dino's, that little test flight off a short cliff. It was enough to satisfy Damien's need to know if Miki could still perform, if he still wanted to perform.

He'd been willing to walk away from all of it if Miki had once said *no*.

Sinjun never ever said no to him. Not when it really counted. Not when things really mattered to Damien, and ever since he'd found the other half of his soul in a bony sprawl on a San Francisco fire escape, Damien wondered what it would take for Miki to stop falling into step beside him.

Kane. He'd thought maybe Kane, but Miki's cop knew both of them well. Deep down inside, Damien and Miki fit into one another in ways neither could explain. Their connection went deeper than brotherhood. Damien'd seen the Morgan boys and their relationships and knew it came close but not quite.

Ever since he'd discovered Sinjun standing in the middle of the Morgans' kitchen, surrounded by Celtic warriors with fierce eyes and tender hearts, Damien knew he'd come home. He'd been brought home by the one man who'd not asked for his heart but simply took it anyway. And in that tumble of familial chatter, out came Sinjun, as wild and broken as ever.

The set list was printed out on a riser for Damien, and he hated having to check to see what song they'd be playing next. Necessary since they were still finding their rhythm but hateful just the same. His heart ached a bit. He couldn't deny expecting to see Johnny flailing away on the opposite side of the stage or having Dave's Zen-chant murmuring behind him so he could keep track of the changeups in their songs.

It wasn't the same—it could never be the same. And it wasn't better. Damien refused to hang that word on the energy building up between the band. But it was new. And good. Especially when Sinjun flashed his sexy, wild grin at Damien to warn him he was about to lob another song at the crowd.

"Since we're back on the road… after such a fucking long time," Miki purred. "We want to take you all with us. This one's called 'Whiskey and Rye.' Sing along with us if you know the words. But dance the fuck along with us even if you don't."

Damien no longer heard the crowd. The shuffle of feet, slap of bodies, and hoarse cries fell away, an orgy he heard in passing through an open window slowly being closed by the band's music. He felt the moment Sinjun hooked his soul, belting out a song they'd fallen into without Damien even realizing he'd started the first chord.

"*Miles of black, whiskey and rye,*" Miki growled into the mike. His foot was on one of the risers, knee crooked and his body bent over the churning crowd. Hands reached up out of the blackened pit, touching the light pouring off the stage. "*Keeps the band warm, and our damned souls dry.*"

There were more words. Most of them shouted back at the stage in a soup of voices he only heard while playing a gig. In every town, and no matter where they played, that *voice*—that singular meshing of sound—was the same. It was something magical they'd found under every hot light and in front of every thumping sound system, a voice that followed them—followed every musician, really—the echoing, hoarse, slightly off-key voice of the crowd joining in to sing their hearts out.

"*A million miles to go, a million miles to get right here. We've drank from every bottle, and more than our share of beer,*" Sinjun crooned, pulling out their voices, challenging the crowd to match his unearthly sweet bawl. "*At every single show, on yet another stage. We find you in the dark. Ready to rock and rage.*"

Sinjun's pale face glistened under the light, rapturous and seductive, and Damien laughed when a red bra came flying up onto the stage. Rafe hooked his boot tip under a bra cup and flicked it up over one of the mike stand legs. Forest didn't skip a beat, his expression both beatific and humble. He mouthed the words along with Miki, a song written in another time when Sinjun needed to remind himself why he was up on stage.

Written in the dead fatigue of a three a.m. pancake breakfast at a diner with more roaches than grains of salt in the condiment shakers, he'd poured his heart out onto white napkins and children's menus while they'd waited for their driver to finish banging his waitress girlfriend in the back of their bus. They'd gotten drunk after that, drowning in Jack and a half-full bottle of Prichard's, all the while complaining their seats smelled too much of sex and not enough of rock and roll.

Rafe and Forest were here with them to change all that. Rafe's husky purr slid under Sinjun's lower range, giving their singer a platform to jump off of. Forest thundered on, picking up the bass line and weaving a trill in between the chorus and Damien's solo. It was a light tease, something he did to poke at Damien's ego, and Forest winked when Damien shot him a fake scowl.

Their drummer wasn't intimidated one bit. But then it probably was hard to intimidate a guy whose lover could crack Damien's head apart like a walnut with two fingers and have the whole family—including Damie's Sionn—forgive Connor because it was, well… Damien.

The solo flew by, a crunchy blues riff he'd cobbled along to go with the sweet of Miki's ode to their life on the road. Bokeh spangles formed on Damien's eyelashes, the hot spotlight on his face grabbing at the sweat, then falling away, a rain of hexagons and spots as he twisted about to shout the chorus. Sinjun slid over, nesting into Damie's shoulder, and sang—pure, simple, and sweet—of debauchery on the road and the bond between four souls up on stage.

Then the bottom fell away.

It started small. Something odd and off. Damien felt it strike, a stealthy bite into the delectable meat of the pit's chanting crowd.

The sound of the audience shifted, a dark thread working through the bright. Damie caught the tail end of a scream, a ripping tear of horror. Then the yelling began and the shoving started, bodies pushed up against the stage in a wave of flesh and panic.

A security guard, one of the ten men they'd shaken hands with earlier, ghosted out of the mass, his bright yellow shirt bloodied and gaping open. His eyes were rolled back, massive arms flailing about under the roll of the tide, his chest slamming into the riser Miki'd been standing on a moment ago.

Chittering feedback roared through the speakers when Rafe slung his bass off and grabbed at the guard's arm. Damien tried to get across to the other end of the stage, but Miki—oh God, Miki—went down as people rushed onto the platform to get away from whatever was behind them.

Not now. Not in a crowd like this. He couldn't lose Sinjun to a boot heel and panic. Damie'd be fucking damned if he'd ever lose Miki St. John again. He pulled off his guitar and flung it aside, worrying more about the man he called brother than the expensive piece of wood and steel he'd gotten from Gibson only a few weeks before.

He'd rather lose his music than lose Sinjun again.

"Sinjun!" It was like yelling into a hurricane, but Damie screamed himself hoarse and dug in his heels, pushing at arms and legs as they came scrambling past him. He'd lost sight of Rafe, and Forest was nowhere to be seen, but a flash of a Blue Sun logo under the black light was enough to get Damien moving.

The logo was bleach dappled, glowing where the blue-toned light hit it. Those spots were burned into Damien's brain, and not just because he'd been staring at the constellation splatter for the entire night. He'd made those spots, ruining Miki's shirt in a spritz of bathroom cleaner, and at that moment, in the flashing-light panic around them, Damie didn't regret it one bit.

Miki was lying on the stage facedown, but his head was up, his arms stretched out and straining. A foot kicked at his shoulder, then another at his temple, but he jerked up, dragging something heavy out of the pit and onto the stage.

That something was a kid, or maybe a short adult. Damie wasn't sure, but like the bleach spots, he no longer cared. Catching at the slender arm Miki already had a hold on, Damien pulled until he could reach the young girl's torso. Her body was dead weight, too still and too limp to respond to Miki's shouts asking if she was okay. The shirt she wore was black, but Damie's hand pulled away crimson, wet with blood where he'd touched her ribs.

"I've got her!" Miki yelled.

Damien struggled to help his brother stand up, but Miki shook him off.

"She's hurt. Get me one of the towels."

That much was obvious. Blood seeped out of a wound on her side, a long red streak of parted flesh peeking out where her shirt rode up. Damien nearly lost his teeth when someone's fist struck his mouth, but he snagged one of the towels they'd left on stage to wipe down their equipment.

Miki pressed down on the girl's wound, staunching the blood flow. The two-foot risers gave them a little protection from the fleeing crowd, but not enough for Damien to feel safe. Whatever—whoever—was causing the panic was still out there. He could hear more cries, horrific gasps and screams, and he couldn't tell if they were coming from the pit or near the club's front door.

"Find the guys. Then get out!"

Sinjun cradled the girl against him. She moved. Then her eyes rolled open, but they were unfocused.

"I can get her outside without you. She's not heavy."

"Get her outside? Get *you* outside! Use the back," Damie shouted in Miki's ear.

His brother winced at the piercing yell but growled back, "Okay! I'm going!"

The heat of bodies was oppressive, and a high terror ran through the crowd, needle sharp and prickling through the scramble to safety. Other bouncers were there, shouting and herding people toward a green-lit sign. A few feet beyond lay the promised land, a rectangle of sky, brick, and streetlamps.

"Head to the parking lot, people!" someone screamed above the rumble of scared voices.

It sounded like Forest, but Damien couldn't be sure. The crowd shifted, slowing into a bottleneck, but the fear was lessening.

"Don't panic. Head out to the parking lot!"

Rafe was a few feet away. Damie could see the bassist's blond head bob up and down above the crowd. He staggered in and out of view, and when the crowd parted for a second, Damie spotted the heavy security guard Rafe was dragging alongside him. Shoving into the stream, Damien caught up with Rafe and worked his shoulder under the man's other arm.

The bassist snarled at the drag for a second. Then he nodded when Damien fell into step. They got to a break in the flow, and Rafe shouted, "Can you see Miki?"

"He's coming!" Damien craned his neck, hoping to find Sinjun. "He's right behind us. Do you see Forest?"

"No! Let's get this guy out first. Then we can look. He's really bad, D."

Rafe didn't need to say anything else, but fright iced over his face. The fear of not knowing where their drummer was nipped at their heels, and they struggled to get the man to the door. The guard was heavy, nearly driving Damien to the floor when he regained consciousness and tried to fight his way free.

Primed by years of living with the burly Morgans, Rafe handled the massive man easily, a quick step-shuffle forward, and then they tumbled out of the back door, into the astringent stink of the club's side alley. Outside was as bad as the bramble they'd just left. People scattered as soon as they reached the door, fleeing some unknown predator behind them. Sirens were wailing around them, the bricks bleeding red and blue from flashing lights, and somewhere close by, a man shouted directions through a bullhorn, urging the crowd to gather near the street.

"We need some help here!" Damien spotted an EMT at the edge of the crowd, a blue-uniformed woman trying to snag people as they ran by. She met his eyes and shouted for her partner, pushing through to where Damien and Rafe struggled to keep the guard upright. A few seconds later the man's weight was lifted from their shoulders, his bulk folding down into a sling and a pair of scissors making quick work of his bloodied shirt.

It was then the panic hit Damien in the gut. He couldn't find Forest. And Sinjun… he'd just gotten Sinjun *back*.

"What's going on?" Rafe pressed at a cop wading through the thick crowd. "What happened?"

"Head to the parking lot," the cop ordered, shoving at Rafe's shoulder. "Just get your fucking ass over there."

"I'm going to go find Sin—"

Miki stumbled out of the club's open back door, and Damien swallowed the fear-ripe bile coursing up his throat. Slapping Rafe on the shoulder, he jerked his head toward Miki.

"Find Forest! Meet us by the van!"

Miki's sleek features were splattered with blood, and his enormous hazel eyes were tired, still carrying the weight of the girl he'd handed over to a medic. The girl was limp, her face deathly white, but her chest moved, shallowly rising and falling with each stuttering breath. Miki hadn't spotted him. Damie could see that from the confusion and fret on his brother's face. He was about to scream Miki's name when Sinjun turned to the same cop who'd pushed Rafe.

In the harsh sharpness of their youth, cops were something to be avoided for one reason or another. Sometimes it was because they were too drunk from a gig to walk properly or had shoved packets of ramen down their jacket fronts so they could survive the few days until they got paid for one thing or another.

Miki'd had other problems—deeper issues—with authority figures, especially after being passed around by people who should have protected him. Irony brought Miki a cop to fall in love with, challenging his distrust and shaking him down to his core. Still, that wariness remained, lurking under the surface of Miki's too-pretty face and wild snarl.

It was wariness that kept Miki on his feet when the cop's baton flashed and struck downward.

Damien was through the crowd before he could think. The mass fought him, closing in its ranks, mindless cells clustering around his viral rage. Screaming Miki's name, Damie lost sight of his brother, but he could still see the cop, his arm raised over his head and the baton clenched tightly in his thick fist.

"Miki!" Damie's throat went raw and slick with fear. "Fucker, you—"

The cop turned, caught by the wrist by one of the bouncers, a black man who'd chattered about New Orleans when they'd finished their sound check. Damien couldn't hear what they were saying, but something the man said turned the cop's face sour. His fist punched out, catching the bouncer on the arm, but the man stood firm, stepping into the cop until they were shoulder to shoulder.

He got through the dispersing crowd as the cop turned away from the bouncer in disgust. Miki was half leaning on the brick wall, his bad knee at an odd angle and his lips peeled back into a fierce snarl. Damie's stomach twisted when he spotted a large piece

of cinder block clenched in Miki's hand, the amalgam-
ated beige chunk tucked back and ready to fly.

"I got him, man," the bouncer drawled when he
spotted Damien coming out of the crowd. "I've got
the boy's back."

"Let go of the—" Damie leaned over to pry the
cement chunk out of Miki's hand, but someone jostled
him from behind, driving his shoulder into the wall.
"Fucking bloody hell. Come on, Sin, let's get you up
and out of here."

"Yeah, that's not going to happen."

Miki looked up, a trail of tears cutting through
the dirt and blood on his face. His olive shirt was
splotched, dark splatters across his belly. His hand
shook as he let go of the cinder block, and Damie's
panic grew when he saw one of the blotches on Miki's
shirt start to spread.

"I can't fucking stand up, D, and I think I've been
stabbed."

THREE

My blood has whispers of you
Stars caught in the red
I've held on to every memory of us
Held on to everything you've ever said
I can't live without you
I breathe, I eat but it is all gray
Baby, can't you see that without you
I'm dying a little every day
—Dying Without You

THERE WAS a moment—a dark, bleak, and gray moment—where Miki wasn't certain exactly *when* he was. He'd had this dream before. A faint echo of Damien's voice; then a warm Irish brogue washed over him. There was a hint of anger and fatigue in the Emerald Isle drawl, but Miki was more worried about Damien and why he was arguing with a leprechaun.

More importantly, why was D arguing with Miki's leprechaun?

"Huh, I have a fucking leprechaun." The idea staggered his brain, no small feat since Miki couldn't seem to get a handle on its floating bits. "I don't like the cereal bits. Those marshmallow things. Those rock. Hey… hey… did you know they're not really marshmallows? They even have their own name. It's *marbits*. Which kind sounds like wombats if you're drunk, but…."

Miki couldn't find the end of his thought, but he'd gotten a hold of the Irishman—his Irishman—who was standing next to his bed. Or *a* bed. It wasn't his bed. It didn't smell like vanilla soap and leather. And it sure as hell didn't have an eau de dog pillow. The wall wasn't to his right. There should have been a wall there instead of the Irishman, because he felt safest when Kane slept on the left, leaving Miki a cocoon of warmth on the other side of the bed.

"Hey, my leprechaun's name is Kane. And he's mine." His eyes weren't working right, or at least he didn't think they were, because no matter how much he blinked, the world didn't snap into focus. His fingers were numb and for some reason tangled up in something, but eventually Miki found Kane's mouth. "I am so fucking in love with you. You know that? Like it hurts to just fucking look at you. Do you know when we are?"

Kane's laugh was warm, coating Miki's heart in honey.

"You're in Boston, baby. And kind of hopped up on the drugs they gave you."

"Not where, K. *When*. Because you're here, and I'm scared you're like some ghost I made up, but you're here. Is Damie here? 'Cause he's not dead. You know that? He's not dead."

"Damie's right here. Me, Damien, and Sionn." Kane's lips were gone from Miki's fingers, then reappeared on Miki's mouth, leaving a gentle kiss. "How are you feeling?"

"I want noodles. *Chow fun*. But not… not the squid kind. Okay, squid if that's all they've got, but if there's chicken, I want chicken. No scallops. If there's only scallops, then I want only the veggies. But squid only if that's all they got."

"I don't know where I'm going to get you noodles around here, but I'll be giving it my best shot."

Kane's fingers roamed over the back of Miki's head, and he nearly purred at Kane's touch.

"How are you *feeling*?"

"Okay. Kinda floaty. I think I hurt my knee. And some fucking son of a bitch…." Until Kane's thumb brushed over a tender spot on the back of Miki's head. He sucked in his breath, trying to take away the pain. "Oh God, that fucking hurts. Did you know about the cop? Fucker hit me. *Fucker*."

"Yeah, that cop and I? We'll be having a little talk once I've got some time. You've got a bump where you hit the wall."

Kane gently rubbed at the spot, soothing away the pain. There was something dangerous in Kane's voice, a thread of dark Miki'd not heard before. It wrapped around Miki's soul, a slither of barbed wire meant to keep him safe. Miki felt… comforted. Wrapped in the darkness of Kane's voice, he *knew* he was safe.

"Trust me, baby. That cop's not going to like our little talk."

"Fucker. Such a fucking… *cop*. Not like you. Or Connor. Or Donal. Not a real fucking cop." He couldn't think, not with Kane looking at him. His cop was too damned… everything, much too much for Miki to take in. "You have such blue eyes. I could drown in them, you know? Well, 'cause I can't really swim, but they're like… Slurpees. Blue raspberry Slurpees. Dark. And sweet. And sometimes I just want to fall into them and let you fill me until I can't breathe anymore. And oh man, I'm stoned."

"You're very stoned, and you're probably going to pass out in a little bit. Don't fight it."

"You gonna be here when I wake up?" Miki heard himself slurring, and he tried to right his tongue, but it wasn't cooperating. "'Cause I'm stoned. And bad things happen to me when I'm stoned, Kane. You and Damie…."

A terror too big for Miki to fight off grabbed his nerves, working its icy talons in his guts. He felt small, warped around the pain blooming in his knee and side. Kane's fingers closed on his, anchoring to the now instead of the then. The barbed line of Kane's growling anger snagged the ghosts in his mind, and Miki felt his panic whisper away.

"Don't let anyone get to me, okay?" Miki pleaded. His voice was rough, scraped raw and needy. It echoed in his ears, but he didn't care what anyone thought… if anyone thought he was weak. "You watch over me, right?"

"I'll be here, Mick. If I'm not in the room, I'll be nearby. Probably looking to find you some noodles," Kane reassured him. "I've got you."

"'Kay," he muttered. Leaning back into the pillows, Miki sighed, relief flooding through his body. The tension seeped out of his bones, and the light coming from a pair of windows bent and fractured when he blinked. "I really don't want squid. I mean, if that's all they have, then… but chicken. Or that red pork stuff. Or fries. Maybe…."

KANE WATCHED Miki fall asleep. He saw his lover go under. Miki's expression softened, and the brash edge of his features slipped away, leaving his face as angelic as his voice. As he tucked Miki's hand under the cold, crisp hospital bedding, Miki sighed, shifting on the mattress and curling in around his pillow.

"He's got the IV around his—" Damien reached across Kane's shoulder to grab at the clear plastic lines attached to Miki's arm.

"Don't fucking touch him, *áthán*." Kane stood up, punching a finger into Damien's chest. He fought to keep his voice down, scared to wake Miki but at the same time enraged to find his lover battered and pale. His anger—there was no stopping the rage building up inside him. The room got small, tightening around them. "You've had him for one goddamn week, and… look what's been done to him. I shouldn't have let you take him. I should have let him—"

"It's cute you think you've got a fucking say in what Sinjun does or doesn't do," Damien cut in. "You want to get mad at someone? Get pissed off at the asshole with the knife. Or that fucking cop who tried to beat him down. Start with those fuckers, Kane, before you come looking my way."

They were chest to chest, and while Kane might have had at least thirty pounds of muscle on Damien, the guitarist wasn't backing down. Fists clenched at his sides, Damien Mitchell was wrung out and as torn open as Kane felt, but he definitely wasn't stepping away from a fight.

Kane needed to be sick. Worn down to the bone from flying and fright, he'd turned on the one person he thought had sway over Miki. Taking a good look at Damien, Kane remembered no one told Miki St. John what he could or couldn't do. The world had taken away Miki's willingness to compromise, hedged him into a cage of pain and grief, and there was no herding him anywhere he'd feel trapped.

Even if it meant he was safe.

Damien looked like he hadn't slept. Probably none of them had. There'd been a horrific phone call, one with stumbling words and constant reassurances about Miki's health, but Kane hadn't listened beyond the words *hospital*, *Miki*, and *stab*. The first flight out of San Francisco was a long, torturous one. Sionn's quiet reassurances did nothing—helped with *nothing*. It wasn't until Kane pushed through the hospital room door and saw Miki breathing and groggy that the knot of razors and fear unraveled in Kane's belly.

Kane didn't want to apologize. Fuck, he didn't feel like he had to, but there were choices and compromises he'd have to make if he wanted to keep Miki in his life. There would be no coming between him and Damien, but the same held for Miki and Kane. Damien walked as fine a line as Kane did. They both knew it. Any compromises that had to be made, it was going to be the two of them making them, because Miki never wavered.

Push him once too hard, and Miki would break. Especially if he had to choose between his brother and the man he loved. He'd choose neither or both, forcing them to work it out. For someone who'd had no one and nothing, Miki loved fully and fiercely. It would be Miki who'd walk away, trusting them both to be there for him once they'd figured things out.

Kane just didn't think he was strong enough have his lover walk away—even briefly—because he couldn't be man enough to share Miki with the one person he considered family.

"We can't do this. You and me." Kane choked on his words, forcing them out. His stubbornness fought with his reason, slinking back off into the shadows in the glaring light of logic. Damien hadn't put Miki in that hospital bed. "I shouldn't have gone after you, but God fucking damn it, Damien, look what they've done to my Miki."

"He's my Miki too, Kane. Don't forget that. What they do to him, they do to me." His shoulders slumped when Kane stepped back to sit back down. "Is that going to be your 'I'm sorry'?"

"Probably as good as you're going to get right now. I'm still… I need the scared to go away, Damie. Maybe once that demon's left, I'll have room in my throat for apologies." Kane hooked a chair by its leg, then dragged it over for Damie to sit on. "'Sides, fighting over him isn't going to do any of us any good."

"It'll just piss him off. I try to spend my life *not* pissing him off." Damien sat, sprawling in the rigid plastic seat. His black hair was a rat's nest around his face, and the bags under his eyes were nearly as bruised as Miki's swollen knee. "I know you're angry. Trust me, K. I'm as angry as you are, but there was nothing any of us could do to stop this. Shit, we don't even know who the hell was in the crowd with that knife."

"What did the cop tell you? That detective Castillo? Anything?" There'd been little time between the airport and the hospital to get any information. What little he'd gotten from Rafe was more questions than answers. "Andrade told me about the uniform who'd struck him. We got a name to go with the asshole?"

"First off, Castillo doesn't have shit, but not for lack of trying. The first person who got stabbed was the security guard, and he's in ICU. I don't know if they talked to him. You might have better luck getting information out of the police than I would. Mostly they pat us on our heads and tell us not to worry. The club won't be suing us for damages." Damien laughed when Kane scoffed. "Dude, it's a real threat. We have to carry insurance on all our gigs. Can't have too many people. Can't give away X amount of free tickets compared to paying customers. Shit, when it's all said and done, I think we're all making a buck fifty a show each."

"Then why are you doing it?" It'd been a question for Kane from the moment Damien rolled up in the pimped-out touring van.

"To make music, K." Damien leaned forward, scooting his chair closer. "Because it's what we *do*. You've seen Miki when he's on stage, haven't you? Because I have. Because I can tell you there's nothing like having the music pour out of you and then filling back up again. It's taking everything you had inside of you and sharing it, like sex only with thousands of people—or even just ten. It's the best damned orgy you can have without catching anything or hurting anyone's feelings because you didn't spend the exact same amount of time with every dick on the bed. It's just what we *do*."

"Well, not this time, Damie. This time someone got to Miki, and I don't know if this thing you guys have to do is worth his life." Kane scrubbed at his face. He stank of sweat and fear, dead tired of the ignorance he'd carried with him from California. "I know I can't tie him down. Shite, don't I know that? But at the same time, I've got to be knowing that he's going to be safe."

"You're not going to know that no matter where he is, K. Look at all the crap that happened to him when you first hooked up with him," Damien retorted. "Shit's going to happen. Look at it this way—the slice was shallow and didn't get down into his gut. Shit, they don't even know if it was the guy stabbing people or Miki dragging himself along the riser. That cop outside? That was shitty. And Miki was probably two seconds away from bashing that guy's head in with that chunk of cement in his hand."

"Oh God, last thing I'd be needing is having him in jail for assaulting a cop."

"Yeah, not high on my list either, but that was taken care of. His knee? He fucked it up a little bit and overextended it. Crappy luck there, too, but nothing's broken. Nothing's torn."

"He's supposed to take it easy."

"Easy doesn't include a riot."

"So then less riots. I've got to depend upon you, Damien. I can't hover over him, but at the same time, I've got to know you'll be watching over him." The air in Kane's lungs felt too hot to hold in, and he exhaled. "Because he'll kill me if I spend the next couple of months living in his back pocket."

"Dude, I promise this will be the last riot… stabbing… whatever… we're going to have on this tour," Damien said, raising his hand up in a mock salute. "Besides, who the hell would want to kill our Miki?"

"HERE." FOREST held a tall paper cup for Rafe to take. "The cafeteria's not even charging me anymore. I think they're just sick of seeing us."

The coffee smelled sweet, black, and probably strong enough to rip apart Rafe's already tender stomach, but he took it anyway. A red vinyl couch took up part of a wall in the private room ward, and they'd claimed it as Crossroads territory nearly as soon as Miki came out of surgery. It was too short for Rafe to stretch out on, more a love seat than an actual sofa, but it was comfortable enough to slump into and nap if he pushed it.

And God, did he want to push it. Oblivion would be welcome, and his skin itched, drawn too tightly and begging for release.

The last thing he needed was oblivion and release.

Seeing Kane and Sionn coming down the hall had shaken him. It was as if he'd been handed something precious and had broken it. The bleak expression on Kane's face reminded him too much of the long, cold halls where he'd paced outside of Quinn's room. He'd snuck off back then, finding a quiet corner to get a couple of pills into his belly to take away his fear.

There was something about the chemical-sharp air with its blend of sick and overcooked brown gravy undernotes. Rafe's teeth ached, his gums itching along with the throb of his nerve endings along his arms. He needed something—anything—to take the edge off what he was feeling.

Coffee wasn't going to do it. Not by a long shot.

He sipped it anyway, his eyes stuck to Miki's hospital room's door.

It was wood. Or faux wood. Rafe couldn't be sure. If Connor were there, he could probably tell them it was oak or whatever else kind of wood was a pale golden color with a ruddy grain. Rafe knew next to nothing about anything besides music. The Morgan boys were into everything, from turning bowls to crafting beers. Hell, Donal probably fucking knitted afghans out of albino pygmy sheep for starving war orphans. Rafe had none of that. Just his music… and his need.

His addiction.

"Hey, I'll be right back." Rafe set the cup down on a steel side table by the couch. "Sionn said he'd be by after he gets us all actual hotel rooms. He didn't want to slum it like we've been doing. Something about not sharing his bed with roaches."

"Damie's not going to like it." Forest grinned and raked one hand through his blond hair. "You know he's trying to do this tour as broke-ass as he can."

"Yeah, well, Damie can suck it," Rafe shot back. "I'd like to bathe in water that's not rusty and ice cold."

It took him about fifteen minutes to find a spot where he could breathe. Space was a premium in a hellhole, especially somewhere quiet and small where a person could think... or even stop thinking... if that's what they wanted.

Rafe badly needed to stop thinking. Stop feeling, really, when he thought about it. His blood was on fire, licking at the underside of his skin, and he couldn't do anything about it. There was temptation in the search for someplace he could simply be. A nurse carting meds around would have been easy enough to stumble into, and a grab of anything would have been even easier.

He had something he could use. Something strong enough to peel back the dryness in his mouth and put the air back into his lungs. Rafe just needed to find a spot where he'd be safe enough to do what he needed to do.

Sanctuary came in an unexpected place—a small closet filled with buckets and cleaning supplies. It was oddly cramped, bristling with mops, buckets, and shelves of paper towels and tissues. There was a lock on the inside of the door, a simple turn switch, and a light bright enough to burn his eyes out, but even smelling of eco-friendly antiseptic, it was bearable.

Digging through his leather jacket's pockets, Rafe found what he was looking for and sighed. Staring down at his hand, he took a deep breath. "Okay, not the end of the world here, Andrade. Just fucking do this and get it done."

"Hello, this is Doctor Morgan." Quinn's voice held a kiss of stained glass and moonlight in its warmth.

"Don't you have caller ID? Or a special ringtone for me?" Rafe teased, knowing that his lover would say life didn't need to be complicated by different noises for different people.

"You called my office phone, Rafe." Quinn sniffed. "And no, no ringtones. Although Miki did offer to have my mother's number come up with the Imperial March, but I told him no. With my luck, she'd hear it, and I'd have to explain why it says Darth Brigid on the screen. How are you? How is Miki doing? Did Kane kill anyone yet?"

"Miki's doing good. Small slice, about as long as a pencil but shallow enough. There was some metal in it, so they put him under and dug it out. His knee's a bit blown up, but the doctor said it'll be okay in a couple of days after some meds," Rafe rattled off. "If Kane was going to kill someone, it'd be Damie, because they're in Miki's room right now. Or they were when I left. I'm…."

Of all the people he loved, Quinn was his center, the foundation he'd built his new life on. If there was anyone who understood what Rafe needed, it was Quinn Morgan.

"You haven't told me how you are," he said softly through the phone, finding Rafe's self-doubt and plucking at it. "Are you doing okay? Are you hurt?"

"No, not… hurt. Just…." Rafe looked up at the ceiling, a bright white rectangle dappled with strips of peeling gypsum-board tape. His muscles cramped in on themselves, pulling him down, and Rafe sat down hard, his ass hitting the cold floor. Pulling his knees up, Rafe tucked himself into the curve of his body and held the phone in close to his face. "I need you, magpie."

A whisper of a breath, then Quinn said, "Do you need me? Or do you need the idea of me?"

"I always need you, baby. And I always need the idea of you."

Only Q would lay out what he thought in a bit of riddle. Rafe waited a beat, then held back a chuckle when Quinn continued, "Sorry, that was… I meant, do you need me to go there? Because I can if you want. If you need. I should have gone with Kane and Sionn, but you said… you told me it was okay."

"It is okay. It's finals week, and I get it. I just needed to hear your voice. I needed to know you're here, with me. Inside of me." Rafe scraped at the raw of his soul and flung it from him, an inky, mewling blob he couldn't shake from his mind. Not until he heard Quinn. Not until he'd found a bit of sweet Irish and fractured brilliance on the other end of the line, and then all his want—all his craving for a sick oblivion—whispered away. "Shit just got a bit too crazy, and my brain decided it wanted to go down the rabbit hole again."

"No more rabbit holes." It wasn't an order. Quinn wouldn't scold or push, not like the other Morgans did. As much as Rafe loved Brigid and her sons, they liked to push, shoving the world around until it did what they wanted it to do. Donal's gentle third son was different and exactly what Rafe needed. "I can fly out there in a couple of days. Friday's my last test day."

"We'll be in Jersey in a couple of days. Maybe," Rafe amended. "I don't know if we're going to continue the tour. Damie wants to see how Miki feels. Forest is good either way."

"And you?" A pinprick of a thorny question drew just enough blood for Rafe to wince. "What do you want to do?"

"If Miki's up to it, I want to keep going. It would be too much like quitting, you know?" It was a relief to say it out loud, and Quinn would keep his secrets. There was never any doubt of that. "I think if we end the tour, I'm never going to be able to do this… to play again. Damie and the guys, they're doing this because they want to bond as a band. Me? I've got to kill off a few demons. The road's where it's the worst for me. If I can't take a tour—even a small one—then I've got to walk away. From this. From everything. From Crossroads."

"Just remember, Rafe…." Quinn's breath caught, a telling hitch carried into the small broom closet Rafe hid in. "No matter what happens or what you decide, I'll be here. Or there. I won't let you walk away from me."

"That's what I'm counting on, magpie. Exactly that," he said softly. "I love you, Q. When it's all said and done, that's what's keeping me going. No more playing Alice for me, babe, because you're worth every single goddamned rabbit hole in the world."

FOUR

Cherry pop lipstick
Black leather jacket dreams
Seeing my baby next Sunday
Good times, know what I mean?
She better stop her cheating
Better put that man to the side
Shotgun loaded, double barrels
Bastard better run and hide
—Cheating Woman, Cold Heart

BOSTON STANK of rusted iron, old hot dogs, and regret. Too tired to think and too wired to sleep, Damien'd followed Sionn down to a coffee shop holding one of the hospital's corners up. Begging for a minute to grab a bit of quiet and a smoke, Damien settled down on a curve of thick chain strung up between two heavy posts and rocked in time with the biting cold wind whipping through the parking lot and under his skin. He'd lost his lover to a reconnaissance mission of the coffee shop's bathroom, but Damien hadn't minded until the wind picked up. Sionn's leather jacket was thick enough to ward off the chill, but the icy bite lay in his bones, leftovers from the feast of fear he'd consumed over the last fifteen hours of his life.

"Longest fucking day *ever*," he informed a skeptical bird when it landed a few feet away from his legs and gave him the evil eye. Not being well versed on avian species, the thing could have been an albatross or seagull, he couldn't really tell which, mostly because he was on the wrong coast and everything somehow seemed upside down. "Hell, I don't even know what fucking day it is."

A massive greenscape in the middle of the hospital's grounds was a lifesaver of sorts. At least it gave Damien someplace to sneak in one of the last clove cigarettes he'd taken from Miki's jacket. Their things had been taken out of the Rocking Oyster's green room while Miki went under the knife, then packed into the van by the club's staff. He couldn't remember who'd given him the keys, but he remembered thanking a very skinny guy with brittle, corn-silk-fine hair for something.

He'd gone through the motions of trying to organize the band's detritus while not losing his mind over Sinjun, but he'd only held it together until the moment the surgeon came out and told them Miki was fine and the damage wasn't as bad as everyone in scrubs had said it was.

Damien remembered crying. Fuck, he'd soaked Forest's and Rafe's shirts and was handed around like a fussy toddler until Miki'd been shoved into a hospital room and could have visitors. When he wrung himself out, his face was sucked dry and crusted with a thin dusting of salt. As far as Damie knew, he'd sobbed out enough tears and sweat to raise the Atlantic Ocean a few feet.

Which probably explained the disgruntled gray-and-white feathered thing sizing up his sneakers. It was mad about the high tide and, from the looks of it, still pissed off about the crates of tea being tossed into its harbor.

When he'd heard Miki call his name, a plaintive mewl of mangled *D*s and *N*s, Damien knew it was time to lock everything away. Miki couldn't see him crying. Nothing shook his brother off his already shaky foundation like Sinjun seeing Damien cry over him. Damien'd shoved everything he was feeling into a small dark hole, turned his back on it, and refused to deal with anything other than Miki and the band.

It worked. Or so he'd thought, but in the loneliness of a rain-soaked green lawn, Damien was feeling the effects of his taut emotions straining to break free. He just had to keep it together for a few more hours, and then he could let go.

Or at least that was the lie he'd been telling himself over the past half a day, reaching for *one* more hour and making false promises to himself to get through everything blowing up around him.

"Shoo. Go away." Damien flapped his hand at the bird.

It shuffled about on its flat feet, wagging its black-tipped tail, but remained firmly planted on the lawn.

"Go find someone else to peck at, you damned menace."

"Bird's got as much right to the lawn as you do, boyo."

The Irish pouring over him was a douse of hot against Damien's chilled blood, and he sighed when Sionn slid one arm around his back.

"Up you go. We're going inside. I'll be getting you something hot to drink, and then you'll be telling me about the sour you've got spread all over your face."

"I'm going to puke if I drink any more coffee." His stomach curled into a little ball, its lining blackened with bile and fear.

"Then tea. Something calming." Sionn helped Damien up off the chair. "And maybe a little something to eat. When was the last time you've had something in you, *a ghra*? And don't say the last time you were in bed with me. *Food*."

"You're food," Damien griped. "Sort of."

"Come on with you. You can chew on a scone or something," Sionn suggested with a wink. "*Then* I'll let you chew on me later."

THE COFFEE shop could have been any hole-in-the-wall scrabble of worn-out people in scrubs, hand-wringing college students, and the occasional pair of nattily garbed soccer moms chatting about their lives over a couple of lattes and a shared brownie.

Except for the accents. Damie listened in fascination at the clop-clop rise and fall of native Bostonians enthusiastically arguing everything from the weather to the price of gas on Southside. Once inside, Damie shed the leather jacket, slinging it over the side of a love seat he'd commandeered. Sionn left him with a kiss on the cheek, then sauntered to the counter to order.

Damien didn't try to hide his smirk when the two women at the table next to him sighed over Sionn's ass and shoulders. He'd sighed plenty of times while watching his lover walk away. Broad shoulders, narrow waist, and long legs, Sionn was a rugged sprawl of muscle and manners with a dash of wicked Irish pirate thrown in for good measure.

"God, I know we don't talk." Damien looked up at the ceiling. "But fucking thank you for sending me a hot Irish guy."

And for letting Miki be all right, he added silently.

The smell of hot coffee startled Damien, and he blinked, furiously trying to clear the darkness from his eyes. Laughing, Sionn patted his thigh as he sat down beside him. The cushions of the love seat were soft from years of people's asses, and Damien tilted into Sionn before he could stop himself from falling over.

"Shit!" The grogginess remained, stuffing Damien's head with cotton. "I must have fallen asleep."

"Aye, the line was fairly long, but you got in a good nap while I was up there." Sionn handed him a tall ceramic cup. "There's an egg and cheese thing in the bag. I'll be expecting you to make short work of it."

"You're not my mother, asshole." He grumbled mostly on principle, refusing to be herded, but the savory pastry was hot and delicious, easing away the knot in his stomach after a few quick bites. After licking his fingers, Damien finally took a sip of strong black tea, then sighed. "God, that's so fucking much better than that shit coffee they've got in the cafeteria."

His stomach gurgled, suddenly aware of its less than empty status, and Damien pressed his lips in tightly, refusing to let his nerves purge his belly. It was a quick, short battle… one he lost. A hasty sprint to the bathroom, and Damien lost everything he'd gotten down.

"*Fuck.*" His guts were churning, spitting out what he'd held in over the past twenty-four hours. Now wasn't the time to break down. Not out in public. The band couldn't chance any bad publicity. God knows the knifing at their first official show was bad enough. One whisper of Damien puking up his breakfast, and the press would have a field day.

Not that they'd be the first ones to crucify him that day. Kane's ass-chewing was an unexpected slap of anger and hurt, something Damien nursed in his heart until it grew edges sharp enough to cut him every time he thought about Sionn's cousin standing over him and blocking the light.

"Goddamn it, Kane," Damien swore at his reflection in the mirror. "Why'd you have to go and fuck things up between us?"

After rinsing his mouth out with ice-cold water from the tap, Damien staggered back to the shop, only to find Sionn'd moved them into an alcove off the main floor. A bottle of ginger ale and another tea were waiting for him on a table. It felt more like he was choosing which poison was going to kill him than soothing away the sick. Shaking his head, he sat down on the low floral couch facing a narrow window, his hands trembling when he laid them on his thighs.

"I don't know if I should drink anything, babe. My stomach…."

"Get the ginger ale into you. Do that at least. I had to call Aunt B for advice, so you'd better drink some of it." Sionn popped the bottle open, then handed it over. "She said to sip at it. Then for you to call her when you're up to it."

"Hell, I'm never up for it, but sure, later."

The ginger ale helped. Or at least the bubbles did. Something in it worked, because the green bitterness in his throat eased off, and Damien's nerves began to unknot.

"Hell. This whole fucking thing is pure hell."

Sionn reached for the jacket Damien had discarded. Tucking it around Damien's shoulders, he edged in closer and pulled his lover into a loose one-armed embrace. The coffee shop's lights added a golden warmth to Sionn's chestnut-brown hair and deepened his steel-blue eyes to a simmering ocean hue. Wrapped in Sionn's warmth, Damien huddled in closer.

"Better?" Sionn stroked Damien's black hair, tickling at his ear.

"Yeah. Stop that. You're making me nuts. Like bothered, horny nuts, so let's not go with the escaped-from-an-asylum quip I'm sure you've got all ready to go."

"Wasn't even thinking about it."

It was a lie, but Damien was willing to let it slide by.

"And as for this all being hell, it's not on you, Damie. Not like you'd planned on some crazy asshole at your show."

"We sort of do. Part of our insurance policy covers shit like this, because shit happens. Edie said she'll take care of it." Damie saluted the band's manager, hoping he was at least facing Los Angeles, where she tirelessly hacked away at the monsters rising up to do battle with Crossroads Gin. "I can't even fucking imagine what Miki went through… after the truck, you know? This is just one damned day and he's okay, but I'm fucking wrung out, Sionn. How the hell did he do this for two fucking years and not kill himself? Because I wouldn't be able to…."

He'd hit a wall at some point, unable to brick off any more emotion away behind it, and Damien thought he could hear himself crack open, a fracture in the control he'd locked himself in.

"God *fucking* damn it," he choked out.

A tear slithered down his cheek, a hot, betraying damp gremlin fleeing the overfull bucket of his anger and hurt. Another followed, and he wiped it away, biting on the inside of his lip, hoping the pain would keep his sorrow at bay.

The sharp burst of anguish only reminded him of Miki moaning as he lay on a hospital bed's too-stiff white sheets, and Damien's tears broke free, a deluge of release shattering the fragile dam he'd erected in order to survive the sight of Miki's bloodied body.

"I fucking can't do this here, Sionn," he muttered, scrubbing at his eyes with the heels of his hands. "Jesus fucking Christ, I just fucking *can't* do this."

It took everything Damien had to pull himself together. Spackling at the cracks in his soul, he took a long, shuddering breath and reined in his emotions. Sionn rubbed at his back, long strokes against every knuckle of bone along his spine. Bed sounded like a great idea, but he wasn't ready to leave Miki to the tender mercies of the world. Until Miki was alert and awake without a storm of drugs in his system and he heard Miki grumbling at him to go away, sleep would remain a speck on a far horizon.

If only Damien could stop the hot threads of tears weaving down his face, stitching at his skin with sorrowful trails.

"No one can see us. Look, the place is pretty empty now, and we're tucked off here. Just me, you, and the couch. If you be wanting to cry, there's no shame in it. Hell, some of the best men I've known cry without hiding their tears. And you're definitely one of the best men I've known, love." Sionn's deep Irish thickened, wrapping around Damien's trembling body. "Just sip at the gingery stuff and catch your breath. Once you're on your feet, I'll get you to the hotel room, and you can crash for a bit."

The ginger ale burned his tongue, but Damien sipped at it anyway. His throat was raw, too tender to swallow more than a little bit of the stinging liquid at a time, and the lukewarm temperature wasn't helping. When Sionn opened a small plastic bag of gourmet marshmallows, Damien thought his lover'd lost his mind.

"Really? Marshmallows?" He eyed the bag. His eyes stung a bit and were still hot with moisture, but the absurdity of marshmallows made him smile. "What the fuck, Sionn?"

"They're good for when your throat hurts. It's got actual marshmallow root in it, not like the fluff you get for cocoa here. Best I could do, 'cause I'm not knowing where to get the lozenges Aunt B buys at home." Sionn turned the package around. "The bag says it'll

be tasting like vanilla and caramel, so here's hoping.
Just take one and chew on it."

"Just eat it?"

The marshmallow helped, as did the gentle sweep
of Sionn's mouth over his, and Damien pressed his
hand against Sionn's chest, pushing lightly.

"What now?"

"I threw up. You don't want to kiss me."

"Babe, I've kissed you after you've done a lot
worse things." Sionn's grin was a wicked slide of sin
on his handsome face. "I'll be back with some ice.
Don't go anywhere."

"Wasn't planning on it." Damien snagged Sionn's
shirt, tugging on it.

"Still again, what?" The frown was slight, more
worry than annoyed, but Sionn's pout was adorable.

"Nothing. Just… thanks." He tugged again, smiling up at his lover. "Because I know I'm an asshole,
and you put up with my shit anyway."

"Yeah, well, it's good you're hot and a rock star."
Sionn pulled free. "Now sip at the ale. We've gotten
all treacle here."

"Yeah, well, I'm not feeling very treacle." Damien
nibbled on another spongy square, washing the sweet-
ness down with a bit of tea instead of the gingery soda.
"I'm kind of pissed off at your cousin, but I need to
talk it out."

"So talk."

"Did you miss the part where I said your *cousin*?" The marshmallow was turning gummy between
his fingers, and Damien pulled on it, mushing it into
a stringy mess. "And I'm not sure how much of it is
nerves and tired or if it's something really fucking

serious. What I don't want is to put you in the middle of it. We've already got Miki between us. That hot seat's going to be getting pretty small if I toss you in there too."

"D, anything you need to talk about, I'm here for it. It's what boyfriends… lovers… the two of us do." Sionn grew thoughtful. "I don't want you to think you can't talk to me about how you're feeling. Even if it's about one of the Morgan boys."

"It's not so much about Kane as… well, me and Kane. And Sinjun." More knots unraveled, spooling out his worries and fears, loosening his heart from its tethers. "We got into it. Kane… not Sinjun. He's pissed off because Sinjun got hurt on my watch, like I'm not already mad about that—"

"I think it's adorable how the two of you some- how think you can *watch* over Miki, but go on."

"Shut up, 'cause I said that too. That's one of the problems. I think we lash out at each other because neither one of us has a say or control over what Miki does." He sighed at Sionn's judgmental side-eye. Damien sucked his fingers clean of the gooey marsh- mallow, then said, "Look, yeah, I get it. No one has control over anyone else, but—"

"Neither one of you is used to sharing him," Sionn interjected. "When Kane came around, you weren't there. It was just him and Miki. And before the whole evil uncle trying to keep you in a crazy house, it was just you and Miki."

"I'm not used to sharing *anything*," Damien whis- pered between them. Shifting to face Sionn, he raked his hands through his sweat-dirty hair and grimaced. "I was an only child. Which, all things considered, thank fucking God no one else had to go through my parents' shit, but I also didn't have to split anything with anyone. You're an only kid. You should know."

"No one's an only kid in an Irish Catholic family, D. You're always wearing someone's hand-me-downs or trying to get food at a busy table. If you're not watching little ones, it's because you're a little one and there's a bigger one lording it over you." He smirked at Damien's long sigh. "It's the truth. Sharing's something you learn when you're a kid, and when you get older, you just don't want to do it anymore."

"So Kane's right for growling at me over Sinjun?"

"No, not saying he is," Sionn remarked softly. "It's one thing if you're talking about a box of cookies from the store, but you're talking about a human being here—Sinjun—and the two of you are going to butt heads unless you learn how to avoid it all."

"I thought we were doing fine," Damien complained. His palms were itchy, and he scratched at them. "We were good. Not a damned drop of jealousy until this shit hit."

"It's all pretty big shit there, D," he agreed with a nod. "But the way I see it, you and Sinjun aren't something a normal guy's ever had to deal with. You can't blame Kane for not knowing how to step around the two of you."

"What's that supposed to mean?"

"It means that when a guy thinks about the relationship he's going to have with his boyfriend, he doesn't really take into account a symbiotic musical half is going to come along with the deal." Sionn slid his hands over Damien's, stilling them. "Think about it. The two of you are like emotional Siamese twins.

It's who you are. I knew that going in. Kane didn't, though, did he? He thought he was dealing with Miki's loss and how to stitch your Sinjun back together to fill that hole he had."

"Then I walked right back in." It'd been a damned good day then, a heart-stopping, nerve-pounding day, but his world had righted itself. As much love and support as he'd found with Sionn, Damien'd known he wouldn't be complete without Sinjun. Miki falling in love with someone wasn't even remotely on Damien's radar. Hell, he hadn't even imagined Miki *could* fall in love. "Kind of like rolling over and finding someone else in bed with you."

"Good analogy." Sionn shrugged his massive shoulders. "Well, good enough. Me? I've got it easy. Your Sinjun's gone over for one of the guys I'm used to sharing with, and I love you, Damie, but your brother's a bit of a porcupine. We're good how we are, and I'm not going to be sticking my nose in there to give a brotherly sniff and hope we can be closer buddies."

"I would pay good money to see you bend over and sniff Sinjun's butt." He chuckled. "I'd put money down on Sin handing you your ass before Kane even got up off the couch."

"Yeah, I don't have that down on my to-do list. Now see, there's also a little bit of a problem between you and Kane. Both of you want to fix things. Take care of him…. Miki, anyway. And as much as both of you say you understand he doesn't need or want coddling, you follow and hover anyway."

"Hey now, I don't—"

"You two are worse than Aunt Brigid. At least she *knows* she's bugging the shite out of him." Sionn pressed his fingers over Damien's mouth before he could speak. "Now here's what I think. Since neither of you can give up watching over him, how about if the two of you come to an agreement on *how* to watch over him? Might make things a little bit easier."

"Might work," Damien muttered behind Sionn's index finger. "Maybe."

"Just one word of advice." He lowered his fingers, then handed Damien the bottle of ginger ale. "Don't let Miki find out what you two are up to, or there'll be hell to pay. God knows, there's not enough coin in the world to get you out of *that* dance with the Devil."

FIVE

*I came into this world, not knowing
    where I've been*
*You came into my life, working down
    into my skin*
*I fell in love once, with a man who loves
    me still*
*You've been loving him since birth, and
    probably always will*
We dance around each other
A mongoose and a snake
You grab and hold and cherish
So tight that I might break
*Can't you see your love, is as poisonous
    as your bite?*
*You tell me to let you love me, and I'm
    afraid I one day might.*
—Orange notebook #3, page #5

THE NEXT time Miki opened his eyes, the room was dark. Or as dark as a hospital room could get. Light slipped in from outside, long stretches of buildings dappled with bright windows while froths of headlights flowed by on roadway streams. Water splattered across the glass, turning the cityscape into fractured bits of stone, night sky, and light. The rain was a gentle patter, rapping at the window before running down the sill.

His eyes adjusted slowly, bringing things in and out of focus with every blink. A few machines beeped and dribbled sounds to the right of him, while a clear plastic IV snake had its fangs sunk into his left arm. Normally rain made him sleepy. This time the sound of the falling water only made Miki realize he had to pee.

"Crap. How do I get out of—" He searched for a button, anything to call a nurse to help him out of the bed. A tightness across his crotch brought back a wincing memory of waking up in another hospital, his bandmates dead and gone while a tube was shoved up his cock to help him piss his guts out during his brief stint in coma-land. Lifting the bed linens, Miki sighed in relief. "No catheter. Just… tape. Tape pulling."

The tape was interesting. A cut. There'd been a bad slice across his side, and his knee—the joint in question began to complain, a sharp, steady ache twisting through the bone and tendon. His knee felt a bit fucked-up.

"So what's worse? Knee or side? Can't check on the damned knee. Where's the fucking call button?" His bladder chimed in, and Miki bit down on his lip to control the press of liquid bearing down on him. "Okay, bathroom first, then…."

He didn't know what *then* would be. The room was empty of people. Just square light-bouncing machines playing a hearty mariachi while the rain set up a steady backbeat. A closed door usually meant a bathroom, and Miki carefully tried to swing himself to the side of the bed.

Which turned out to be a spectacularly bad idea.

His foot barely touched the floor when it seemed to slip out from under him. A blink, and the lights spun around him, turning into cobweb streaks across the room's buttery paint. Miki tried grabbing at one of the bed rails, but he was either too far or too late. He couldn't tell which. The stuffy head he'd woken up with swelled, filling his sinuses and eardrums until the ceiling became a wall and the bed turned to mush beneath him.

When he fell, he went down hard.

As noises went, it was a cacophony of chimes, rattles, and steel hitting tile. He might have sworn when he tumbled, but he sure as hell let loose once he struck the floor. The pain was incredible, shooting up from his leg and grabbing at his side, clenching in tight over his ribs. His breath was floating somewhere about the hospital room, because Miki was sure he'd lost it when the floor smacked him in the cheek. Gasping, he rolled over onto his side and simply let the pain ripple out to where it needed to flow.

A second later a light flared on, and Miki lay on the sparkling white tiles, wondering who'd needed to put a spotlight on his clumsiness. He didn't have to wait long. In the moment his lungs decided to begin working again, a shadow fell over his prone body, and a pair of red sneakers filled his watery view.

"Now why'd ye be doing that, Miki boy? Are ye trying to finish off what that rat bastard tried to do to ye?"

Ireland held its grip on her dulcet voice, a stronger, deeper roll than her American-Gaelic sons had in theirs. She was a terror, a miniature nightmare packaged into a curvy Irish Venus with a mane of deep red curls and Quinn's green eyes.

"Motherfucking hell," he gasped. "Brigid. What are you—?"

"Did ye think I'd not be coming to yer side? Yer my son. For all yer anger and grousing, right now, ye need a mum. And I'm the one yer going to get." She stroked his hair, rubbing a bit of it between her fingers. "Worst part about being in the sick house, isn't it? Yer hair gets all grimy, and they're not be letting ye wash it proper."

He held it all in until her fingers ghosted over his cheek, and then Miki began to cry. Frustrated and angry, he pounded at the floor, hurting his hand in the process, but Brigid only bent down farther, kneeling beside him, then hooking her hand under his arm and helping him sit up. He tried shaking her off. It was too much… she was too much… and Miki knew he wouldn't be able to deal with breaking down in front of Kane's mother. Not when he was too injured to do anything but curl up into a ball and hope not to break into little pieces.

He didn't dare let Brigid get her arms around him. Something inside him already hurt, already ached and crinkled from finding her in his room. Kane, he'd expected. Hell, he'd imagined Damien bought Kane tickets before even calling home to tell him what happened. But Brigid? She was a surprise.

Exhaling a ragged breath, Miki fought to get himself under control, then asked, "Why is it every time I start crying about you, I'm on the fucking floor?"

"Well, ye seem to have yer greatest epiphanies when yer on yer knees." Her arms were around him before Miki could stop her, but the hug was brief and fierce. She wiped away the scant tears on his face, then said, "And don't ye go making that dirty in yer head."

"I just didn't…." He couldn't find the words he needed to explain away the pain inside his heart. It was a prickly swell of emotion, clouding his judgment and muddling his thoughts. It grew from a seed lodged deep in his throat, then spread its roots down to his chest and belly. Miki struggled, then sighed out the one thought he'd tucked deep inside him, an undiscovered thread of wonderment woven into the darkness he'd spent years fighting. "You here? Not for me. Not *ever*."

"I'll always be here for ye, Miki love. Of all of ye, ye might growl and snap the loudest, but that tells me ye're the one who needs a mother's love the most." She sniffed. Her lips quivered, then firmed into a smile. "I had to fight Donal for the honor, though. I'm going to have to pay up deep for it, but someone's got to stay with the house and kids."

"I—" The words Miki needed to say stuck to the sides of his tongue, refusing to come out. "Brigid…."

"I know, love. I know. Now come on," she crooned, a warm chocolate slather of comfort on his bruised heart. "Let's get ye upright at least, and maybe then we'll be calling someone to come help ye to the loo. 'Cause that's where ye was heading, right?"

"Yeah." His knee hurt, and his ribs were creaking, but the bathroom was a much greater worry. "I couldn't find the button thing to call the nurse, and if I don't pee soon, it's going to be bad."

"There's the plastic bottle thing. I can help—"

"I'm not pissing into a bottle while you hold it," he protested. "And does Kane know you're here?"

"Boy knows I was a few hours behind him. Probably thought it'd be best not to tell ye." Brigid's smile wavered, teasingly fragile. "In case you crawled out the window. And we're about ten stories up."

"No, I'm good. We're… good. He could have told me I'd turned into a unicorn, and I'd have believed him. They had me on some massive fucking shit." Miki shook his head. As bad ideas went, rattling his noggin around was up there with sliding off the bed, because whatever marbles he had left were off and running, bouncing about on the inside of his skull. "Oh God, bad move. Head's icky. I think I'm going to throw up."

"Let's not have ye be doing that just yet." Brigid fumbled at something dangling at the side of the bed. "But if ye have to, just let it go. Yer probably not going to be the first one to lose his stomach on this floor. What's the matter? Ye've gone pale. What's wrong? I'll find ye the bucket—"

"No, I think I'm good. Not going to hurl," Miki croaked, then realized he was sitting with his naked ass on the floor and his hospital gown spread wide open. Scrambling to cover his bare skin, Miki couldn't find an end of the gown to pull over himself. "Fuck, I'm…. God, just kill me now."

"Please, ye think yer the first block and tackle I've seen?" Brigid grunted, steadying Miki while he struggled to get to his feet. "I've raised six boys. There's been peen flying about the house since before ye were born… and not all of it my sons'. Now get yerself going here. I'll help you to the loo, and then we're going to be finding out why there's not a nurse in here. When I push a button, I'll be expecting someone hopping, or I'll be finding out why not."

THERE WASN'T anything he could do for pants, but a pair of loose boxers was enough for Miki to feel he'd held on to his dignity while a broad-faced nurse chattered with Brigid about apple pie filling and silly offspring who thought they could go to the bathroom by themselves.

A painkiller, the bathroom, and then warm sheets were enough for Miki to sink back down into a soft blur. He didn't *hurt*, and more importantly, he couldn't quite focus on Brigid's face as she started telling the soft-voiced black woman in SpongeBob scrubs about the time he'd tried to help her make brownies for movie night.

He discovered he didn't mind it—being the center of one of Brigid's rollicking tales. It was odd. Any time in the past, he'd have felt mocked and demeaned, but he half listened to Kane's mother tell SpongeBob nurse about losing the microwave in an earth-shattering kaboom because he'd put an egg in it instead of the bowl of chopped-up chocolate he had in his other hand. Brigid spun out the tale like a master weaver, adding flourishes of the family's fear and then laughter as they officially declared the appliance a fallen warrior in the war of the brownies.

There was… *affection*… in her voice. He sat and heard not only her words but the music beneath the Irish. She sounded like every other time she told someone a story about one of her kids: a bit of teasing, a dash of humor, and a lot of… *love*.

Time and time again, Miki found it hard not to compare Brigid and even Donal to the men who'd caged him in their perversity and mindless cruelty. There were still times when he winced and recoiled if Kane raised his hand too quickly. Hell, even Dude didn't react as violently to sudden movement as Miki did, but it was something Miki was working on.

It was just so damned hard to hear the love in the *now* when he'd drowned in pools of mockery in the past.

Miki heard it now. In the half slumber of drugs, eased pain, and a cup of ice chips, he finally *heard* Brigid's heart in her words.

This time he let his few tears fall without shame. Without any regret.

"Here now, Miki boy," Brigid asked from across the room, "are you okay?"

She sounded alarmed. He hadn't wanted to alarm her. He just wanted her to continue talking, to lull him into a safe, warm place where he didn't have to worry about pissing someone off because he didn't know how to be an actual person.

"I'm fine." Replying was a bit difficult, but Miki focused on moving his tongue properly. The ice chips were nice. As was Brigid's hand on his. "I just realized I'm fucking Pinocchio."

"I'll just be leaving the two of you alone. The doctor will be by shortly to take a look at that knee." The nurse pointed at the call button lying at Miki's side. "You need something, you have your momma ring one of us. No getting out of bed, young man. Not for anything. If you're good, they'll let you go tomorrow. If not, I'll be seeing you this weekend."

"She makes it sound like a bad thing," Miki grumbled under his breath. "Much better than the torturers I had in Los Angeles."

"Lorraine left ye some juice cups, but if ye want food, I can get one of the boys to bring ye something up." Brigid settled into a chair near Miki's bed. An odd expression fluttered over her face, slightly troubled and hesitant. "And here I go just sitting down when ye might want me gone so ye can sleep."

"No, it's nice. Good." His tongue still wasn't cooperating, but Miki figured Brigid could deal with it. Having been in the middle of a Morgan argument where English and Gaelic flew about in fiery streams, Brigid could understand if he slurred. "Did you tell Kane to crash?"

"For a little bit. It was hard going, but he needed it." She popped a straw into the foil top of a juice cup, then passed it over for Miki to sip at. "He'd been running on fumes. Would have been no good to ye otherwise. Do ye mind?"

"What? No. Not like he'd have listened to me." He grinned. "Guess we've got that in common. We both don't listen for shit."

"It's a Morgan trait. I'd say they get that from their father, but we all know it's my door that blame is laid at." Tucking a strand of flaming red hair behind her ear, Brigid smiled. "And ye should know that Donal sends his love. And for ye to get better. We have a bet, my groom and I, on whether or not ye'll continue the tour."

"Who bet against me?"

"Neither. He says ye'll pack yerself up out of the room tonight and head over to Jersey like the Devil's chasing ye." Brigid laughed at Miki's wrinkled nose. "But I say ye'll stay at least long enough for the docs to have a look at ye so Damien and Kane can't argue with ye, and *then* ye'll go on yer merry little way."

"Got a lot of money riding on this bet?"

"No money. Just bragging rights," she said with a shrug. "We've been married long enough to know sometimes the best prize from a bet is being able to say *I told you so*."

"Yeah, that's not something I hear a lot from Kane." He smirked.

"Only because yer not the teasing sort. Took me a long time to understand that about my Donal. We had to bend, he and I." She nodded when Miki snorted. "It's the truth. He was so very serious and wound up tight, like the weight of the world was on his back, and me? I was scattered and flighty. But oh, I wanted that man so badly I could feel it in my teeth. He was worth growing up for. I have no regrets on that. No regrets on any of it, really."

"I can't see Donal not laughing." Hell, it was hard to imagine the Morgan patriarch being anything other than easygoing and steady. "He laughs a hell of a lot now."

"Connor taught him how to laugh." She dug her elbow into the bed and rested her chin on the heel of her hand. "Baby boys are a wonder. Girls too, but it took us a while to find that out. Kane, now, yer lover's the one who showed Donal there's five sides to every story. If there was any question of Donal becoming a detective, it was answered when Kane started talking. Pulling the truth out of that one was like finding a long needle in a haystack of short needles."

"Kane. A liar?" Miki scoffed.

"'Liar' is a bit of a strong word to use there." Brigid pursed her mouth. "Think of it more as ye had to know what question to ask if ye wanted the whole story. He wasn't one to give up his secrets. Not like Quinn. That one is an onion. Kane was… he cherished his secrets. That's how I knew ye were precious to him. He wasn't having any sharing of ye until he was good and ready."

"Yeah, I kind of feel that way about him too." The confession was out before Miki could stop himself, but he found himself rambling on. "D keeps after me about love songs… because he thinks I should write them now… because of Kane."

"And ye don't?"

"I keep telling him, Kane's… I don't want to share him. Not with the world. Which is stupid. Because they won't really have him, but…." He sighed. "He's *mine*. I write them. The songs. I'm just not going to record them. Not yet."

"That's fair, love. Ye should only give out what ye want to lose." Brigid's eyes grew dreamy. "See, I always think yer writing away bits of yer heart and soul when I hear yer songs. Slices of yerself, like one of Alice's tea party cakes. And ye can always make more, but they'll not be the same taste. Not every time. If there's one that's only for ye and Kane, then that's how it should be. I'm sure there are things ye share only with Damien."

"Damie's different. The world fucking owns us. We sold ourselves a long time ago. Anything I make for Sinners… for Crossroads, it's not mine. Once that button hits Record, the song isn't mine anymore." Miki tried to catch his thought before it escaped him. "It's like once there's a song, then it… it's like no one owns it. Everyone's got a piece of something that's theirs because no one hears the same song. But when we get all together, under those lights, in front of those speakers, we're all singing each other's song. It's like thousands of voices singing a piece of you back. It's intimate, but at the same time, you're spread wide open for everyone to see. Even if they don't know what they're seeing."

"Ye love doing it, then, the singing?" she asked softly. "Because I'll be telling ye, Miki love. I worry for ye. Up on that stage. I worry yer doing this only for Damien, but Donal, he's got a better hold on yer heart and mind than I do. He says ye can't *not* sing."

"He's right," Miki whispered after a moment. Touching Brigid's arm, he continued, "The first time I heard the crowd sing my words back to me, it was like someone saw me… *knew* me. Someone other than Damien. Or Johnny and Dave. My whole fucking life, I wasn't seen. Wasn't heard. No matter how hard I cried or how much I shouted, it was like I was nothing. Invisible. Like my pain didn't matter. Like I didn't matter. But that night… I couldn't see them, but they could see me. And they heard me.

"And I get it now. I didn't so much before, but now I do," he said softly. "It isn't just them singing at me. It's everyone singing *with* me. Because in that moment, none of us are invisible. We're all just in that moment together… and it's safe and it's good. So yeah, I'm heading to Jersey. Because maybe somebody out there needs that bit of song to remind themselves that they're still alive."

SIX

*World's gone too dark, too dark for me
    to see
I turn and reach out, but there's no one
    there for me
Every time I hear a heart break, I die a
    bit inside
I cry for every child, I cry for every
    bride
Atlas carries the world on his shoulders,
Jesus hangs for our sins on a tree
White doves for peace are in the air
But something whispers we'll never be free
Light a candle for the darkness
Light a candle for our sin
Hug your nearest neighbor
Don't forget to let love in
—Candles Burning*

"To the left, Miki. No, my left," Kane murmured, his hands sliding over Miki's hips. "Turn over. No, not that way. Come on—"

"I can fucking walk, K," he growled between his gritted teeth. "It's a damned soft brace. I didn't break anything. It's just swollen a bit. I just want to sit down on the couch."

"How are the stitches? Pulling?"

"They're fucking fine. No swelling. Not hot." Miki slapped Kane's hands away, irritated at being guided to one of the suite's couches. "It's not even that deep. Even Castillo said I probably cut myself on one of the riser brackets."

"Castillo also said they don't have a suspect for the knifings."

"Not her fault. Club stopped checking bags at ten. That's on them." His knee was better but still tender. Standing wasn't the best thing for it, but he was sick of sitting down. "Remember, she's got a knife they found behind the bar."

"Getting prints matched up just takes fucking forever," Kane grumbled. "Place should have had a camera. Hell, I never should have let you—"

"Keep on with that thought, and we'll see how much I'll *let* you near me," he cautioned. As much as he loved Kane, there were times when the Morgan family motto was less "*Honor and virtue*" and more "*Herd lovers like you're border collies.*"

"I'm fine. Castillo's doing her job, and you've got one night with me before you head back. Couch doesn't look that comfortable, dude."

"You were just… it kills me to see you hurt, *a ghra*. Those days in the hospital about did me in."

"Yeah, wasn't a picnic for me either. Done now. We're good. And finally not fucking stuck in the van. I'd *almost* take the hospital over that any day."

The time Miki spent in the hospital were the longest forty-two hours of his life. When he'd been laid up in Los Angeles, Miki thought the emptiness of his life with only Edie to come by once in a while was the worst thing he'd ever have to experience.

He was wrong. The constant in and out of people coupled with frequent pokes and prods by specialists was enough to make him scream.

Or kill.

When the doctor in charge of his recovery announced he could be sprung, Miki still hadn't ruled out killing as an option quite yet. Kane was certainly getting on his frayed nerves, and he wasn't going to feel right unless he got in a good hot shower and scrubbed the sick off his skin.

Because no matter what put a guy into the hospital, he always came out smelling like death.

The next day following his escape from the hospital had been a whirlwind of people and good-byes. Brigid was off on a plane before the sun rose over the Atlantic, and they'd all piled into the band's van to head to New York. All of them—including Kane and Sionn—because for some stupid reason, they were going to spend a day in the Big Apple. Together. Like some demented vacation flick where a leather-faced guy with a chainsaw would go a long way in making things just that much more interesting.

About half an hour into the trip, Miki was more than ready to be the one with the chainsaw.

Forest at least had the good sense to sprawl over the back row of chairs and spend his time talking to Connor on the phone. From the sultry chuckles and soft *ooh*s coming from the rear of the van, Miki didn't think Forest heard one damned bit of the arguing going on in front of him.

Miki didn't have that luxury. He had a front-row seat to the most convoluted, testosterone-fueled discussion on which way to get to Manhattan from Boston. Despite having the disadvantage of not growing up in the Morgan household, Damien held his own. They'd played musical driver's seats along the way and only once ended up in a state they hadn't planned on detouring through.

And Manhattan was exactly as he'd remembered.

It was loud and a bit pretentious, packed with people from somewhere else but desperate to call themselves New Yorkers. The real New York clung to the edges of the sidewalk, in the faces and voices of street vendors and city workers who watched the streams of people with bemused expressions. The sky was filled with walls, and lines of cloud-streaked cadet blue striped the cityscape, a rare clear day sparkling through the grime. Subway entrances sucked in and vomited out bodies, sending crowds careening along their way. A few long miles into the noisy city, and they'd arrived at the overpriced hotel Kane and Sionn booked over Damien's barely there protests. Rafe had been the first one out of the van, proclaiming his love for the Apple in a voice loud enough to draw stares while Forest simply stood in awe of Times Square.

Miki'd just wanted to stretch out someplace and maybe get Kane in bed, but the Irish cop seemed to be more in the coddling mood than cuddling.

"There's isn't ice in the freezer. Five-star hotel my ass. You'd think they'd have ice in the damned room." Kane stood in front of the couch, caught halfway between the sweep of windows overlooking the square and the suite's kitchenette. "Do you want me to—"

"Kane, just sit the fuck down for a minute." Miki exhaled hard, sinking into the soft cushions. "You guys turned a four-hour drive into a slog through the Scottish Highlands."

"It wasn't that long."

"We left at seven in the morning, dropped your mom off at the airport, then got on the road." He glanced at the clock. "It's now five in the afternoon. You guys took… wait, let me count… I'll even cut some time off for the two-hour good-bye we had with Brigid. Eight! *Eight* hours to get from there to here."

"We stopped for lunch."

"We went through a drive-thru." He shook his head at Kane. "And we ate while Rafe drove."

"You took the longest to say good-bye to Mum." Kane's Irish thickened. "At least fifteen minutes."

"She wouldn't let go of my neck," Miki shot back. "Woman doesn't know a good-bye even when it smacks her in the face. Couldn't wait to get rid of her."

"You love my mother." His lover took a step closer to the couch, looming.

"I'm not saying I don't," Miki countered quickly. "What I'm saying is that it took the four of you assholes eight-plus hours to get us to New York. And for what? One night? You and Sionn fly out tomorrow from JFK while we head over to New Jersey. What good is that?"

"The good here, Miki love—" Kane knelt down in between Miki's parted legs. "is that I get to spend a night with you here. In New York. Without anyone else in sight."

It'd been too long since he'd had Kane's mouth on his, and Miki suckled at his lover's lips with a fierce hunger. Their tongues brushed once, then again, teasing and probing into one another. Kane's body was as familiar to Miki as his own and a hell of a lot more enjoyable to touch. His fingers found Kane's waistband and then the button he'd been looking for. His thumb dug against the metal disk, and an amused chuckle stopped him dead in his tracks.

"Oh, fuck me," Kane muttered under his breath.

Miki rested his forehead against his lover's chest, sighing heavily. "I was trying to."

"Guess no one told you the living space connects to my room, Sin," Rafe drawled from an open door across the suite's main room. "You guys up for Italian? We're going to meet in the lobby in about forty-five minutes. Damien says it's a bonding experience. Notice the air quotes."

"I'll go get you some ice for that knee, and you get a painkiller in you. No arguing about that." Kane buttoned his jeans back up, to Miki's deep disgust. "Maybe you can work on getting Andrade out of the room."

"Can't argue about the pills," Miki replied. "I fucking flushed them. Well, the pain shit. The anti-inflammatory ones I kept, but I've got tons of those from before we left home too."

"Why the fuck would you flush—" Kane bit his lower lip, frustration working over his face. "Miki, they're for—"

"Rafe doesn't need that kind of crap around him." It'd been an easy decision, one Miki made nearly as soon as he'd left the hospital. "Drug-free band. Drug-free backstage. It was one of the conditions for this tour. I'm not going to fuck my friend up because I can't deal with the shit I've already been dealing with."

For a second, Miki thought Kane was going to argue. It was a moot point. The pills were probably already getting a sewer alligator stoned, but moot points were sometimes what Kane liked to latch on to and grumble about. This time he took a long, hard look at Rafe, then picked up the silver ice bucket he'd left on the coffee table.

"I'm going to get ice for your damned knee. Andrade, we may or may not be down for Italian." Kane bent back down to give Miki a kiss. "You, love, decide if you feel up to it. I'm good with room service and a movie. And it doesn't even have to be a dirty movie."

Rafe waited until Kane left, then sat down on the couch. "You didn't have to do that, Mick. I'd have been… fuck, I don't know if I'd have been okay. I'd like to say yeah, but I just don't fucking know."

"Why risk it?" Miki shrugged.

The pain in his joints was something he'd learned to live with, a price he'd paid for waking up after the accident that tore his life apart. What happened in Boston strained his knee, but it wasn't anything he couldn't endure, and with a steady supply of anti-in-flammatories, he'd be fine in a few days. Providing he didn't engage in hot rock-star sex in the bathtub, al-though the stubble across Kane's firm jaw and his lov-er's strong hands on him every time he turned around wasn't helping.

"What'd they give you for the pain?" Rafe asked.

Miki rattled off what he'd read on the bottle be-fore dumping them in the toilet. "Fuckers wouldn't flush. It was like a zombie hoard, shuffling back up to the surface. I'd have fished the damned things out, but they get all gummy and fall apart in your hand. I'd probably have ODed scooping them out into a bag. How'd that have looked?"

"Shit, you'd have gotten some bucks on the street for that crap. What'd they give you? Ten?"

"Thirty." He smirked at Rafe's low whistle. "Yeah, probably could have paid rent on a Chinatown trash can or something with it. But it's pining for the fjords right now."

Rafe stretched his long legs out, resting his feet on the coffee table. He looked as rumpled as Miki felt, stained with the slight rank of hours spent in a car and eating junk food. It was the smell of being on the road, an intimate, familiar scent coupled with the oddness of it being on unfamiliar skin. A long silence yawned between them, the puzzle piece of quiet turning as it tried to fit into the space between them. Something must have clicked in on Rafe's side because he cleared his throat, then spoke.

"You didn't have to toss that shit, you know. Not for me." Rafe's raspy, deep voice was threaded tight with emotion. "I should be strong enough to deal with you having stuff around. I can't be crippled by this crap I've got going on."

"You pissed off about it?" That was something Miki hadn't thought of. He'd taken away Rafe's choice to stay clean with one flush of a Boston toilet. Well, several flushes, but it didn't matter. The pills were gone, and he'd pretty much cut Rafe's balls off with a dull knife when he pressed the handle. "Figured it was better to just get rid of them."

"Truth?"

"Always a good thing," Miki replied.

"I'm fucking terrified of having any kind of shit around me," Rafe muttered, dropping his head back to rest on the couch cushions. "I'd like to be all big man about it and say I wouldn't come breaking into your bathroom if you're not around, but thing is, I fucking can't promise that. So while I'm kind of pissed off you thought you had to dump your shit because you can't trust me, the truth is I can't fucking trust myself."

"Okay." He pursed his mouth. "Just so I've got this. Dumping pills is good but shitty because you don't know if you can handle being around them."

"Not shitty. You're watching out for me. Because you don't know what kind of crap I've got going on inside of me." He glanced over at Miki, then bit his lower lip. "I said I can't do this tour unless we're drug-free—not like any of you do shit—but you stuck to that.

"I spent a lot of time hitting up that hospital's damned meetings because getting shit-faced was all I could think about. Like how fucking easy it would be to take something when no one was watching," Rafe continued. "It's going to be fucking hell for you, because a dead raccoon can see you're in a lot of fucking pain, Sinjun, but I'm going to be an asshole and say sorry, but I don't want to end up in rehab again."

"They suck? Those meetings?" He'd been around enough drunks and druggies before. Being on tour pretty much guaranteed that, and he probably would be cock-deep in them again. Drugs and booze were as much a part of the business as music, and Miki wasn't going to lie to Rafe about spending his whole life on stage and behind it as sober as a nun. He'd woken up more than once in a strange place with even stranger people. "We went through a couple of drummers before Dave, you know? One guy—Pedro—he was really cool. Intense, but I liked him a lot. We'd left him at the apartment 'cause he said he was sick. Came back from helping Damie lay tile on a job, and Pedro'd cleaned our apartment out. Guitars, amps… the goddamned forks we'd stolen from that Denny's in Japantown… fucking everything. And you know why our shit was gone."

"Yeah, I've had that happen too. Fucking sucks, huh?" Rafe chuckled. "It's stupid what your brain decides is okay to do because your bones are itching."

"So fast-forward… like, two years later. We weren't huge yet, but we had crowds, you know?" Miki explained. "And we're at a gig down in San Diego, and in walks Pedro, right up to me and Damie backstage."

"Fucking balls."

"See, he'd come by to ask for absolution. Said it was one of his steps, and of all the people he'd hurt, he felt the shittiest about fucking me and Damie over." It'd been hard to listen to Pedro go through his reasons for putting Damie and Miki into the hole for over two grand, even harder to hear him beg them for their forgiveness. "Sorry doesn't cut it, right? I mean, no matter what goes on afterwards, it never goes back to what it was before. He was so fucking good, Rafe. Like a dream to fucking work with, but he cut us pretty deep. 'Sorry' doesn't kiss better a boo-boo that's gone black, you know?"

"Yeah, I know," Rafe murmured. "There's a couple of people I haven't said I'm sorry to. Don't know if I've got the balls to do it."

"Dude, Pedro was scraping the bottom of life when he ripped us off, and I don't think he was much better when he came round backstage. You want to know why I flushed those fucking pills down?" Miki grinned over at his friend. "I don't want us to ever get that deep—that far down the hole—where you feel like you've got to crawl through glass for something you've done. Not you. Not if I can help it, you know? The pills? My knee? It's fucking nothing compared to your life. I've lost enough friends, Rafe. I don't intend to lose you too."

"WHERE THE fuck are we going, babe?" Kane kept his strides short, surreptitiously watching Miki's gait. The sidewalks were wet, the afternoon's clear skies a distant memory, much like the lunch they'd eaten in the van. "We're about a block and a half from where the cab dropped us off."

They were in Greenwich Village, a chopped salad of flashing lights, loud voices, and garish personalities. The buildings were vivid, strong faces poking up into the wet night, brashly seducing passersby to

waltz through their open doors and sample the de-
lights within.

A woman on thin, white stilt heels eyed him
when they strolled by a sushi place. Her eyes clung
to his chest, then flicked over to Miki. As usual, his
lover was oblivious, his full mouth in a slight pout
as he studied the streets. His loose-hipped stroll was
graceful despite the slight hitch in his knee, a prowling feline of a man with more than a little bit of street
grit clinging to his every move. There was something
coiled and dangerous in Miki's presence, a fierceness
Kane loved... and dreaded.

Miki St. John depended on no one, counted on no
one to bail him out, and if there was one thing Kane
could change about his lover, it would be his unwill-
ingness to lean on Kane when times got rough.

It couldn't get any rougher than being stabbed
while performing for the first time in years.

The woman in heels was gone in a blink, faded
off into the chatter around them. It seemed like every
other place they passed was a restaurant or a few parking spaces turned into a battleground for competing
food trucks selling everything from octopus balls in
teriyaki sauce to tofu tacos with kale chips.

His stomach pointedly reminded him it hadn't
seen a speck of food since a handful of cold fries
somewhere in Connecticut. His dick wasn't helping
either. Sex over the past two weeks had been over the
phone and his own hand, so his emotions ran high and
hard every time he so much as glanced at Miki.

Kane'd dropped back to let Miki take the lead
and soon regretted it. Miki's ass looked great, delectable and firm in his worn jeans. He'd filled out a bit

since Kane'd moved in, gaining muscle and weight where he'd gone thin after the accident. Kane's brain hummed with the satisfaction of seeing Miki healthy. His dick, however, had purely nefarious thoughts Kane didn't need to hear as he was walking down a busy New York street.

"We're almost there," Miki promised for what had to be the tenth time. "It's down this street."

"You keep saying that, and then there's another street." Kane nearly lost his lover in the shadowy clot hanging over the corner Miki turned down. "Miki love, where the hell do you think you're heading?"

The road was narrow, larger than an alley, and at least warranted a name. It also looked more like a spot garbage trucks ambled down to pick up dumpsters, a supposition soon proved once Miki jogged them past an alley opening just as a junk truck passed by. A garage did a brisk business to the right of the alley, the attendant sliding vehicles into stacked bays, rolling them up and out of the way. Easing a minivan out to the car park's entrance, a thick-necked woman in a neon safety vest nodded once at Kane, her hand already flicking the keys to another attendant as she headed toward the back.

The alley wasn't as long as Kane thought it would be, maybe a few hundred feet or so from the street, widening out at the far end. The building in front was angled and hosted an Italian restaurant behind its black-and-gold-painted storefront. Despite someone's best efforts, the structure was unable to shake off its birth as a bar during Truman's days and still reeked of cheap booze and unfiltered cigarettes. The line out the door promised either a good meal or a five-star bowl of bacon foam and gold leaf. And it didn't seem like they were going to find out which, because Miki shouted at him to get his ass into the alley.

"Here we go." Miki slid past the dumpsters, wading through the puddles making soup of the back alley's debris.

"Go where?" Kane wondered if the softness he stepped in was rotten food or a rat. Deciding he didn't really need to know, he stomped through a few puddles to get his shoes cleaned off. "Where are you—?"

Once clear of the dumpsters, Kane got a good view of the alley's end. Formerly a small courtyard, it'd been walled off by years of construction until all that remained was a garden space scalloped with deep divots filled with fragrant herbs. A sturdy wooden table stood firm on the brick pavement, its four retro vinyl-and-metal chairs sitting at each of its sides. A pair of novena candles was pushed nearly to the far edge, flickering red and green behind an old glass salt and pepper shaker set with battered steel tops.

They were behind the restaurant, but the aromas coming out of the kitchen were nothing like any Italian food Kane'd ever smelled before. Ribbons of coconut and curries trickled out, splashing a colorful palette of perfume on the slightly chilly evening. A small elderly Vietnamese man stood with his hands out to shake Miki's, fingers trembling with age, and he cackled with undisguised glee when Miki gave him a quick hug.

"Kane, this is Lanh. He makes the best damned *pho bo kho* in the world, and I asked him if he'd cook for us… for you." Miki's smile was nearly as wide as the tiny old man he had in the crook of his arm. "Lanh, this is…."

Miki's eloquence was normally reserved for paper and song, and he always struggled to find the words to express what Kane meant to him… who Kane was in his life. It was something Kane was used to, but standing in a rain-soaked New York alleyway, Miki suddenly seemed to find the something he'd been struggling to say ever since Kane moved in.

"Lanh, this is Kane," Miki said softly, his eyes never leaving Kane's face. "He's the love of my goddamned life."

SEVEN

Mick love, how are you doing? Glad I
        caught you on the phone. How is—
Are you at home, K?
Yeah, do you need to call me back?
No, just... can you put Dude on the
        phone? I kinda miss hearing him
        breathe.
—Saturday morning call

"So I'm eating cow ass." Kane poked at his soup with his chopsticks. "Is that what you're feeding me here?"

"Swear to God, I'm going to cut you if Lanh hears your shit." Miki leaned across the corner of the table. The *chágiò* he shook under Kane's nose dripped gua-va-tamarind sauce, splashing a dusky pink thread over

Kane's wrist. "Cow ass… you're teasing me, right? Jesus, why do I even take you places?"

"Because usually you're the one holed up at home," he reminded his lover. Taking a bite out of the eggroll's tip, Kane chewed to the familiar sound of Miki's muttered outrage. "And yes, I know it's oxtail. I've had oxtail before. Just not like *this*. It's good. Not saying it's not good."

The dish was aromatic and oddly enough, even with its pho name, very much a stew. The *pho bo kho* screamed its French upbringing despite its Vietnamese pedigree. Rich, hearty, and spiced in ways no French chef would consider, it was a surprising burst of anise, chilies, lemongrass, and achiote with a layer of something thicker beneath it. Kane took another spoonful, slurping the broth up, and watched Miki tear off pieces of bread, then dig out chunks of meat from the stew.

It was always fascinating to watch Miki eat. When he'd first come across the reclusive singer, Miki's diet was mainly preservatives and chemically based foods. Not much had changed since then. If left to his own devices, Miki St. John was just as comfortable eating a broken-up packet of uncooked ramen noodles as an average person would a sandwich or microwave meal. But when faced with an actual meal, Miki savored every bite. He *enjoyed* food, his expression as delightful and sensual as when Kane was done kissing him breathless.

Kane couldn't think of a better way to spend a rain-speckled evening than watching Miki mouthfuck a piece of stew-soaked bread.

The night was perfect. Some might not have thought so. A light drizzle fell, soft enough to mist the air, but in the tight confines of the restaurant's alley, a patio umbrella kept them dry. New York shouted and grumbled beyond their brick corridor, a clash of voices and the infrequent blasts of car horns brazenly ignoring a decades-old honking law. Somewhere close by, an aspiring musician practiced their cello, dipping and scraping out long, solemn notes, while above them an open window poured out the sounds of a family dinner full of boisterous Italian and rolling laughter.

Amid all the chaos, their sliver of space held a certain magic. After setting up the patio umbrella and delivering their food, Lanh and his crew disappeared back into the building, leaving the heavy back door open but shutting the metal-mesh security door behind them. Spurts of noise filtered out. A rattle of dishes and pans being washed chimed and clattered above the hoarse chatter of the Vietnamese and Puerto Rican chefs as the kitchen continued its evening service.

A lone floodlight at the back door's frame was the only illumination they had besides the sputtering candles, a golden wash over the area not quite strong enough to shove back all the city's shadows. It was enough for Kane to see the amber flecks in Miki's eyes and the warmth in his lover's face when he looked up from his food to see Kane staring at him.

"Talk to me, Miki love." He slid the bread closer to the center of the table, closer to the stew bowl they were sharing.

"About what?" Miki looked up, cheeks chipmunk plump with bread. He swallowed. "Like how I'm glad you're here even though you're heading home tomorrow? That kind of shit? Because I am. And you are."

"I have a job." Kane chuckled at Miki's eye roll. "What? Do you expect me to live off of my rich rock-star boyfriend?"

"I've got a job too," he replied softly. "Signed up for this tour. I'm going to finish it."

"How are you doing with it?" Another eye roll and Kane added quickly, "Other than the riot and stabbing. Easy living with the guys in a van?"

"Rafe and Damien tell very bad jokes when they drive, and Forest plays meditation music, which I think he does to piss them off." Miki licked a dribble of stew from the side of his hand. "Everyone's got different ways of driving. Forest is pretty calm but too fucking slow. D drives like the city's going to run away if we don't get there quickly, and Rafe's not as bad, but he likes drumming along with the music. Makes it hard to think if I'm writing something."

"So you're not driving, then? Probably safer that way. Considering how much damage you've done to the house." That didn't surprise Kane. Miki's uneasy relationship with his car and the road wasn't isolated to the vintage GTO in their garage. There was something under Miki's words, an undercurrent of tension humming beneath the surface. "What's the matter, Mick? About the van."

For a moment Kane thought Miki was going to blow him off. It would have been classic Sinjun to puff out his cheeks and move on with a dismissive hiss, but this time Kane got a wary, assessing look. Then Miki shrugged.

"There was a deer. On the road. Before Boston." Miki's interest shifted from the stew and back to the plate of deep-fried eggrolls, splitting one apart to dribble sauce onto its pork-and-shrimp filling. "It wasn't really even *on* the road. Just on the side, and I kind of lost my shit."

"Lost your shit how?" Kane had to probe delicately. There were ways to scrape aside the deadness in Miki's emotions, abrading the distance he put between himself and events, but if done too quickly or harshly, Miki pulled back, burying himself back into his silence. "What happened?"

"Nothing happened. Not on the road." Miki popped the end of the eggroll into his mouth, then tapped at his temple. "In here, fucking *everything*."

Silence was Kane's best persuasive tactic. Silence and distraction. As he refilled Miki's glass from a pitcher filled with lemonade and soda water, he nodded, urging Miki to continue.

"Man, the deer wasn't even fucking near us. It was across the road, but I saw it. Right there, and his eyes gleamed. For a fucking second, I felt like I was staring down into that truck's headlights—the truck that hit us, you know? I didn't even know I fucking had that image in my head, but—*bam*—there it was, K, and all I could think was, oh shit, we're all going to fucking die again."

Kane skimmed his fingers over Miki's forearm. "What did you do? What did Damie do?"

"I screamed. Not even a manly one. Maybe. In my head I was screaming. Really fucking loudly, but I don't know." Another shrug, but this time Miki's eyes were troubled, his eyebrows pulled in tight on his forehead. "I must have made some kind of noise, because D asked me if I was okay. I just wanted to get off the damned road, you know? I just wanted to stop moving and get the hell out of the van."

"Did D stop the car?" Kane pushed away the rush of resentment and anger folding over him. Damien wasn't at fault. Not for the deer. Not for the van. Not even for the damned club and the asshole with the knife that may or may not have stabbed Miki. As hard as it was to swallow, Kane gulped down the bitter in his throat. "What happened?"

"I didn't want him to stop. I just wanted to get to where we were going, right?" Miki went back to the stew, deftly picking a piece of meat out from the thick russet broth with a pair of wooden chopsticks. "Hey, there's noodles under here. Fucking A. Usually you get bread or noodles. Not both."

"*Piscín*, focus on this for a bit, okay?"

"Don't call me that. I know what it means, dick. And I am focused. Kind of." His eyes never left the pho, but Miki's words twisted in, edged despite their soft tone. "It's just really fucking hard to look at it, you know?"

"Yeah, love, I know, but what else are you going to do? Keep it inside of you?" That earned Kane a look. It was weighted with complications and trauma he couldn't begin to imagine going through, but the roil of emotions were there in the subtle shifts on Miki's face and in his hooded hazel eyes. "You can't do that, Mick. It's not good for you."

"What the hell else am I going to do with it?" His mouth hardened into a line, and Miki looked away, a flush of anger in his cheeks. "It's so… it's like I'm being dragged raw over glass, but on the inside. I don't know what else to do. There's so much shit inside of my head sometimes. I can't shake it out. I want to, but it's like wet salt in a shaker. All clogged up and clumpy. I can't make sense of it."

"I can find you someone to talk to—"

"*No.*"

A drop of hot anger splashed between them, a fiery sauce muddying the taste of fizzy lemonade in Kane's mouth. Miki's lips twisted, then eased into a small smile.

"Sorry. I just… there were too many damned shrinks at the hospital. Before, you know? And they just kept poking and poking until I wanted to fucking scream. How did I feel? How the hell did they think I felt? My fucking world was torn open and stomped on, and they were feeding on me like maggots and I was a chunk of rotten meat. So no. I'm done with people to talk to. I just need some time to figure it all out."

The urge to touch Miki was strong. Every instinct told Kane to reach out and grab his hand or even his wrist, but Miki's needs were odd. Instead he inched his chair forward, then cupped Miki's face in his hand. Their legs touched, a brush of Miki's thigh on his as his lover moved closer. He placed one hand on Miki's knee, its tenderness lingering with a touch of heat and swell, but Miki didn't flinch when Kane rubbed at the joint.

"You're all I need, K," Miki whispered, icing over the annoyance he'd thrown between them. "You. Damie. The band. Fuck, even your goddamned family and the dog. I don't want anyone else inside of my head but you guys. I can't take it. It's all pressing in on me and shoving me out at the same time. Maybe… later? I don't know. The fucking goddamned deer scared

the shit out of me—more than that thing at the show—
and I don't know how to deal with that. It scared me
so deep inside I felt like my bones were throwing up."

"If something happens again, you've got to call
me, babe." Kane pressed against Miki's cheek, leading
Miki's gaze back to him. "Promise me, Mick. Even if
you feel stupid or silly afterwards. Just because I'm
not right next to you doesn't mean I'm not with you."

"Yeah, I know," Miki replied. His breath slithered
warmth over Kane's palm. "But since I only have you
for one more night, do you think I can get you *in* me
as well as *with* me?"

THE FIRST time they made love, Miki'd known
in his marrow Kane would be gone in the morning.

After the many mornings since he'd taken Kane
into him, he'd learned Kane would never be an empty,
cold spot in his bed. Even on the days when murder
dragged his lover out into the cold, foggy San Francisco night, Miki *knew* Kane lay next to him.

All Miki had to do to find him was to look in his
heart, and Kane melted Miki's icy fears away.

Still, there was nothing like having the heft of his
muscular lover under his fingertips, in his hands, and
filling Miki's mouth.

Their clothes were somewhere in the suite. Hell,
Miki wasn't even sure if anyone'd been in the living space when he and Kane stumbled in and began
tearing off what they'd worn out. He remembered his
jeans being tugged off—Kane was careful there, easing the denim over his tender knee—but the rest of it
could have been turned into unicorn poop for all he
knew.

He didn't care. Miki didn't give a shit about anyone seeing him wrap his legs around Kane's waist
before his cop carried him to the bed or even when
he'd shoved his hand down Kane's pants to cup at his
heavy, furred balls. He only knew he needed to sear
the heat of Kane's skin into his, because after tonight
Kane would be too far away to hold Miki when the
nightmares rolled over him and stole the sleep out
from under him.

"Think I can get you to come fuck me every other
week? Rack up some airline miles? I could even meet
you halfway, and we can do it in an airport bathroom
or something."

It was a silly thing to say, but it made Kane
chuckle. Miki liked hearing Kane laugh. He loved being able to make his blue-eyed Irish cop rumble out an
emerald-tinted laugh, then mutter something naughty
under his breath to make Miki blush.

"Let's worry about the here and now, *a ghra*."
Kane bit at a tender spot on Miki's neck. "I want to
make you limp tomorrow, and not just because of that
knee of yours."

The bed was soft, sucking Miki down an inch or
two when Kane laid him carefully on it. Kane's already undone belt slithered out of its loops when Kane
tugged on the buckle, then tossed it to the carpet. His
jeans and underwear were next, shucked off Kane's
hip bones and down his powerful thighs. About to
climb onto the bed, Kane stopped when Miki shook
his head.

"Just… let me look at you for a second, K. I just
want to *look* at you."

He was used to the begging note in his voice when he was in bed with Kane. The man did horrible, tender things to Miki's independence whenever he was around, but it wasn't anything Miki minded. Not now. Not when he could open himself up and know Kane could delve in as deep as he wanted without tearing Miki apart.

Miki was so very tired of being torn apart.

Kane's ink-black hair was longer than when they'd first met. Not by much, but enough for Miki to get a handful of whenever Kane sucked him down. There were scars from an adventurous childhood and a dangerous profession, but the little nicks and mottles embellished Kane's powerful beauty. He was bulky, not as broad as his older brother Connor who'd decided wearing a badge meant kicking down doors and going in with heavy artillery, but Kane still was *massive* compared to Miki. Thickly muscled and taut, Kane's body gleamed from the light duskiness he'd gotten from the weekends he and his brothers spent reshingling Connor's roof and replacing broken windows.

God, Kane Morgan was a fucking fantasy to look at. His cock was already tight and primed, lifted up from its nest of ebony curls and ready. Kane's legs were lightly dusted with hair, and a trickle of fine black down led from his navel to his groin. He was pale where he'd worn shorts, a lighter stripe of skin across his hips, and Miki ached to lick at the thin spray of freckles running along Kane's ribs and down into the fair stretch untouched by the sun.

"I thought I fed you enough dinner, babe," Kane murmured as he mounted the bed. "You look like you haven't eaten in weeks."

"Couple." He grinned at Kane when his lover pushed him down into the linens. "I got hungry for you as soon as I left SF. Glad you deliver. But your takeout guy is slower than the Chinese food place down the street."

"Funny. Very funny."

The bed shifted under Kane's weight, and Miki tensed when his knee sent a warning tingle down his calf muscles. He must have winced or made a sound because Kane stopped just short of kissing him and frowned.

"We don't have to—"

"Finish that sentence and I'll rip your dick off so I can fuck it myself." It was a good threat, because Kane blanched. His own dick was hurting him, nearly tight enough to split his skin. Its head was already damp and aching, and Miki didn't want Kane to stop. "Trust me, okay?"

"If it hurts too much—"

"Then I'm going to pretend I signed us up for a tantric sex yoga class and push through the burn," Miki promised. "Don't… stop, Kane. Not now. Not tonight."

He'd flayed himself open at dinner, scraping apart the scabs he'd hidden inside him since that night on the road. The past week pushed down on him, and Miki wasn't sure if he could go another night without release. Everything was bound too tightly around him… the band, the hospital, even Brigid flying in like an Irish Valkyrie to slay any invisible demons Kane might have missed. It was too much for his soul to absorb, and it—all of it—needed to go away, burned off by the fires he and Kane stoked between them.

Then Kane to comfort him afterward and tell him it would all be okay.

Miki *needed* it to all be okay.

"Lay on your stomach, love?" Kane whispered into Miki's ear. "It's easier on you? Than on your back?"

"No, I'm good. This is good," Miki whispered back, touching his nose to Kane's. "We'll just not do downward dog, knotted pretzel, or whatever that's called."

"I'll have to go look that up." Kane's fingers ghosted over the ridge of Miki's cockhead. "Right now, we'll stick to the basics."

The basics included a dribble of lube on Miki's balls, then Kane working the slick past the rim of his hole. He dug his fingers into the duvet, fisting the soft cotton sheets while Kane spread him open. Miki mewled, craving the taste of Kane's cock on his tongue, but Kane refused to turn around.

"You're killing me, asshole," Miki groaned. "I just want to—"

Miki lost his mind. Whatever was boiling up in his brain dissipated into the hot turmoil Kane pulled out of his brain when his lover wrapped his lips around Miki's cock and Kane's lube-coated fingers slid into Miki's body.

His knee was forgotten. The world was forgotten. The pressures building up inside Miki were shoved aside to make room for the incredible want he had for Kane. His skin itched, need crawling along each of his nerves, tingling the skin between his thighs and down his fingers. There wasn't an inch of Kane's body Miki didn't want to touch or bite. Maybe both. Probably both, and he blindly sank his teeth into whatever part of Kane he could reach.

"Teeth, boyo." Kane's Irish ran thick and hot, a teasing lilt in his laugh. "I'm going to have to use that shoulder."

"Why does it take so goddamn long for you to fuck me?" He didn't expect an answer. Miki never thought Kane really heard him when he grumbled, but Kane's teasing continued.

The man's fingers were long and rough, burled from handling guns and wood. Kane brought the world in with him whenever he came home, a chaotic mess of sound and scrambled lives, and Miki felt every moment of Kane's life in his hands. As gentle as Kane's touch was, there was no denying the *man* in his flesh and bones. Every tender caress scraped a bit, peeling back another flake of Miki's tearing defenses until he could no longer keep Kane's expansive self out.

Not that he ever really wanted to. Not if he were being honest.

If anything, Miki wanted more. He wanted to smile out in the sunlight and hold hands with his lover. Miki wanted not to care about the shadows moving in the spaces where his mind had tucked away his horrors. He longed to wake up one Sunday morning and not be reluctant to sit at a table of boisterous Morgans a few hours later.

Most of all, he wanted to be able to climb into a car and not steel himself for Death's touch.

If there was anything he was tired of, it was Death stalking him.

"You make me forget all that," Miki whispered into the crook of Kane's neck. "You make all that go away."

Kane suckled again, and Miki flew, breaking apart in Kane's mouth. Those long, skilled fingers were easing in and out of him, working into a slippery glide and brushing along the edge of Miki's control. He wouldn't last long, not if Kane didn't stop, and Miki pushed at his lover's shoulder, sliding slightly away from Kane's questing hand and mouth.

"Gonna lose it, babe," he whispered. "Too... much. Not enough. Fuck... something. Me, maybe?"

"Plan on it," Kane promised. "You let me know if I'm hurting—"

"Swear to God, gonna kill you. Hard." Miki held Kane's gaze for a moment, then relented. "Fine."

His leg ached a little when Kane moved in, but the stretch of his muscles was a good pain. His back arched, and Miki felt himself open up for Kane's cock when he rested his calves on Kane's hips. Hooking a hand behind Kane's head, Miki pulled him down for a kiss, needing another taste of Kane's mouth.

Kane's lips were like his fingers, both gentle and rough, caressing the tender skin of Miki's mouth, then biting at the plump flesh to bruise it. Kane's hand was on his cock, milking him while his tongue gently fucked Miki's mouth. The scent of the lube and their mingling sweat licked at Miki's senses, and his balls churned between his legs, begging for release.

"You like that, babe?"

Kane squeezed again, running his thumbnail over Miki's damp slit. His cockhead throbbed in Kane's hand, beating a soft whisper on his palm.

"Can you hold it in until I'm inside of you?"

Miki wasn't even sure if he could hold his breath much less his control, but he nodded anyway.

Any amount of pain was worth the pleasure of Kane's cock pressing against him. The anticipation of his body clenching, tight and needy despite the pressure of his muscles closing in. Miki's body hummed with the waiting, a low hiss crawling out of his lungs when he felt the first push against his tender ring. His hole was slick, and Kane's cockhead slid up over his taint before Kane guided himself back and dipped in.

The burn was incredible, a mingle of prickly heat and expectation. Kane's ridged head was a thick knob of velvet pulling him apart, and Miki had to remember to breathe while his lover worked himself in deeper. The stretch—God, the stretch—of his body around Kane's length made Miki pant, and then the wait for all of Kane began, a long, agonizing gasp of time that never seemed to end.

Miki never *ever* wanted it to end.

"You okay, Miki love?" Kane bent forward, his weight carefully balanced on his hands and knees, but the length of his body covered Miki, his lean hips spreading Miki's legs apart until he was as open and vulnerable as he ever was going to be.

If it were any other man, Miki would have clawed his way free. This was *Kane. His* Kane. *His* cop. The man who saw into his soul and stroked at the broken bits of him to coax him out of the dark and into the sunlight. For as much as the brightness burned at times, Kane cradled the pieces of Miki's soul, held them up to the light, and taught Miki how to love.

"Don't leave me," Miki whispered, finding his voice in the rampaging folds of emotions crashing over him. Carding his fingers through Kane's thick hair, he tugged at the ends. "It fucking scares me—loving you. Don't *ever* fucking leave me."

Because everyone had. Everyone did.

His tears were hot, as searing as Kane's cock inside him, but Miki choked them back. Kane's mouth found his, laving away the tightness on his lips, and then Kane stilled—so very still—and simply held him.

"I'd die for you, Mick," Kane whispered in the shadows caught between their mouths. "Just like you live for me."

Then Kane began to move, and Miki shattered apart once again.

There was a music to their bodies, a guttural, primal beat born anew every time they joined. Awash in the pleasure of Kane inside him, Miki fell into the sounds of their bodies. It was different every time and once heard lost out into the universe, carried off in the rippling waves of sound to be buried in stardust. This song was slow, a creep of the city edging in from the partially open windows, but mostly it was the rhythmic thump of their bodies rising up and meeting, a wet, hard slap of skin on skin. Their grunts and whispers formed layered lyrics to their joining, nonsensical but vital, the sense of their needs puncturing the deep bass of their sex with a breathy harmony.

In the moment Kane drew himself out, Miki went with him, pulling out of himself and then back in, following each stroke of Kane's cock into his warmth.

The searing burn of his flesh being spread apart was soon replaced by the flush of tingling excitement of his body reaching for its release. Miki's balls were primed, his cock slapping its wet head against their stomachs, trapped between them as Kane's hips rocked up into Miki's ass.

His own hips ached a bit, his ass spread apart and pounded hard, giving when Kane held his ass up and thrust in deep. The tickle of Kane's hair on his ass and belly was a satin slide across Miki's skin, and he reached for his lover's shoulders, urging Kane on.

A snap of Kane's hips, and Miki was near the edge, staring down into the abyss of pleasure he'd needed since the moment Kane darkened his door, demanding a piece of damned wood. He squeezed down on Kane's cock, grinning when Kane swore in a filthy Gaelic torrent at the pressure.

"Keep doing that, and I'm going to lose myself," he mumbled through his grunts. "You're driving me mad there, Mick. Not going to last—"

Bearing down again, Miki felt the rush of Kane's cock surrendering to his warmth. Then the delicious hot fill of his body followed. The slamming grew more intense, Kane's fingers closing in on Miki's shaft and milking it, sliding up to cover his too tender head until Miki's toes curled from the overwhelming bitter-rawness. His own sac boiled over, his control crumbling when Kane's spurting length spasmed in the tightness of his ass.

Miki came, letting go of everything to drift in the cup of Kane's embrace. Sticky and fluid, his orgasm ran over their skin, filling in the crevices where they didn't quite meet and seeping into the seams where they did. Kane continued rocking, holding Miki tight while he shuddered around Kane's cock. They slowed together, letting the sounds die between them, leaving only their gasps as they struggled to catch their breath.

"I can feel your heartbeat," Miki whispered. The thump in Kane's chest was a rapid push against his, nearly in time with Miki's frenetic rhythm.

"Yeah, that's all you, love." Kane chuckled. He shifted, easing out of Miki's body. Ignoring Miki's displeased hiss, Kane moved onto the bed, resting on his side, then pulling Miki in close. "Quit grumbling and let me hold you."

"We're going to get stuck like this," he reminded his lover. "Every time we cuddle, we fall asleep, and it's like pulling tape off."

"I don't mind."

A kiss on Miki's ear, and he was mollified.

"So long as you're the one I'm waking up to. Love you, Mick. Don't ever forget that."

"I won't." Sleep crept up on him, slinking around the languor of his worn-out body. The pinprick ache in his knee was back, but Miki was too tired to scrape up a pill to ward off any swelling. Besides, the last thing he wanted to do was leave Kane's embrace. "I love you too, you know. Just… no matter what… no matter how fucked-up I get, don't forget *that*."

"Through thick and thin," Kane promised softly, then brushed a kiss on Miki's throat. "You're mine, Mick, as much as I'm yours. For better or for worse."

"And Death shall never part us," Miki finished softly, then let sleep slip over him, taking Kane's kiss with him into his dreams.

EIGHT

Mouthful of whiskey
Sweat running down my back
Strings under my fingers
Amp cord hanging down slack
We gather here together
On stage for one more day
Stomp your feet and sing along
Rock and Blues are here to stay
—Roadshow Blues

"STRAWBERRY PLAINS?" Forest turned the town's name over in his head. "Are you sure we didn't miss it?"

"Yeah, it's where the 34 and the 25W meet. An old restaurant. Davis said they've got the place cleaned up and wired for us," Damien replied from the passenger's seat. "Should be about another two miles. On the left. Or was it right? Shit. I've got to see what the map says."

"Isn't there a petting zoo or something down here? With zebras?" Miki'd been silent all through Tennessee, and Forest stopped himself from glancing back to see what their singer was doing behind him.

"Yeah, I think so," Damien said over his shoulder. "Remember that camel? The one who ate Johnny's hat?"

"That was an ugly fucking hat," Miki replied. "Surprised that camel's mouth didn't burn from how bright orange that thing was. Then we had to make sure it all came out before we could leave. Good fucking times. Let's skip the zebras."

Driving the van was like herding an elephant through pudding. It was responsive enough but lumbering, often sucking up a tank of gas before any of them could blink. They'd run out twice so far, going back across the states, zigzagging in and out of borders in a dizzying weave of gigs and bad diner food. He couldn't tell exactly when they'd crossed into Tennessee, but the hills turned blue and misty, and the land ran ripe and green. There was water everywhere, and the wind smelled musty, heavy with pine and maple. The van's dusty exterior blended into the infrequent traffic along the slender motorway, another burdened-down metal speck in a never-ending, stretched-out caravan.

From what Forest could see, Strawberry Plains was a scattered collection of old houses and quarries tucked into whatever cracks and crevices the land would give up. Just outside of Knoxville, it was a blink-and-miss-it kind of town, but people seemed friendly enough, or at least the two elderly women who waved at him when they blasted by in their weathered turquoise Cadillac convertible. A bright spot of leopard print, magenta, and teased bouffant hair, they'd made Forest grin even when Damien grumbled at him for slowing down to let them pass.

"There!" Damien pointed at a dilapidated shambles of a building to the left of a merge in the road. "That's Davis's Pinto. Try not to hit it when you pull in. Smack that thing wrong and we'll all go up in a fireball."

"Who's got a Pinto?" Rafe mumbled from the back. He yawned loudly enough to make Forest's jaw ache, and Miki yelped at something. "Shit, sorry. Didn't mean to spit."

"Like a damned cobra, man," Miki replied. "D, can we not talk about blowing up Davis's Pinto?"

"Can we not talk? At least until I—" The sleepy motorway was suddenly a hotbed of activity. An old food truck grumbled up on Forest's right side, speeding up and edging in as he was trying to move into the left lane. A long-bearded young man on a backfiring dirt bike took up the lane Forest needed to get in to, and as his bandmates continued to bicker about gleeking and zebras, he slowed down to maneuver the van over.

The blaring bass horn of the food truck was something to be ignored, as was the middle finger the kid shot him as he jerkily gunned past the van. Damien barked something back at the kid, and Rafe joined in, rattling off something in Spanish, then Portuguese. The food truck swerved, its top-heavy bulk swaying dangerously to one side, and the smell of burning tire rubber filled the air. Caught in the middle of the tussle, Forest took a deep breath and tried to recall why he chose to leave his studio and Connor behind and submit himself to the abuse he got for his driving.

"Will all of you please… *shut… up*?" Raising his voice to be heard over the rhubarb, Forest kept his eyes on the road. "I'm trying to drive."

The van went silent.

The bike was easy enough to avoid, but the food truck was determined to shove in before the way was clear. Easing into the space, Forest left his turn signal on, then made the left, leaving the food truck and dirt bike to duke it out on their way to Knoxville. Dust kicked up from the restaurant's overgrown lot, weeds and dried mud puddles overwhelming the cracked parking space lines painted on the asphalt. Forest brought the van to a slow stop in front of the single-story building's entrance, waited until the front tires kissed a cement block at the end of a space, then turned the engine off.

"Just so you know, I didn't say a damned thing back there." Miki opened the van's long door. The singer jumped out, leaving the door open for Rafe. "If I'm not driving, then I don't got room to talk."

"Sorry for including you in with their shit, then." Forest met Miki's grin with one of his own. "I'll buy you a cup of coffee. Just not here."

"God no, this place is shit," Miki shot back. "Looks like somewhere rats wouldn't live."

Forest *liked* the irascible singer. With a long-standing reputation for being aloof and moody, Miki'd seemed like the wild card in the band in the beginning, but a few hours in the singer's company, and Forest felt like he'd known the man for years. They shared a lot of silences, long stretches of pure music, and quiet conversations about the stupid things churning over in their minds. He'd found a brother of sorts in Miki, a street-tough, tenderhearted musician who bristled when threatened and was deadly when attacked. There was a strength to the singer Forest admired and a deeply ingrained sad-anger he wished he could help ease.

It was always nice to make Miki laugh. Damien and Rafe were easy. They were like a pair of hyenas cackling and circling their prey. A few snaps from Miki, and they'd leave the singer alone, only to tease and nip at Forest. It wasn't mean—Forest *knew* mean—but there were times when he'd have paid good money to take the pair's volume off eleven and down to zero.

Now was definitely one of those times.

"Just the asshole twins, then?" Miki dodged Rafe's playful swipe at his shoulder. "Truth hurts, Andrade."

"I wasn't telling him how to drive," Damien defended himself, dragging a duffel bag out of the back. "I was—"

"Telling me how to drive," Forest teased lightly.

"How about if we find this Davis guy before a bus goes by and you guys toss me under it?" Rafe hooked an arm around Forest's waist, pulling him into a lopsided hug. "And then we can talk about how shitty you drive, Fore."

"HELLO?" DAMIEN called out into the dank-smelling, shadowy building. "Anyone here?"

After almost slamming into Damien, Miki shoved his brother out of the doorway. "Great, first fucking thing you do in a horror movie, call out to the crazy guy with the chainsaw. Damn, this is a dump. I think we've said that about most places you've taken us, D."

"It's pretty bad," Forest agreed. He kept his breaths low because of the dust they were kicking up as they walked, but nothing seemed to help. A foot in, and he was coughing up mud.

Forest'd lived in dumps. Years spent on the street and in dive motels, he'd always thought he'd seen possibly the worst a place could possibly get, especially after cleaning out the Sound's upper storeroom so he'd have a place to live. God only knew who'd used that space and what they'd been doing over the decades, but whatever happened, Forest never quite got the musky reek out of the walls.

This place went *beyond* reek.

From the outside, it was a run-down ex-pancake house dressed in broken wooden lattice and scrub bushes. A large yellowed red-and-white plastic sign with a pig in a chef's hat was stuck at an odd angle, canted in midturn from either loss of power or its motor giving out. Forest hadn't been able to make out the name of the place. The elements had wiped away most of the building's identity, and time took care of the rest. They'd walked past an open patio roofed with rusted tin slats, but the building itself was cinder block, impervious to the weather. The drywall inside, however, was a different story.

The remains of a few old laminate-covered dining tables were piled up in the far corner, as far away from the door as possible. There was a kitchen—or at

least Forest assumed it was a kitchen—behind a wall
with a pass-through at the back of the building's deep
expanse, and the double doors leading to the patio area
were boarded up with plywood covered in misspelled
graffiti. In the wall next to the kitchen's pass-through,
a set of doors marked Boar and Sow hung unevenly
on broken hinges, and a pay phone's mangled carcass
dangling from a few bolts took up the wall space between them.

Forest only hoped the stench came from the kitch-
en and not the toilets, but he wasn't going to bet on it.

"We're playing here… when?" Forest picked
through the trash on the floor, avoiding a black stain
on the gray industrial carpet. It looked suspiciously
like a body outline, but the shape could have been a
trick of the light coming through the dirty windows.

"Dude, this place is…." Rafe inhaled sharply,
then gagged. "Fuck, what the hell is that *smell*?"

"Bitterness. And failure," Miki chimed in. "*That's*
what failure smells like."

Damie tugged at Miki's jeans, pulling him back a
step. "Nice. Now all of you shut up. Davis's got plans.
And we don't go on stage for three days. It'll be—"

He never got to finish his sentence. Instead the
tallest, skinniest man Forest'd ever seen shuffled out
of the Boar's door. A corona of Play-Doh-yellow hair
formed nearly a perfect sphere around his long face,
his hangdog expression not helped by a bulging pair
of watery blue eyes. The delight on his face when he
spotted the band was obvious, but his smile pushed
into his jowly cheeks instead of lifting them, and when
he raised his arm, his bony elbow caught the knob of
the door. Instead of swinging farther, the door gave

up any pretense of its lot in life and flung itself to the floor in a loud clatter. Surprised, the lanky man jerked to the side, tripped on his partially unbuttoned jeans' legs, then face-planted on the carpet next to the door.

Forest winced at the decidedly wet, squishy sound the man's body made when it struck the floor.

"Davis?" Rafe cocked his head at Miki.

The singer nodded and sighed. "Yep. That's Davis."

"Nice," Rafe muttered and patted Damien on the shoulder. "I'll be in the van."

"Hey, wait… hold up," Davis drawled as he got up off the floor. His pink camo shirt was damp from his chest down, and he brushed at it mournfully while he walked over to the band. "I swear, we'll have this place looking spic-and-span by the time the doors open. Just got the keys today, and people are buzzing to come by and get it cleaned up. You're going to be our first show."

"You don't even have a stage, Davis," Miki pointed out. "Or a sound system or a… bar."

"Oh, no bar. No liquor license yet, but we'll be slinging some nice ice-cold Cokes and teas."

Davis went to hug Damien, but the guitarist held him back.

"Oh right, yeah, the shirt. How're you doing, man?"

"Good." Damie reached in for a shoulder bump, then grinned over at Miki. "Come on. Have you ever known Davis to let us down?"

"I don't know." Miki's eyebrow went up, a mocking curve over his forehead. "Other than that time when he fed our back tire to an alligator? Or when he booked us into a hotel that'd burned down?"

"Could happen to anyone," Davis protested in a spluttering mumble. "Hotels burn down sometimes."

"It'd burned down in 1968, Davis," he replied. "None of us were even born yet."

"Come on. It'll be great." Damien stepped in. "Besides, there's help, and not like we don't know how to wire up a sound system. Forest here owns a goddamned studio, for Christ's sake."

The Sound had its share of problems, and Damien was right. If it wasn't one thing with the boards, then it was another with the wiring. The interior walls were drywall, but he wasn't going to guess what fuckery lay behind it. For all he knew, there were hidden junction boxes and squirrels' nests on every stud, but Davis's eyes were hopeful when Forest glanced over, and he resigned himself to the job.

"If… and I mean *if*… you get a licensed electrician in here to look at the wiring, I'll help put the system in." Davis made a quick move over to hug him, and Forest hastily stepped back. "No hugging. Not until… well, you've got to change your shirt. And maybe burn it. I think you landed in what the smell is."

"Still doesn't take care of a stage," Rafe reminded them. "This 'my-uncle's-got-a-barn' kind of shit isn't exactly going to happen with a click of our sparkling red heels."

A shadowy figure filled the kitchen's doorframe, not nearly as tall as Davis but close enough to make the man carefully watch the trim when he stepped out into the dusty space. He was thick across the chest and thighs, his jeans nearly as old as the carpet and torn at the knees, and his SFPD short-sleeved T-shirt was pitted with small holes. Cobwebs clung to the ruff of his short black hair. A long tendril of dusty silk stuck to his neck and dangled down to his upper arm, curling over the sunset-flamed phoenix inked there. The bird clenched a banner in its claws, *Oro enpaz, Fierro enguerra* written in black on the parchment scroll spread across its belly and tail feathers.

The tattoo on the man's muscular forearm was as familiar to Forest as his own face.

If Davis's delight at seeing the band brightened his homely face, Forest was damned certain he lit up like a star when the blue-eyed Irish cop headed his way. Especially when that cop unhooked the tool belt strapped to his lean hips and let it drop to the floor so he could pull Forest into a tight, smothering embrace.

Forest didn't need to talk. He didn't need to breathe. While the band was becoming his life, the man holding him was his world. Burying his face in the man's neck, Forest whispered with the last bit of air he had left in his lungs, "God… *Connor.*"

"OUR CHOICES are pizza, pizza, and then there's…." Connor made a show of checking the sheet of paper they'd been handed at the check-in desk. "Oh wait, there's pizza. How could I have missed that?"

"I'm good so long as there's mushrooms, cheese, and no fish." The towels in the bathroom were thin, barely enough of a pile to soak up the water on his body, and Forest chuckled to himself, remembering a time when bathing was a luxury and he'd scrubbed himself dry with sheets ripped off a brown paper roll he'd stolen from a taco stand. "Hot water's kind of sketchy, but the pressure's good. The door's got to stay open or the steam gets too thick to see."

Their plans to share a shower were quickly dashed when the shower turned out to be barely larger than a coffin. The motel room wasn't much bigger, and the king-sized bed took up most of it. He'd unpacked their clothes while Connor showered, trying not to laugh when he heard a thump and a string of Gaelic. What little he knew included most of the words filtering out of the bathroom.

"I ordered pepperoni and—" Any thought of pizza slipped Forest's mind when Connor came out of the bathroom, a curtain of steam paisleys trailing behind him.

The white towel was nearly translucent and hung low on Con's hips, his heavy cock clearly outlined under the fabric. Water dewed on his chest, drops clinging to the fine hair scattered across his sternum and nipples. Then Connor smiled, a slow, sexy promise, and Forest forgot how to breathe.

"Hey, you." Connor caught Forest's wrist and drew him close. Kneading Forest's ass, Connor laughed when Forest leaned in and inhaled deeply. "And what do you think you're doing there, love?"

"I love the way my soap smells on you." He licked at a drop poised on Connor's collarbone. The water tasted of male and peppermint, and Forest swallowed, taking a bit of Connor into him. Biting at Con's lower lip, Forest left his lover with small bruising kisses. "Can we forget the pizza? You're all I want to eat."

"When was the last time you had food?" Connor scowled playfully. "Real food. Not microwaved hot dogs and a Mountain Dew you got from a gas station. God, I'm pretty sure this is the kind of conversation Kane has with Miki."

"Does pizza count as real food? Because that's what I ordered."

"More than the hot dog," Con replied. "But not as good as a steak."

Forest shook his head. "Steak's out. Unless someone delivers it. I think I fell asleep in the shower."

His lungs and bones were tired. They'd tackled much of the former restaurant's filth, working around a pot-bellied electrician who'd proved to be a master at wiring. Forest wasn't certain he'd gotten all the bleach smell out of his skin, but it was a damned sight better than the wretched stink Davis carried with him after his fight with the carpet.

"Yeah, I think I'd rather go through a door than swap out another damned toilet." He made a face. "Let me get some sweats on. This towel is going to slide right off my arse, and I'm freezing my balls off."

"You're going to have to let me go," Forest reminded him. "Unless you want to do this like the potato sack race at your parents' house."

"God no. I was scared I broke you."

Connor let him go, then edged around the bed. Forest got a quick glimpse of Connor's firm ass before it disappeared under a pair of gray sweats.

"What time did the pizza guys give?"

"Anywhere from forty-five minutes to an hour." He checked the clock on the nightstand. "And that was about five minutes ago. I ordered one double pepperoni and one sausage and mushrooms."

"No pepperoni and pineapple?"

"Mock me all you want. You *know* that's some good shit." Forest climbed onto the bed to sit against the headboard. "And no, they didn't have any pineapple. Who doesn't have pineapple at their pizza place?"

"Sane people, that's who." Connor nudged Forest over, then stretched out onto the bed next to him. The tufted headboard wiggled in its moorings behind them, and Connor shifted, easing some of his weight off it. "Okay, so who's next door? Damie and Miki?"

"Yeah, Rafe's got a solo. Why?"

"Because we're going to have to move the bed away from the wall. The headboard hits pretty hard when we're just sitting against the damned thing. I'll not be hearing crap from those two if they hear knocking. You know how they are."

"Not as bad as Rafe and Damien. Miki's pretty quiet." He leaned forward to let Con drape his arm behind him. Tucked up against Connor's side, Forest let the tightness leave his body. "I'm so fucking glad you're here."

"Damien asked if there was a way to get a contractor to fix up that club quickly. I told him he'd have to find someone who can crack a whip." Connor's dimples winked when he grinned. "So I offered to hold the whip if he could get all of you to Tennessee ahead of time. I have a lot of leave I need to burn off. Can't think of a better way to use it than seeing you."

"Good," he sighed. "And honestly, that club's a shit hole."

"Bones are good. Plumbing is decent, and the electrical is okay. Just needs some good scrubbing and, well, a band to open the place up. It'll be nice to see you on stage without the family all around me. Hard to scream your name like a little girl seeing a pony around my kin. They'd never let me live it down."

"It's kind of surreal, you know? Being up on stage with them. I keep waiting for someone to tell me they made a mistake. Like I'm not… I don't know… like it's all just a joke or something."

"Your name went on a dotted line, love." Connor's lips brushed Forest's temple. "You're a quarter owner of a band called Crossroads Gin. It's no joke. You're a good drummer, and you fit in with them. Odd as it is, because I'd not have said it would have worked if I hadn't seen the four of you together. Besides, you and Miki are close, yes?"

"Yeah, I think so. Hard to tell with him sometimes."

"How's the knee? Kane about lost his mind over Boston. Da's still talking him down."

"Good, I think. It's hard to tell about that too." He turned, resting his head on Connor's shoulder. "Miki doesn't talk about being in pain. You've got to watch him, because he doesn't say anything. I used to think it was pride, but…."

"Fear, I think. Like a hurt wild animal. If predators know they're hurt, they become targets." Connor's deep voice slowed, saddening. "It's because of how he was raised. Well, of the men who had him. He's not who'd I'd have wanted for Kane, but now I can't think of anyone else I'd see Kane with. My brother is stupid in love with his Miki. Kind of like how I am stupid in love with you."

Connor's lips were gentle, a lingering caress of his mouth on Forest's lips, then the dip of his tongue on the slight nick on Forest's front tooth. It was casual, simmering with a little heat, but most of all it was comfortable, soft and sweet, a bit of San Francisco held in Connor's mouth and passed on to hold Forest until he came back home.

"That's good," Forest said when he could finally breathe. "Because I'd hate for it to be just me stupid in love. Between the two of us, we probably have enough common sense left."

"Oh shit. Speaking of two of us," Connor grumbled, digging into his pocket. "I'd meant to give you this. I got the rings from the jeweler. And I know we talked about tungsten or platinum, but… the more I thought about it, I found something out about us. We're kind of old-fashioned—you and I—so I went with, well… the kind my grandfather bought for my da when my mother finally wore him down."

"You're mean to your mother. She's adorable."

"She's about as adorable as a Tasmanian devil, but she loves you. Nearly as much as I love you, but close. She's glad to call you son. Ah, here we go." Connor pulled his hand out of his pocket. "Because I'd like it if we were…. God, you take my words from me. Here, Forest love. I hope you like them."

Forest couldn't breathe. His lungs were refusing to work, and damned if he was going to cry, but Forest felt the threat of tears in his eyes. The small black velvet box Connor handed him felt so heavy—*so real*—he couldn't find the words to say. *Thank you* seemed hilarious, especially considering it was the first thing to pop into his head, but eventually he settled on simply smiling until his face hurt from its grin.

The rings were wide with a slight barrel and brushed gold. They looked old, heritage pieces to be passed down from one couple to the next, and Forest felt his heart dip down deeper in love with the man next to him. Solid and sturdy, the rings grabbed at the light and held it as tightly as Connor hugged him in the morning before they went about their day.

"They're perfect, Con." He picked up the larger one, then shifted on the bed, sitting cross-legged at Connor's side. "Your mom's going to kill us. Are we really not going to tell her?"

"How do you want to be telling my mother that her firstborn got married in Vegas? Without her there? You're the one that thought of this. I'm agreeing it's a good thing to do."

Connor slid the smaller ring onto Forest's right hand. It was heavy and solid, and the metal warmed up quickly against Forest's skin.

"Besides, you said yourself, we're not really married until there's a priest and the family. We'll be doing that when you get back from being a rock star. Until then, it's on our right hands, love."

"It seemed like a really good idea then. Just no more whiskey crawls. God knows what other shit we'd end up doing." He couldn't stop grinning. Fitting Con's ring over his finger, Forest pushed past a knuckle and slid it down, nesting it against Connor's palm. "There you go. We are now officially… what are we calling this?"

"Hand-fasted," Connor replied softly. "Best I could come up with. I see your point of not saying we're… legal… but I don't like it. I'd rather the world know you're mine. At least in case something happens, you'll—"

"Don't fucking borrow trouble. No jinxing shit," he warned. "They're great. Perfect. I love you."

"I love you too, *a ghra*," Connor murmured. "Always."

"I'm sorry we won't be marrying in the church." He'd wrestled with his dislike for the Morgans' church. Religion had never been a presence in his life, but for the Morgans, their faith was fierce and a foundation for their family. "I know… it's important to you. It sucks. I feel like—"

"We're not going to mourn it. One day, maybe, but I'll rather have the man I love in my life, and the church and its men will have to deal with that. God and I are fine. I have no quarrel with him. The vows say, 'What therefore God has joined together, let not man put asunder.'" Connor twisted his ring around his finger. "He brought me you, and if other men cannot see that and treasure it, then the sorrow is theirs, not mine. The rings. You and I. That's all that matters, Forest."

"Yeah. And so we're old-fashioned. I'm good with that." He squeezed Connor's hand. "No minivans. Or bake sales. Or whatever the hell else housewives used to do. Fuck, I'm going to have flashbacks about driving the band's piece of shit for the rest of my life. It's like maneuvering a blind sea lion through an obstacle course."

"I don't know. You could make a mean cupcake, eventually."

"I microwave bacon and you wince. You're going to trust me with a cupcake?"

"No one's perfect, love. But you're an easy cross to bear." Connor glanced at the clock. "What time did you say the pizza's going to be here?"

"They were loose with the exact time, but we've got about half an hour. Why?"

"How about if you'll be helping me pull the bed away from the wall?" Con whispered into Forest's ear. "So I can show you how much I am going to love you for the rest of our lives."

NINE

*Q, you know you're the best thing I've
        got in my life, right?*
*I was always here, Rafe... okay, not al-
        ways, because you're older than
        me, so there were a couple of years
        when I didn't exist. And if you want
        to be technical, you didn't meet me
        until you were—*
*Babe, just come here so I can kiss you.
        Doesn't matter when you came into
        my life. Now is all that matters.*
—Bathroom conversation after a show

TENNESSEE WAS a blurry memory after another two weeks and four more shows. They'd eaten at
nearly every dive diner along the way, and everyone
except Miki sported some kind of scruff on their faces,

a morning shave being a luxury as they dragged themselves from gig to gig. Showers were mostly cold, and the beds were hard. Coffee ran from weak to bitter, all of it soured and ripe with acid, but every gas station packed enough cold drinks and Cheetos to keep them fueled until the next motel.

There was always a next motel. A next gig. With no end in sight.

And Rafe loved every fucking minute of it.

"It's going to be on our right. After we cross East Austin Street." Miki was slung over the passenger captain's chair, one leg up over the arm and his back against the window. "It's next to a store or something. Sells candy and sundries. What the hell are sundries?"

"I have no fucking idea." While Damien and Forest slept noisily in the van's back seats, Rafe took a good look at the stretch of bleached-out road and black-barked trees around them. Every few feet, a line of straggly bushes fought for its miserable existence alongside the highway. He counted yet another house of worship, reaching a full twenty since they'd turned off onto North Llano. "There's a shit-ton of churches. Have you noticed that?"

"Yeah, kind of feels like we're running a gauntlet or something." Miki scratched at his knee, poking out of a rip in his jeans. "We get to the end, and we'll have to fight a boss or something. Too early for Jesus. Maybe one of the saints? You're Catholic. Is there a Saint Frederick?"

"If there is, I wasn't paying attention." Rafe smirked, remembering the long days in Religious Studies he'd spent trying to work out the bass lines on sheet music he'd shoved between his books. "I remember the big ones, like Michael and Gabriel. But after that… oh wait, Saint Cecilia is the patron saint for musicians, but no Frederick."

"I know Christopher. Kane gave me a medal with him on it. For traveling, he said." Miki stared out of the window, his gaze drifting across the road. He held up his arm, his wrist cluttered with black and silver bracelets. A familiar oval dangled from one, its jump ring thick and closed tight. "To keep me safe."

Rafe slowed down when a cement truck pulled out into the lane next to them, and Miki grabbed at the dashboard, his body rigid with tension, but his expression remained placid. Or as placid as Miki St. John got.

It was hard to read Miki's expressions. Most of the time, Rafe didn't have to. St. John's emotions were always on the tip of his tongue, and he shared them, laced with profanity or wisdom, depending on his mood. He was always Damien's lanky, pretty-faced shadow, a long-legged, chestnut-maned quiet man who poured his heart and soul out into dark words and turned into liquid sex once his boots hit the stage.

It was odd knowing the actual man. They were certainly older now, considering he'd first met Miki when they'd both been teens, but Miki's world-weary eyes never changed. He'd seen it all, rolled in the shadows and came up with its stink long before Rafe ever picked up a bass, but Damien's Sinjun had never been afraid before.

Not like he was right then when a cement truck eased in beside them.

Fear rolled off Miki in waves so strong Rafe could taste it in the air. A moment later, it was gone, dissipating quickly amid the snores coming from the two sleeping behind them. All that was left to show of Miki's tenseness was the white across his knuckles and the softening divots in his chair's leather armrest.

"You doing okay there, Sin?" Rafe had nothing to lose in tossing a drop of water on the hot oil of Miki's personality. They'd worked into each other's dips and dives, finding common ground in music and Quinn, but trespassing into Miki's personal hells was always risky, especially when the singer didn't feel like talking.

Today was apparently a talking day.

"Yeah, it's just... I really fucking hate being in a car sometimes," he said softly. "Kane thinks it's a lack-of-control thing. Says I don't like not having control over my environment so I get all... wonky."

"I think he's got you confused with Damie." Rafe risked a quick glance behind him, assuring himself that their band's leader was still passed out. "Love him, but your boy D either has to have a stranglehold on things, or he lets them run wild like Dude right after he's had a bath."

"I can see that."

Miki went silent again, and Rafe wondered if he'd lost the man to the music constantly rolling through his head.

A few minutes later, he murmured, "I hate being on the road. I like the stage and the music, but getting there? Fucking hate it. It's worth it.... I know it's worth it, but I still fucking hate getting there."

"Right now I'm right there with you, man."

A flatbed zoomed by them, burdened with a dark green tractor, but this time Miki remained a boneless sprawl.

"But you've got to admit, it's been a hell of a lot of fun."

"It's always fun." Miki looked up, his hazel eyes hooded and shadowed. "Until it's not."

"WOW, I didn't think you could find any place shittier than the last one, but…." Rafe took a good look at the broken-down theater he'd pulled up in front of. "Just… fucking wow."

"Anyone ever tell you you're kind of a dick, Andrade?" Damien slanted a disgusted look his way, but Rafe ignored it. The guy wasn't telling him anything new, and truth be told, there was no denying they'd pulled up in front of an aging crap hole.

"It's not so bad." Forest shoved his hands into his jeans and rocked back on his heels. "There's no graffiti on the walls, and there's a lot of parking."

"It's like I'm traveling with one glass half-full and the other one half-empty," Damien replied, then exchanged glances with Miki. "Don't give me that look. Your glass is cracked."

"Love you too, fuckhead," Miki replied. "How about if we go pound on the door, dump our stuff on the stage, and go find our hotel? Because if it doesn't have AC, I'm sleeping in the van."

The Box was a wooden building, old enough to have grandchildren who voted and drove motorcycles down the wrong way of a one-way street. Sitting on the corner of Fredericksburg's two thoroughfares, the building wore a thick patina of dust and grime like an aging showgirl wore her false eyelashes to go shopping for support hose. Once a cornerstone of Southern rock and hard blues, the Box slumped into its foundation, waiting for yet another band to come hammer away on its bones.

Still, there was something magical about the place, even standing in the white-hot sun and the sweltering heat. Miki'd stripped down to a tank top and jeans, his black leather boots nearly as old as the theater, while Forest and Damien seemed unaffected by the clotted air, thick with dust and humidity.

A knock on the front door yielded no results, but a walk around to the back did. Damien found Jasper, the Box's owner, leaning against the wall near a propped-open fire door. A time-worn, sun-weathered man in jeans and an old Iron Maiden shirt, his beard was yellow from nicotine, and he spat a line of tobacco juice out when they came around the corner, but he grinned broadly when they introduced themselves, shuttling them inside to get out of the oppressive heat.

"Okay, screw the van," Miki said once they got inside and the Box's chilly interior gripped them tight. "I'm sleeping backstage. Naked floor's gotta be better than a motel mattress."

"You haven't even seen the place," Damien protested. "And you're not sleeping backstage for three nights."

"If you're staying down at the Traveling Gypsy Inn, then you're in a good place. Beds are soft, and Doris puts down a good breakfast spread." Jasper trailed after them as they walked out onto the stage from the back. "'Course, she's been my girlfriend for the past twenty years, so maybe I've just gotten used to her cooking."

"Could be. I've gotten used to Sionn's." Forest turned, then nudged Rafe in the ribs with his elbow. "Man, look at that space, Andrade."

The struggle to get from the small stage to arenas had been a glorious rise of sex, drugs, and rock and roll. Rafe'd climbed those stairs and danced on the highest peak of his personal rock-star mountain, simply to leap off armed only with the wax wings of his ego. While he didn't remember much of the last few steps he'd climbed, he clearly remembered his flaming descent, and his soul still bore the bruises and scars he earned on the way down.

If there was one good thing about Damien's low-rent, guys-in-a-van tour, it was Rafe remembering why he'd picked a bass up to begin with.

In the beginning, there hadn't been fame. Even less fortune. He'd cut his fingers apart learning chords while his friends tried out for sports teams. When the others began dating, Rafe'd been begging bands for a chance, covering for sick musicians, and playing *everything* just for the experience. He was decent on the guitar, okay on the drums, but when he settled a bass around his neck, he'd known he'd found his first love.

After Quinn, his heart whispered, there was no other love before Quinn.

He'd hitched himself to Jack Collins, and they'd played every sleazy bar and club willing to let them hit the stage. The stages grew bigger. So did the audiences. And, Rafe admitted freely, so did his ego, but nothing had ever dimmed the tingling, magical feeling of a *stage* beneath his feet.

The Box's stage was no different. Like all the venues they'd played at since they left San Francisco, there was a silent magic there, an anticipation, as if the building was merely holding its breath, waiting to exhale at the sound of the first buzzing thrum of a pickup or the rattle of a cymbal. Rafe could feel the history of the place in its walls, murmuring old stories of blues men and long-haired Southern boys bending a guitar to their will. Ripe with the scent of stale alcohol and lemon wax, the Box's stage sang back as Rafe walked over it, his footsteps rolling mellow thumps across the vast empty space.

"Tell me you can't feel the music in this place's bones, Andrade." Damien came up behind him, his voice dropped to a low whisper. "Fucking legends played here."

"*We're* playing here," Rafe replied, giving Damie a wicked grin. "And we're going to bring this place to its knees."

"Not without our shit." Miki snorted. "Fore, want to help me get the van unloaded while these two jack off together?"

"Yeah, I got the spare set of keys." Forest headed across the canted floor toward the entrance. "Jasper says we can use the front door. Just have to prop it open 'cause it'll lock behind us."

A rectangular block of light cut into the interior's shadows when Forest opened the front door, burning out Rafe's eyes with its intensity. Blinking away the echoes of lines and blotches dancing across his vision, he looked away, hoping to regain some sight before schlepping their gear in.

"You know, next time you want to do this backwater tour shit, bring a roadie along with us, Mitchell." Rafe wiped at the tears forming on his lashes.

"This bonding shit could still work with a few minions, you know."

"See, it's all about teamwork, Andrade," Damien said, following Miki down the short flight of stairs to the left of the stage. "Roadies would just get in the way of that. And besides, it's about time you put in an honest day's work."

"Says the fucker who slept his way across Texas," he shot back. Rafe was about ready to jump off the stage when Forest's silhouette cut into the light coming from the open door.

"Hey, guys?" Their drummer's voice sounded strained. "Um… someone took the van."

"LOOKS LIKE they popped the driver's side door lock and got in that way. We've got a witness who was drawing cash out at the ATM across the street. Said the alarm went off for a few seconds but then stopped. She assumed the guy climbing in was the driver and just forgot to disable it." A thick mustache dominated the cop's face, a bristle of salt-and-pepper under his long nose. Tapping the van's hood with his pen, he nodded curtly at the band. "Good thing you had that lockdown switch activated, or they'd have stripped this thing down to the bone before you hung up with dispatch. We've already got as many prints as we can off of it. We'll want you boys to get printed so we can exclude you, but we're pretty much done with it. You can have it back."

A call to the car service hooked up to the van, and it'd come to a shuddering stop about a mile away from the Box. The cops beat them to the spot, scrambling to catch the thieves, but they were gone before the first police car pulled up to find the van's rear doors left wide open and its storage space nearly empty. They'd taken turns pacing the sidewalk, waiting while the cops went over the van. In the meantime the day cooled off quickly, and a curtain of dark clouds threatened the clear sky, lingering at the edge of the town.

Rafe's heart started pounding when he saw the van's ravaged storage racks. Forest's drum kits were still locked down in place, but the guitars were gone, their bindings cut loose and dangling from their struts. A few amps remained, bolted in with heavy straps, but the guitars—the empty slots for their cases dug holes into Rafe's belly.

"Oh fuck no." A sour bite of bile burned Rafe's throat, and his soul twisted in his core, a spiraling black thread of fear. He approached the back slowly, unable to believe what he was seeing. "My bass… Donal gave me… oh fucking hell no."

Forest clasped his shoulder, squeezing tightly. "Shit, we can get it back—"

"Hey!" Miki called out from inside the main cabin. "Fuckers didn't take it. Or Damie's Phenix. I put those behind the back seat and locked them down. They're still here."

"Jesus *fucking* Christ." Rafe exhaled hard.

The rest of his equipment he could part with, but he'd cut off his left nut rather than lose the bass Donal bought him when he'd first decided to throw his life out onto the road and play. Rafe's lungs unclenched when Miki extracted the bass's flat rectangular case from behind the far back seat.

"God, Sinjun, I am never going to mock your fucked-up squirreling away of shit ever again," Damien said, taking the case from Miki as he unbent from leaning over the seat back. "God love your fucking paranoia, Sin. God just fucking love it."

"Remember Johnny always saying hide your stash and prime shit? And since I left *my* really good guitars at home, I stashed yours." Miki shrugged, curling over the seat for another case. "Back here can hold two cases. So I shoved them there."

"Boy's not wrong. Those looked like they were just part of the wall. I'll tear my crime guy a new asshole for missing them. Let me call someone back to grab prints. Just to cover asses all around." The cop's chest rumbled with laughter. "We'll get back to you with what we find. Got your numbers. They can't have gone far. Not many places to hide out here, and you boys will be here for a few days, right?"

"Yeah, but we've got a gig here in a couple of days," Damien replied.

They all caught the cop's rueful expression.

"And yeah, we know you can't promise anything, but we can't play a gig with only one guitar and bass. Don't suppose this place has a music store?"

"If we did, that'd be the first place I'd look for someone to dump your gear." The cop's mustache twitched. "Austin's an hour and a half out. You boys probably want to head there. Might want to have a locksmith look at those doors first. Know a guy who'll come out and swap them out pretty cheap and fast."

"Hey, so long as he wasn't the one who popped them to begin with, I'm good with anyone." Damien grinned. "Especially since it looks like we're heading to Austin."

IT WAS cold, a bone-biting, spine-cracking cold, sharp enough to slice a man's skin open with its dry razor's edge, but Rafe felt nothing other than the music pouring out of the band and slamming into the loading bay's cinder-block walls. The back of the guitar store faced an empty field, long grasses dancing in a furious breeze, their seed-heavy tops slashing at a chain-link fence separating the building's back parking lot from the grassy sprawl. Once the manager'd pulled the rolling steel door open, the stuffiness eased out of the boxy cement bay. The large space was never meant to be used for anything other than intakes for a now defunct warehouse store, and the staff at the store had turned it into a lounge of sorts, setting up amps and spare equipment to play during breaks and after work.

Which made it the perfect spot for Crossroads Gin to whip themselves into a frenzy and play their hearts out for no one but themselves.

There were other people, shadows really, lurking at the edges of the dank space, but Rafe didn't see them, didn't hear them. He and Damie'd worked through four or five instruments each, pulling guitars off the walls and stringing them up with Ernie Balls. Miki'd fallen in love with a semihollow Gibson Memphis, and Forest merely walked behind them, laughing softly at their crooning and random strumming.

When the store manager offered them the space to test out their finds, it seemed like the perfect excuse to fuck around and let off steam.

Little did Rafe know, it would be the exact thing he needed to fall in love all over again.

The mic setup was a good one, enough for each of them to have one, and despite its humble beginnings as an intake room, the store's lounge had fantastic acoustics, a clean, pure sound with only the slightest bit of bounce back. With the amps set up and everyone wired to go, they'd hit their first chord and took off running.

"*Bled onto my hand, shoved his fist into mine. Stood tall against anyone who'd break through our line.*" Miki slithered over his lyrics, punching in a bluesy rasp through the melodic stack of Damie's wailing six-string. "*No matter what they do, no matter what they say, Death's already tried to part us, and we've already made him pay.*"

A half skip later, and Rafe took a breath, adding his voice to the chorus. "*So lift a glass to the Sinners. Lift a glass of cheap-ass gin. Put your lips on the Gates of Heaven, 'cause we're taking you to sin.*"

His skin hummed with the power of their connection, the rightness of how Miki fit into the weave between his bass and Damien's guitar. Beneath them, Forest laid out a heavy beat, forcing them to keep time and not to wander, driving the band forward. In the pop and crackle of beat-ass amps and torn nails on new strings, Rafe *felt* the others on him… in him… and a snarling refrain from Miki's hot, sensual growls led them on.

Miki and Damien played around each other, throwing themselves into the sheer sound of the music. It lifted Rafe's blood, stretching his spine and grabbing at his balls when Damien leaned against him, playing through a riff slick enough to tear off anyone's pants.

The music was raw, a searing mouth-fuck of a sound as coarse and bawdy as any overpainted whore with a heart of gold. Outside the bay door there were more shadows, lengthening, then spilling over one another until the day dropped off the horizon. At some point Rafe's fingers began to hurt, and Miki pulled off the mic and changed gears, throwing them into a slow song to wind them down.

"*The prophets and the wicked both wear black. How do I tell one from the other?*" Miki rasped into the mic, his fingers slick and nimble on the Memphis while Damien reached for the upper licks of the song. "*When both want to kiss me, and ask for my soul.*"

When the song was over, they all took a breath and stilled the music, letting it seep back into the cinder blocks and wisp away into their blood. Rafe laid his palm over his bass's pickups, taking one last slide of his skin over the coiled strings before he flipped off the power.

There weren't any words for what they had. Nothing could explain the orgasmic roller-coaster rush of a tight play and a synced-in band. He'd almost had that with Jack Collins, but they'd never reached the stratosphere of emotions he'd run through with Crossroads. It filled Rafe with a peace, one he normally felt only with Quinn, a stilling of the frenzy in his soul and quieting the world's chaos until he could hear the sky turning slowly above him.

"*Fuck*," Forest whispered behind them.

And Miki broke out in a full-bellied laugh.

"Shit, we've still got to break stuff down and get it into the van." Damien glanced at his watch. "And it's almost ten."

"Better yet, we've got to pay for this shit." Miki sounded hoarse, reaching for one of the bottled waters lined up on an amp. "I've got to get some lemon drops or something."

"I don't think I can walk." Forest steadied himself with a hand against the wall as he extracted himself from behind the store's drum kit. "I'm for getting a few rooms here and heading back in the morning."

"Sounds good," Rafe choked out. He'd have to steal some of Miki's lemon drops. His throat was a little raw, and his hands hurt like fucking hell, but the burbling simmer in his belly was calm. Dead tired and worn out, he slung the bass off, then tried to shake the feeling back into his fingers.

The bubble popped, and the space quickly filled with people. The bass he'd been playing was being wiped down and packed up before Rafe could blink, and someone was helping Forest take a few tentative steps out of the hole he'd been in, his legs wobbly from hitting the pedals for hours on end. It was suddenly loud, everyone talking at once and on top of each other. One of the guys chattered on about recording the session and offering it up for Damien to take with him. There was the standard scurry and weave of Miki avoiding someone's hands on his newly acquired guitar, and then Damien stepped in to herd the crowd.

"Kind of weird seeing you with these guys."

A voice pricked through the chaotic jumble, and Rafe turned to find a skinny-faced blond man coiling up the cord Rafe'd unplugged from his bass. Rafe stared back at the guy, who shrugged at Rafe's blank look.

"You probably don't remember me, but we hooked up the last time you came through Austin… when you were with your own band."

"Sorry." Rafe gave him a small, tight smile. Of course he didn't remember the guy. He'd been too lit to remember his own name back then. It was no wonder Jack left him at the curb like the trash and every miracle Miki, Damien, and Forest picked him up out of the garbage pile. "It was kind of a crazy time back then. Shit's gotten to my brain."

"Yeah, I didn't think you remembered, but we had a really good fucking time." The blond looked around, then dug something out of his pants' pocket. Turning so his back was to the rest of the room, he opened his hand, flashing Rafe a glimpse of embossed green pills. "Got some clovers. What'cha say we split, and I show you what a really good fucking time you had when you were here?"

TEN

Brick covered in blood
Face painted with spit
Skin the wrong color
Suck cock, called unfit

So many ways to kill us
So many ways to make us less
When's it all going to stop
That's just anyone's guess

Don't pick up that stone
Just unclench your fist
Turn the other cheek
We're all better than this
—Bathing in Hate

LAS VEGAS'S lights drowned out the stars, bleaching the night sky to a pale dove gray. Hints of amaranthine and goldenrod flickered and lapped at the edge of the horizon, a saturated wash of radiance stealing away the dark. The strip itself bled fractals into Miki's eyes, leaving art-deco sunbursts behind when he blinked.

There were people everywhere, a low hum of chatter fueled by the clash of horns, the clatter of a roller coaster on the side of a building, and the rushing *swoosh* of what seemed like a million fountains. Lights did battle to push back even the faintest of shadows, and the early-evening crowds ebbed and flowed in waves, forming into pools at each corner before the traffic lights sent them scurrying on the next tide. Double-decker busses edged in and out of the way of frantic cabs weaving through the thick traffic.

"Where the fuck are they all going?" From his spot in the passenger seat, Miki watched as a scatter of silicon-breasted, scantily clad women tottered past them on high heels. "It's like being caught in a giant outdoor mall or something. Like one of those hamster trails."

One lagged behind, her nosebleed-high cork wedges clopping over the crosswalk's broad white lines. Wiggling her fingers at Damien, she nearly plowed into a round-bellied man in khaki shorts and a *CSI* T-shirt lumbering in the other direction, his hands clenched around a soda and a hot dog. They did a shuffling dance, exchanging smiles, then continued on their way, but not before the man snuck a backward peek at the woman's plump asscheeks.

"Welcome to Vegas, Sinjun," Damien replied, pulling the van into a stream of traffic when the light turned green. "And yeah, it's less of a Habitrail and

more of a theme park, where everything is fake smiles
and set dressing."

"Food's good, though," Forest said as he stretched
his legs out. "Con and I had a great time last time we
were here."

"Yeah, I saw Connor's neck when you got back."
Damien chuckled. "Looked like he fell into a lamprey
nest."

"He bruises easily," Forest defended himself.
"'Sides, not like Sionn doesn't wear turtlenecks on
Sunday during the summer."

Damien spared Forest a quick hot glare. "Fuck,
that one time. And it was cold."

"It was over seventy-five. Who wears a turtleneck
past seventy?" Forest prodded.

"Who wears a turtleneck?" Miki tossed out.

"We're not staying at some broke-ass dive, right?"
Rafe cut into the teasing. "Because I'm kind of sick of
the no-tell motel shit, D."

Miki's spine knotted, and he risked a sidelong
glance at Damien. D's knuckles were white as he
flexed his fingers around the van's steering wheel.
His mouth went a little tight, and then he took a deep
breath, cocking his head, his mouth opening slightly. Knowing Damien as well as he did, Miki knew he
wasn't going to like what came out of his brother's
mouth, so he did them all a favor and gave Damien a
swift kick to his shin.

"Fuck, Sin! What the hell?" Damien unwrapped
one hand from the wheel to rub at the dusty shoeprint
on his jeans. "What was that for?"

"Shit doesn't need to be smeared around," Miki
growled, flicking his eyes once to the back of the van,

where Rafe sat in a sullen slouch on the rear seat. "Let it go."

Their bassist had been carrying an attitude since they'd left Texas, and the gig they'd played in Arizona was good enough but missed that elusive something they'd had up until their gear'd been stolen. It'd been one thing after another following the Box gig, and everyone's nerves were stretched tight enough to pop.

Damien hissed softly, "Fucker's been—"

"I took care of it. Just fucking get us to the Venetian." Miki tapped at the dashboard's GPS, changing the van's destination address.

"We're not staying—" Damien cut himself off at Miki's disgruntled growl. "Okay, did you at least cancel the other reservations?"

"Where? At Ass-chaps Inn and Marriage Chapel?" He pursed his lips at Damien's soft protesting sigh. "No, because I didn't know where you had the goddamned reservations. It's like a fucking scavenger hunt with you. Pay for the fucking no-show and pull into the Venetian. Their top floor suites were open… well, they got opened up for us. So just find us the fucking hotel, and we can get our brains on straight again."

One thing Miki'd never gotten used to was the Strip's smell. It permeated everything, getting down under his skin and then filling his nostrils with its odd mix of booze, cotton candy, and sex. Despite the early-evening hour, the sidewalks were already littered with plastic cups and cardstock flyers advertising the hottest places to see naked women.

"When'd they get an M&M store?" Damien craned his neck to stare up at the building.

"It's been there for years," Miki said, shoving him back into the driver's seat. "You've always just been too drunk to notice every time we came through."

"Shit, I'd have crawled in there and ate myself sick if I'd known." He twisted around in his seat. "When did this place get so fucking busy too? I don't remember it being this busy."

"You've never driven the Strip before. Last time we were in Vegas, we got in at four in the morning, and they shuttled us in through the back. Don't you remember trying to hump that happy Buddha they've got over at Planet Hollywood?"

"I can't even remember being at the hotel." Damien sighed. "God, I was so fucked-up back then. Now look at me, yawning my ass off, and it's not even seven o'clock at night."

"It's over to the right." Miki's stomach was a mess. "Do valet."

He'd made a call before they left Arizona, pleading his case as quickly as he could before the others made it back to the van. The tension between them was odd, tight in spots around Rafe and sometimes, he had to admit, even himself. Forest and Damien seemed to be holding up, but there were signs of cracking, especially when the drummer audibly growled at D when his hand drifted too close to Forest's bacon at the roadside diner they'd stopped at for breakfast.

"So the whole hard tour thing we'd agreed to is kind of out the window for Vegas, then?" Damien grumbled.

"Once again, only you wanted to do this shit, Mitchell," Rafe grumbled.

"It's been good," Forest interjected. "A couple of shitty things but mostly good."

"I don't think Miki getting stabbed the first time we hit the stage qualifies as shitty. That was more than shitty," their bassist shot back. "And did you forget the shit someone smeared all over our windows in Georgia? Or the asshole who spray-painted crap all over the sides of the van in Phoenix? 'Cause waking up to someone telling you to fuck off and die is really fucking great."

"Yeah, just park, D." Miki shook his head at Damien before he bitched back at Rafe. "Look, a couple of paint cans, and then it was all good."

"It was kind of fun to tag up the van," Forest offered. "Come on. At least it looks like something a rock band would own now."

There were still flecks of gold, blue, and purple under Miki's nails from their impromptu art project to cover up the neon pink death threats they'd found on their van after the Phoenix gig. The van wasn't any prettier—none of them ever claimed to be an artist—but it definitely was going to go down as the most unique thing he'd ever ridden in. Razor blades got the paint off the glass, but there was no fixing the car's finish. Now the van had the band's name in thick print on either side, with flower-eyed sugar skulls and flames filling up the spaces in between. Miki'd gotten a tortured smile from Rafe when he'd been handed the gold paint, and Miki told him to do the lettering since he had the best handwriting.

Miki hadn't been disappointed with the results, but Rafe's apathetic shrug at the band's praise had him worried. The Rafe he knew couldn't even spell *apathetic*. He was passionate about everything and anything, and when asked what was wrong, Rafe simply shrugged again, tightening his mouth up, then handed Miki back the empty gold-splattered cans.

The Venetian was busy, and the band's van stood out like a sore thumb among the limos and smartly dressed people milling about the front entrance. A sign pointed them to general parking and valet, but Miki pointed to the main driveway.

"Wait, the Palazzo or the Venetian? Where the fuck am I going?" Damien groused.

"Right there. You see that guy up there? Head over to him." Miki smacked Damien's arm. "Just pull up."

"It's on the wrong side. I can't—"

"You're fucking part British. It's on the right side for you. Just go over there." He sighed heavily while Damien maneuvered around a stream of people in their way. "See? He's waving you to go over."

"He's not waving for me to go over," Damien replied sharply. "That's the universal sign for get your piece-of-shit van out of our driveway, you skanky whore."

"I swear to God, if you don't fucking park—" Miki sat back in his seat as Damien slid the van into a space between two taxis, then brought the vehicle to a stop in front of the doorman. "Jesus, was that so fucking hard?"

Damien turned to glare at him. "Some days—"

The driver's side door opened, and a beaming young man nodded at them. "Welcome to the Venetian. We've been expecting you, sirs."

"What did you tell them to look for? Something that looks like a clown threw up on it?" Rafe asked, reaching for the van's side door handle. Another hotel employee got to it before he did, and Rafe nearly tumbled out of the open door. Forest grabbed his waistband, pulling him back. Patting Forest's shoulder, he mumbled, "Thanks, man."

"No problem." Forest scratched at the sparse golden scruff on his chin. "I really want a shower and a shave. If you bashed your head on those cobblestones, we'd have to go to the hospital smelling like armpit and ass. Not something I want to do."

"Again," Rafe added. "Because I'm pretty sure that's what we smelled like in Boston."

"What the hell's going on, Sinjun?" Damien grabbed Miki's arm, holding him back while the others headed into the hotel lobby ahead of them. "You don't give a shit where we stay, and you sure as fuck don't call ahead for ass-kissing."

"Just fucking get inside the damned hotel."

If his stomach was in knots before, it was goddamned macramé by the time his shoes hit the hotel's marble floor. He scanned the lobby for his Hail Mary's response and found it quickly in the four broad-shouldered men standing to the right of the front door.

"Fucking A."

"Shit, Miki," Damien exhaled. "What the fuck have you done?"

They were a broad wall of Irish aggression and toughness, sharpened to a keen edge by an Irish woman's wit and a solid man's granite sensibility. Dwarfing the crowd, the Morgans and their Murphy-Finnegan cousin were all smiles and Gaelic charm, animatedly talking to one another and oblivious to their lovers, who stood near the door. The youngest of them turned, his hyperaware senses catching a shift in the crowd, or perhaps Quinn was so tied in to Rafe's heart he could feel the other man close to him. For whatever reason, Brigid's green-eyed son shifted, and his face lit up brighter than the Vegas strip.

"Rafe!" Quinn's uncharacteristic shout stilled the others, and they turned nearly as one, grins plastered on their faces.

Kane was in front of Miki before he could take another breath, and the marble and gilded lobby spun around them as Kane wrapped his arms around Miki's waist and held him tight. He breathed in Kane's scent, burying his face in the crook of Kane's neck and then struggled to get in another mouthful of air around Kane's embrace. Fingers were in his hair, a strong grip cradling the back of his head, and Miki let himself be spun around again, wrapping his own arms around Kane's shoulder and torso.

He felt so fucking good in Miki's arms and against Miki's skin. The knot in his belly began to unravel, leaving only a sop of sourness behind. He didn't give a shit if they were kicked out of the hotel. Miki fully intended to chew Kane's face off in a long kiss. Thankfully, Kane obliged. Kane's lips found his, and Miki bit at them, nipping to get a full taste of Kane's laugh when he pulled back.

"God, you look a mess, Mick," Kane murmured, then brushed his mouth over Miki's cheek. "Still, it's damned good to see you."

"Don't get me wrong, K," Miki whispered in his lover's ear. "Because you know I love you and everything, but I'm really fucking glad you got Quinn to come over. There's something wrong with Rafe."

RAFE WASN'T sure how someone cheated at Rock-Paper-Scissors, but he knew Miki somehow had. The suite… the goddamned penthouse suite… was bigger than every single one of his childhood homes combined. Standing in the middle of the fussy living space with its eight-seat dining room and grand piano, Rafe wondered how the hell he'd ever thought he wanted more than what he already had.

Especially since he seemed so willing to throw it all away.

"Do you want coffee?" Quinn called from a room deep in the suite. "Or… water? There's, like, a small gym in here with about ten cases of water. This is nuts. I can just hear Mum complaining about the waste. Do you think they throw it all away every time someone leaves? How would they know someone didn't contaminate it all?"

Rafe swallowed, listening to Quinn's gentle patter. His lover's familiar wandering through subjects and words, examining the world, with its constant stream of visual stimulation and noise. He could hear Quinn getting into everything, opening drawers and picking things up only to put them back down. The household staff would be driven crazy by the time they vacated the suite, probably stuck spending at least half an hour putting things back where they belonged because Quinn would carry something from one room to the next.

His eyes stung, watering with hot tears, and Rafe gagged on the lump growing in his throat. Shoving his hands into his jacket's pockets only made things worse, especially when his fingers brushed over the lump of Kleenex he'd balled up and tucked away.

Quinn found him there, leaning against the window and facing the long corridor leading to the penthouse's double doors, staring at nothing and wondering how the hell he was going to tell Quinn he'd made a mistake falling in love with a fuckup like Rafe.

"What's the matter, Rafe?" Quinn'd lost his shoes somewhere in the suite, his bare feet barely making any noise on the living room carpet.

His green eyes were troubled, shrouded in worry, and Rafe ached to reach out to him but knew if he so much as felt Quinn's skin under his fingertips, he'd lose every ounce of shaky control he had over his emotions. Crossing over to where Rafe stood, Quinn studied him with every step. Coming up close, Quinn twisted his fingers into Rafe's thin T-shirt and leaned into him.

"Tell me what happened. Did the guys say something? Do something to make you mad?" A heartbeat later and Quinn asked the one question that would always break Rafe's heart. "Did I?"

"Oh God, fuck no, Q." Rafe uncoiled and reached for Quinn. Cupping his lover's handsome face, Rafe hitched his breath, and his tears tore apart his defenses, dampening his cheeks. He kissed Quinn gently, then murmured, "There is never ever anything you can do to make me mad. Okay? Nothing."

"I don't know about that." Quinn's smile wavered like Rafe's voice, but he attempted one anyway. "People can get pretty mad at me. Hell, someone even tried to kill me because I couldn't remember his name."

"Guy was fucking crazy," Rafe whispered, pulling Quinn in close. The lump in his pocket seemed to burn into his side, but Rafe didn't want to let Quinn go. Not when he seemed to make the world quiet around them. "That was so not on you."

"My mum's got a bullet wound that would say otherwise, but it's nice of you to think so," Quinn replied. Returning Rafe's soft kiss with one of his own, Quinn sighed into Rafe's open mouth. "Now, tell me what's wrong, because I know you, Andrade. You're carrying something on your shoulders that's heavier than a fallen angel's wings."

There were few times in Rafe's life when he couldn't dance away from the truth. He'd spent a lifetime conning and dealing to get just that little bit more to make it through another day, and his instincts told him to lie, to reassure Quinn Morgan with soft words and comforting noises. His mind laid out everything for him, how to seduce the soul-shattering questions being thrown at him and feed Quinn's deep passions with a night of hot sex and cold beer.

He could do it. Rafe knew he could. Quinn's trust glimmered in his face, his guileless, open expression full of a love so unconditional it hurt Rafe to look at him. Quinn would take anything Rafe said to heart and defend it to his last dying breath if he had to. There was nothing Quinn wouldn't do for him… including swallowing every bitter lie Rafe told him.

Taking a deep breath, Rafe opened his tear-hot eyes and trusted the tiny voice in his heart telling him Quinn would do *anything* for him… including stay.

"I did something really fucking stupid in Austin," he heard himself say softly. "And I don't know what to do now, because I fucked up so bad, Q. So fucking bad."

"You're going to have shit happen, Rafe."

Quinn's expression changed to one Rafe'd only seen on Donal's face, a mix of affection, tolerance, and a readiness to kick ass if needed. His arms tightened around Rafe's waist, and Quinn stepped into the space between Rafe's legs until they were snugged up close. "You're going to *do* shit too. If you took a step off of where you need to be, it's not going to be the end of the world. Not for us. Not for you."

"You don't know what I've done, Q," Rafe spat back. "And this fucking crap—"

"Maybe less flogging yourself and more telling me what happened?" He cocked his head. "Because right now, I can't help you if I don't know what we're dealing with."

Such a simple word… *we're*… and it was enough to unman him.

He buckled, and Quinn caught him up, holding Rafe's weight easily. Catching his balance, Rafe stumbled over to one of the suite's couches, letting Quinn guide his steps. The tension in his muscles made him stiff, and he hurt everywhere, wound up too tight around a nest of worry. His ass hit the cushions, and Rafe fumbled with his pocket, trying to extract the tissue wad. His fingers were cold, unresponsive, and Rafe's guts felt like they were shredding with every breath he took.

"Let me help," Quinn said softly, moving Rafe's hands out of the way. A second later, Rafe's pocket was empty, and Quinn was unwrapping the tissue. Staring down at the nearly fluorescent-green pills in his palm, Quinn examined them, then turned them over. "Ecstasy? Why do you have E?"

"Surprises me as fuck you'd know what they are," Rafe confessed in a hot rush.

"My dad's a cop. You don't think he's shown me what stuff looks like so I don't take it?" Quinn leaned over, placing the tissue and its contents on the table in front of them. "Now, why don't you be telling me exactly what happened so we can work out what we need to do?"

Once Rafe started talking, he couldn't get the story out fast enough. His phone rang a couple of times, burbling from its spot on the dining room table where he'd left it, and Quinn's chirped once before he turned it off and tossed it across the couch. With his legs crossed and his hands wrapped around Rafe, Quinn simply listened.

"Fucking him never even crossed my mind, but the pills, damned if I didn't want them," Rafe confessed. "That's worse, you know? I don't know if that makes any sense, because I'd fucking sooner die than cheat on you. You know that, right?"

"Yeah, I know. But taking the pills would have been cheating on yourself," Quinn replied, squeezing Rafe's hands. "Why'd you keep them?"

Quinn never asked if he took any. So fucking like Quinn to ask about why he still had them and not if he'd swallowed one. Rafe exhaled the fear he'd been holding inside him and shook his head.

"No fucking clue. Every time I go to toss them, I just… can't." He couldn't explain the trembling in his body when he'd held the wad over the toilet. "It's like I just need to make sure I've got them every fucking day and *not* take them. And it's pissing me off, Q. It's seriously fucking pissing me off, because suppose one day… one fucking day… I just say fuck it and pop them? Then what? I mean, it's goddamned fucking E, of all things. How stupid is this?"

"Because it's safe. Or your brain thinks it's safe," Quinn said firmly. "It makes sense. It does. Like Mum's Dead Sea chocolate ice cream container. The one she's had in the freezer since we were kids but she'll never eat because if she does she's admitting she's given up on her diet."

"I've seen her eat ice cream. At your birthday party," Rafe reminded him. "You're telling me she's still got that damned pint sitting in the back of the freezer?"

"For years. And I ate that ice cream fifteen years ago and filled the container back up with water so it had weight." Quinn grinned. "But it's like a shrine to something she's not fighting anymore. She's never going to be that size zero, and that's okay because she's eating healthy and working out. You're always going to be an addict, and that's okay too, so long as you keep the poisons out of your body and talk to me. Or go to a meeting. Did you go to one?"

"No. Because we were… I don't want… the band, Q. The guys. Miki knows, but…." Rafe scrubbed at his eyes, wiping at the grit in them. "I fucking hate talking to them about it. Asking them to stop their whole damned lives because I've got to go hook up with some people sitting around in a circle because we're too damned weak to stop doing drugs."

"You are not weak, Rafe."

Quinn surprised him, cupping Rafe's face and forcing him to meet Quinn's gaze.

"You're genetically screwed up. Just like me. I need chemicals to help me keep on the tracks, and your body wants chemicals because it's an asshole. Our bodies need things, some good and some bad. Yours is just on the bad side. And as much as I hate taking my meds, I take them because I know life gets too tight around me if I don't."

"And if I do, life just gets too fucked-up," Rafe whispered. "So you think I held on to the pills because I've got some masochist thing going on with my head?"

"A little bit. That and you're kind of stupid about complicating things when sometimes the easiest thing to do is ask for help," he replied, dropping his hands. "The guys know you're an addict. It's not a surprise. If Damie's willing to stop and look at the world's largest wasp nest, I'm pretty damned sure he'd be willing to put the tour on hold for an hour so you can hit up a meeting. But you have to tell them, Rafe. Just because you got into this on your own, love, doesn't mean you have to stay in it by yourself."

"Miki'd kick his ass if he said no." Rafe chuckled. "And yeah, he'd never say no. I'm a fucking idiot, Q."

"Yeah, sometimes," Quinn said, snagging the wad up from the table. "Now I'm going to toss this in the toilet, and you've got to go apologize to the guys for being an asshole to them."

That brought Rafe's head up. "What? Someone told you I was being an asshole?"

"I've known you for years, Rafe. When you get pissed off at yourself, you're an asshole to everyone around you." Quinn stroked his thumb over Rafe's lower lip. "I love you, but asshole is kind of your default setting. It's probably why you and Damien get along so well."

ELEVEN

Pretty pretty baby, legs so damned long
Stop for a little bit, hear some of my song
You've got a twitch in your hips
Something sparkly in your hair
A twinkle in your eye
And not a damned care
Watch who you tease
Watch who you break
'Cause maybe one day
Gonna be your heart that aches
—Sweet Little Tease

"I THINK you broke me," Damien gasped. "Bloody hell, Sionn."

His blood stampeded through his veins, and he could feel his pulse in his ears. His chest couldn't seem to move fast enough to draw a single full breath, and he was halfway convinced he'd snapped his knee in half. Or maybe his back. Either way, he wasn't going to be moving any time soon.

"You were on the treadmill for fifteen minutes, you whining git." Sionn leaned over him, his smile tinged with playful disgust. "And don't think you'll get any sympathy from me acting like you're dying on the floor. It's marble. You're only lying there because it's as cold as shite and you're a damned sweaty mess."

"If you loved me—"

"I love you enough to tell you to get your lazy ass up off the floor and into the shower, boyo." Sionn nudged Damie with his toes. "And get out of the way so I can get a run in."

"You just biked, like…." His brain hurt trying to calculate how many miles Sionn could have done in the time it took him to get dressed, stretch, then run on the treadmill. "Like five hundred miles or something. What do you need the treadmill for?"

"Going to cool down," Sionn said, stepping over him. "Go hit the shower, D. I'll join you in a few minutes."

"Yeah, like I'm still going to be in the shower by the time you're done hiking up the Alps," Damien grumbled, rolling over onto his stomach.

Getting up was painful. Cramped up from hours of sitting in the van, Damien winced when his back complained louder than his legs. The treadmill was probably a good idea to loosen his muscles, but Damien wasn't going to give Sionn the satisfaction of agreeing with him. Especially since he didn't seem like he was going to be rushing to the shower.

"Do you need some help there, D?" Sionn didn't even have the grace to sound breathless as his feet pounded along the treadmill.

"No, I've got it, asshole." Staggering to his feet, Damien flashed Sionn a *V* and ignored Sionn's hearty, boisterous laugh. "Yeah, funny. We'll see how much you giggle when I pass out on you before you can get your rocks off, fucker."

The hot water on his tortured body felt good, but not as good as the travertine tile under his bare ass. Damien felt every inch of the past two thousand miles in his bones and under his skin. Despite the brutal slog on the treadmill, he felt looser than when he'd walked into one of the hotel's luxurious suites and stripped down to just a pair of briefs. The run pushed him to the very end of his limits, and soaking his sweat and stress from his skin seemed like the best way he could spend the evening.

Although it came in a far second to fucking Sionn, but Damien wasn't sure he had the energy to even make it to the bed.

"We could fuck here," he muttered to himself, examining the enormous glass-enclosed shower.

It was larger than most bedrooms, and the wraparound bench held an allure to it. There was even a handrail to hold on to if they needed it, and Damien debated testing it with a firm tug but gave up hope of ever lifting his arm again.

The place was discomforting, styled so much like his childhood home Damien half expected to find his father waiting with a switch around every corner. The delicate wood and brocade fauteuils in the sitting area were nearly an exact match for the ones he'd squirmed in while his father paced the study's floor, berating Damien over the slightest of failures in his school-work or music. A missed note during practice merit-ed a barrage of angry screaming. Flubbing a section meant not sitting down for a week without something soft underneath him.

Everything around him reminded him how small he'd been, how pushed into a corner and whipped un-til blood ran down the back of his legs and soaked into his socks. The heavy silver chargers under the fine porcelain plates were too much like the ones the housekeeper spent hours polishing to a sparkling sheen, only to have his father throw one at Damien's head because he'd cleared his throat at the dinner ta-ble. Everywhere he looked the suite held echoes of nightmarish hours spent wondering when the next burst of pain would come or if the silence around him meant he was alone or simply being stalked.

He nearly jumped out of his skin when Sionn opened the shower door and stepped in.

"Jesus, warn a guy." Damien sucked in a mouth-ful of steam from the jets blasting his back and legs. "You almost gave me a heart attack."

"I think that's from the running you did," Sionn murmured, sliding around Damien to sit on the bench beside him. There was more than enough room for his lover to walk around. Hell, the damned stall was big enough to hold a tiny rave in, but Sionn seemed to take great delight in slithering his hard, toned body over Damien's shaky legs.

Naked, Sionn made Damien's mouth water. Or dry. Depending on what he had in mind. But it eventu-ally led to one of them being on their back or stomach and both of them screaming each other's name. Sionn's flat belly was banded with muscle, and a faint sketch of hair caught at the water drops, turning them into tiny streams coursing down to Sionn's sinewy thighs. His cock swung loose, cowled and dipping to the right. His balls were flushed pink and dappled with fine brown hair, rolling to the side when he sat down.

Everything about Sionn touched off every nerve in Damien's body and set him to humming whenever Sionn was near. There were childhood nicks and scars on Sionn's lightly tanned hands and arms, along with a few dings from battling kegs and rousting drunks. The scars on his knee from being blown out and rebuilt were cleaner than Miki's, but then Sinjun's injuries bordered on crippling while Sionn's larger, healthier body shook off most of the damage as if it were nothing.

Damien knew better. There were days when Sionn ached, but suggestions he slow down were usually met with a slow smile and then a long, sensual lesson on how Sionn could still give as good as he got.

Sucking at Damien's lower lip, he lengthened it into a kiss, then let go. Patting Damien's leg, Sionn teased, "If you could call what you did there *running*."

"I ran. And it got me nowhere but on my ass in the shower." He wasn't going to admit he felt better for doing it, even as his thighs ached. "And there are a lot of better places I could have put my ass."

"That I'm not arguing, boyo." Sionn laughed, turning the hot water up. "There's quite a few places I'd rather have your ass than on a treadmill, but sometimes sacrifices have to be made."

"That's it. I'm a sacrifice for the great…." Damien eyed his lover. "What kind of fucked-up god do you guys have over in Ireland? One of the older ones. Like that thing that grabs you and drags you down into the water."

"It scares me that you've got a tally of murdering spirits in your head, love." Grabbing the plastic soap carrier he'd tossed in earlier, Sionn nodded at the long scrub cloth hanging on the rail near Damien's shoulder. "Pass me that, will you?"

"Only if you promise to use it on me too." Damien fought off a yawn, but it triumphed, cracking his jaw when he succumbed. The soap Sionn brought with him was a pungent, familiar rush of sweet citrus, vetiver, and cliché. Tossing the cloth into Sionn's lap, he pulled a foot up off the tile floor and dramatically plopped it on Sionn's thigh. "You know, I still can't fucking believe you use Irish Spring. It's so… who the hell uses Irish Spring?"

"I do. You do too when it's around and all we've got in the shower. Besides, it's nice," Sionn protested lightly, lathering the cloth up, then grabbing Damien's foot. "And it reminds me of you, Cowboy. Back when you were scraping up coins just to do laundry. All scruffy, worn down, and sexy. Kind of like you are right now."

"Shit, don't call me that. And that's my favorite hat."

"Yeah, I know. You look good in it, D," Sionn said, winking. "And I love when that's all you wear too."

He was too old to be embarrassed, or so Damien told himself. Still, he couldn't ignore the light heat working across his face and down his chest. Soap bubbles frothed over his foot where Sionn scrubbed.

His lover slid his way up Damien's leg, then did the other, gently working over his body until Damien was a slithering mess in Sionn's hands.

He was also harder than the tile under their feet.

"Hey, babe, I've got to get some food in me. I haven't eaten in… well, since the Hoover Dam." Damien gasped when Sionn's hands found the inside of his thighs. "You keep doing that, and I'm going to—"

"Just let me finish. Then you can complain some more." Sionn bit at Damien's thigh, sinking his teeth into the spot he'd just rinsed. His wet hair tickled Damien's hip, and Sionn licked the spot, then bit again, working Damien's skin between his teeth. "Sometimes, D, the only thing I'm hungry for is you."

"Can't believe you can taste food with the shit that comes out of your mouth, Murphy. I've heard Kane say that to Miki too. You guys just swap cheesy pick-up lines?" Damien tugged at Sionn's hair, loving the feel of the silken wet strands between his fingers. "And I'm going to get heat stroke in here. And—"

"And there's a bed out there. And room service," Sionn said, tweaking Damien's left nipple with his fingers. "So we should move." Sionn circled Damie's throbbing nipple with the tip of his tongue. "Out there. Where the bed is."

Out *there*.

Outside the steamed-up shower stall where the nightmare of his childhood lurked in every couch, rug, and sconce. Damie hated every damned pretentious, delicate curve of the chairs and loathed the tasteful flower arrangements sprouting up in every damned room like a floral fortress of solitude. The place was making him jumpy, wound up tighter than Miki when someone else's fork strayed too close to his plate. Sionn's hands on him were a distant sensation compared to the memory of his back's skin being shredded, then having to mop up his own blood from the floor so the housekeeper didn't find it when she came in the next morning.

The ink on his back couldn't mask all his scars, just like Damien ignoring the suite's overblown gold, white, and brocade decorations couldn't make it all disappear so he could focus on the one man who'd found his way into Damien's heart. It was stupid and childish. His brain rebelled at the thought, but Damien was past arguing with his own mind. Logically, he should be able to handle anything the world threw at him. He fucking escaped from an asylum and a serial killer. A few couches shouldn't even be a blip on his radar.

But they were.

"Can I ask you a favor, Sionn?" Damien caught up Sionn's hands, stilling their journey over his ribs.

Sionn frowned and stroked Damien's cheek with his thumb. "Yeah, love. What do you be needing?"

"Can we just…." He kissed Sionn's thumb pad. It tasted of soap, Sionn, and the flat water only found in Las Vegas pipes. "Can we just get the fuck out of this room? This place gives me the creeps."

THEIR NEW suite was smaller, but then the mini apartment they'd just left was bigger than a lot of clubs Sinners played when they were first starting out, so *smaller* was relative. Damien slung his bag onto the red velvet chaise at the end of the bed, then walked over to the window, taking a deep inhale of the cold canned air the hotel pumped through its ducts. A king bed was plumped and readied for them, the covers pulled down, and a towel swan squatted in the middle of the duvet, its beak slightly off-kilter from its hasty creation. There was a sitting area in the main room right off the entrance with a dining table large enough to seat four people. A peek through the bathroom door showed a shower much like the one they'd left behind, luxurious and massive enough for him and Sionn to shower together.

But not a damned faux-Rococo or fake Renaissance Revival piece in sight.

"I literally hate that I know what all that shit is," he muttered at Las Vegas's skyline. "Who the hell teaches their kid about furniture? Oh yeah, my sick asshole father."

Off the strip, the city was mostly flat, racing out to the horizon in a cobweb of flashing lights. The windows were too thick for him to hear anything, but he could still feel the scrambling pulse of thousands of desperate souls dancing as fast as their devils could play. They'd come to stay for a few days, intending to hole up someplace where no one could find them and do nothing but eat, play music, and sleep.

Miki, for some reason, changed all that, throwing Damien's plan out the window, a piece of wadded-up paper soiled with the grease of their disparate personalities. But Sinjun definitely knew what he was doing, because he hadn't heard a damned peep from the others in hours.

"You talking to yourself over there, boyo?" Sionn called out from the kitchen. "Think any of the guys are looking for us? Or can we call it a night?"

"I left messages with the guys that we were done for the night. I'd say it's weird no one but Sinjun picked up, but I've spent weeks with those bastards, so I guess I can let their boyfriends have some time with them." Remembering the dazed expression on Forest's face when Connor bear-hugged him, Damien smirked. "They're probably all having hot rock-star platypus sex on every flat surface in their rooms. I'll be lucky if my rhythm section can walk by the time we head out."

"If you're lucky, you'll be saying that about your lead guitarist too."

His lover's laugh warmed away the rest of the chill in Damien's soul.

"Would you be wanting any of the leftovers? Or should I stash them in the fridge so housekeeping finds their dead, rotting corpses after we check out of here?"

"Nah, I'm good." The air was still canned, but Damien found it easier to breathe. It became even easier when Sionn came up behind him, wrapped his arms around Damien, and rested his chin on Damien's shoulder. "Yeah, I like your plan for the guitarist. He's had it rough these past weeks. Probably could use a bit of downtime."

"Not to put too fine of a point on it, but I'm hoping for an up time." Sionn's low murmur was rich with the hint of rolling green hills and whiskey. "But right now, love, this is very nice. Even if I had to wait two hours before we had a place to sleep again. And then you ate chocolate cake in front of me."

"You ate it too," Damien pointed out. "Can't believe you bitched at me because I wanted to eat dessert first."

"It's just not how things are done, love. Pudding comes after meat." Sionn's reflection in the glass grimaced at Damien. "I was all right with it until you started licking the cream from your fingers. Then… things got interesting. Pretty sure the waiter kept that serving plate of his in front of him to hide that hard-on you were giving him."

"Left him a tip." Damien leaned back, curving his body into Sionn's. "A really good one. And please don't say you'll give me more than a tip."

"Ah, Mitchell, you know me so well."

"Did you miss the part where I've been stuck in a van with your best friend?" He stroked the fine hair on Sionn's forearm, reveling in the tickle on his palm. "Man, do I have a few stories about you in high school. Rafe can talk for days. And does."

"Talking. We should be doing less of it, because I've got to tell you, D," Sionn whispered. "I'm kind of hoping I'll not be walking too well either."

DAMIEN WOKE up screaming.

Or at least he tried to.

His mouth was open, throat straining to break past the thick membrane of sleep, but there was no sound. No *anything* but a pitch-black pressing in on him and his past unleashing a herd of nightmares to ravage the already muddied landscape of his broken mind.

The dark clung to him, wrapping him tight and oozing into his mouth until he choked on the gloom around him. Phantom searing pains slashed across his back, legs, and chest, his body jerking at the flashes of heat his skin remembered all too well.

"*A ghra*." A thin silvery thread wrapped around the tentacles of fear shoving their way down Damien's throat and *yanked* at the stygian terrors. "Damien love, wake up. God in Heaven, please."

Damie's world shook, rattling his bones and rapping at his skull. His breath was being stolen away, shoved out of his lungs by the rapacious tendrils his mind sent out. The fight to survive the attack was real, a betrayal of thoughts buried so long ago Damien'd thought they were dead.

Instead they were merely stewing in the hatred and violence that forged them, waiting for a moment when Damien's walls cracked and they could push through, intent on sucking his will to live until it was nothing more than dust on his soul.

"*Damien*." A familiar voice urged him to follow its brightness. "*Wake up!*"

He surfaced, breaking the sticky black bubble encasing him in his dreams. Grabbing on to Sionn's voice, Damien forced himself up out of the tar he was drowning in. The air he sucked in was stale, deader than what he'd shoved out of his lungs, but at its edges he found Sionn.

His lover smelled of his damned soap and the sex they'd had, a sweaty, messy romp where they'd run out of lube and fell asleep midcuddle. Sionn was solid under Damien's hands, a buoy he could cling to in the storm of his panic. A single blink, forced but necessary, and the inky shroud covering him fell away, leaving only Sionn and the lingering sandpaper feeling of drying fear in his chest.

"I'm good," Damien gasped, stroking his trembling fingers across Sionn's worried face. "Awake now. I'm good."

There was enough light to see, a bleed from the still-churning Strip despite the early-morning hour. They'd forgotten to close the drapes or hadn't really cared if anyone saw them fucking, Damien was never sure which, but it was something to bother him now. Sex was a celebration. This fear—his fear—was a haunting too intimate for him to bare to the world.

"Close… can we close the curtains?" Damien struggled to sit up. His legs and torso were trapped in the bed linens, and he couldn't find an end to begin unraveling himself.

"Stay there," Sionn ordered softly as he got up. "I'll be getting the curtains and some water for you. You going to be okay while I'm gone?"

"Yeah, I'm fine." His stomach hurt, and Damien tried to swallow around what seemed like the mouthful of sand he had in his throat. The bedroom fell back into shadows, but they were softer, warmer than the hard-edged ice he'd woken from. There was still enough light to see, a faint hint of gold coming from the windows in the next room, but the dimness helped soften the worry aging Sionn's face. Smiling brightly, Damien said, "Water's good. I could use water."

His dreams were whispers, half-seen and barely heard nothings lingering at his memory's horizon. Damien didn't want to chase them. It would be a futile trip to the edge of an abyss he'd stared down more times than he cared to count. Suppressing the urge to shower the creep of sweat from his body, Damie pulled his legs up and waited for Sionn to come back.

Sionn came back with tea. Scalding, delicious-smelling English breakfast hot enough to scald the sweet off a virgin's tongue and sugary enough to convince the Devil he'd gotten his wings back.

"God love you," Damien whispered, taking the dish-towel-wrapped mug. "God just fucking love you for the rest of your life for bringing me this."

"That's what I love about you, D." Sionn chuckled, climbing into bed next to Damien. "You're a slut for a good steeped leaf."

"Sometimes you just *need* tea." His first sip was a brief slurp of molten heaven. "Must be a genetic thing, because for as much as I love coffee, there's nothing like a good black tea." Another sip and Damien sighed. "Thank you, Murphy. For… everything."

The concern tightened Sionn's gentle smile, and he nodded curtly. "How about you get some of that in you, and then you tell me what's got you screaming in your dreams."

"It's Sinjun's nightmares. They're contagious."

He tried a laugh, but its acidic hiss only succeeded in creasing Sionn's brow further.

"No, really—"

"I don't mind you lying to yourself, D," Sionn said gently. "But don't you be lying to me. Not after everything we've gone through and probably some shite we'll be going through in the future too. Don't you be cheapening us with some tinfoil lies you've got on that silver tongue of yours."

Music was easier than words. Sure, he could talk nearly anyone into doing what he needed, but if there was one thing Damien couldn't do it was speak for himself. The darkness helped. The feel of Sionn's fingers down his naked back went a long way in stilling his jangled nerves. But his tongue lay thick and still in his mouth, a heavy, damp lump unable to form a single word to explain away the ghosts he dredged up in his sleep.

"I don't know where to start," he confessed. Biting back the sour rising over this tongue, Damien shook his head. "I don't know, Sionn."

"How about if you start with why we had to move rooms. That's as good a place as any," he suggested, his hand trailing down Damien's spine, caressing each bump. "Because that's not something normal, D. And don't talk to me about the spoiled-rocker crap you pulled on the front desk. You didn't give one shit about the view."

"It was the whole fucking place, Sionn." That was the best he could come up with, and Sionn's hand stilled. Once he started, Damien found he couldn't stop talking, and he caught himself stumbling over the words pouring out of him. "I don't know if I am just really worn out or what, but it was like pieces of my life were coming up out of my childhood and slapping at me. I couldn't look at anything in that suite without flashing back to when I was a kid, you know?

"Every bloody shadow in the hall was suddenly my dad, waiting for me to go into his study or the living room so he could beat the shit out of me because I tied my shoes the wrong way or didn't write my name neat enough on a fricking test. I couldn't fucking breathe in that house… or in that room, Sionn."

His hands began to shake, and Sionn took the mug out of Damien's hand and set it on the nightstand.

"I don't *feel* real when everything around me is thousand-dollar chairs and silverware on gold plates.

It's why I like the warehouse. Shit, probably why I love you and Sinjun. You feel *real* to me."

"We love you too, D. So long as you know that, yeah?"

Sionn pulled Damien into his arms, an ungainly wrap of limbs and skin, but Damien reveled in the heat of his lover's body and the comforting brush of Sionn's lips on his cheek.

"You know you don't have to be afraid to talk to me, D. Anything you need out from your soul, you can depend on me to help you muck it out."

"Most of the shit there is caked on and dried, Sionn. And it's what I'm standing on. I don't think there's anything good under there to dig out." He curled up in Sionn's embrace, bathed in Sionn's warm breath and soft words. "I lived in my dad's toy box, babe. He took me out and pulled me apart whenever he was bored."

"And your mum?"

"Mom. My mom kind of floated around the place, drunk off her ass and buying these spindly fucking gold chairs, like if she made the horror show we lived in prettier, no one would see the blood on the floor." He exhaled, hard. "That penthouse? It was like being right back there, Sionn. It's why I don't *like* staying at fancy hotels or eating dinners where I need escargot tongs. There wasn't a silver spoon in my mouth when I was born. That metal taste was a loaded gun shoved past my lips, and my dad's finger was always on the trigger, squeezing."

"You're safe from that now, love. No one's ever going to do that to you again."

"Babe, I love you, but that's exactly what they did when they put me in that loony bin and told everyone I was dead. That was just another little box where they could poke at me whenever they wanted to. Look at the mind games my uncle and dad pulled on me." He bit down at the anger growing in his gut. "They paid a couple of people to pretend to be my parents. Tried to convince me I wasn't even *me*. He wasn't happy with just locking me up, Sionn. He had to unmake me, fuck with me so much I couldn't even be sure of even Sinjun. I can't go back into that kind of box and not feel him beating me down, Sionn."

"Staying in motels with roaches the size of a dog doesn't fix that, D." Sionn laughed at Damien's disgusted snort. "It doesn't, but I can see where you'd be wanting something earthier. And as that earthier something, I'm glad for it."

"I wanted to do this trip with the guys because I really fucking *needed* to feel like this was genuine. It's because you guys make me feel like I'm not some goddamned wooden boy puppet who can't get anything right. With you guys I'm not my dad's goddamned Pinocchio. Although Miki says he's the puppet, he ain't got shit on me." Damien grinned despite the chill in his blood. "I *like* the bad food and the long drives because I know at the end of it, I get to climb up on a stage and play with some of the best fucking guys there are to be with. Then when it's all said and done, I get to crawl home and have you. I'll take that over a plate of escargot any day, Sionn. *Any* fucking day."

"Just one thing wrong with that, D," Sionn drawled slowly.

"What's that?" Damien sniffed.

"You never have to wait to crawl home to have me, love," his lover said, lowering Damien into the pillows, then covering him with his long, hard body. "Whether I'm there by your side or not, you'll always have me with you. *Every* fucking day."

TWELVE

I've come a long way
Cried in the dark
There's been times when I've screamed
Times when my soul's barely a spark
You touched me then
Kissed my bleeding heart
Showed me the sunshine
Promised never to part
Wake up in the morning
You are still near
The world's only beautiful
When you're right here
—Beautiful Day

CONNOR FELT the air change when Kane spotted the matching rings he and Forest wore and then the ripple when, a second later, his baby brother made the intuitive leap to their meaning.

Mostly because, as they strolled down the Vegas strip behind Miki and Forest, Kane looked up at something Forest was pointing out, glanced back down at Connor's hand, then said, "Mum's going to fucking kill you both."

Connor had about fifteen pounds of muscle on Kane and maybe an inch or two of height, so he figured he could take his brother down and bury his dead body someplace out in the desert before Kane spilled the beans to their mother. The biggest complication in that plan was Miki. As dirty as the Morgan boys fought, Miki was dirtier and meaner. A normal person would take one look at Miki St. John, see a lean, silky beautiful man inclined to sidestep trouble, and think he'd be a pushover, especially against Connor's mass and strength.

Yet Connor knew better. He might have the brawn to do serious damage, but Miki had years of living on the edge, an unnatural ability to turn anything into a weapon, and no fear of death. He'd go all in where a fight over Kane was concerned, and that made him doubly dangerous. So while Con knew he could best Kane, he'd live in terror of Sinjun for the rest of his life. Which would be about five seconds after he popped Kane in the mouth.

Funny thing about Las Vegas—something Connor hadn't noticed before—there were a lot of things an enraged rock star could use to kill a man lying about on the road. The newsstands were bolted down now, their curved forms randomly dotting the sidewalks, but there were other dangers, like street entertainers with canes or women with impossibly tall stilettos. He wouldn't put it past Kane's Miki to upend a woman in a tight gold lamé, rip off her shoe, and bury its knife-like heel into Connor's eye.

Since Miki and Forest were about ten feet ahead of them, Connor decided he'd take his chances.

"Say one damned thing to her, and I'll rip your fucking balls off, little brother," he ground out through a smile he gave Forest when his lover glanced back at them.

It was a good threat. Solid and delivered with enough menace to leave Kane weak in his knees. Nearly two years of living and loving Miki St. John, however, changed a man, and Connor was disgusted when his baby brother laughed at him.

Literally laughed in his face, then kept walking.

"I'm serious, Kane." Connor snagged his brother's arm, yanking him to a stop. "You whisper one word in Mum's ear, and you'll be giving Sinjun toothless blowjobs."

"Should have thought about that before you married him." Kane shrugged him off. "'Sides, she loves Forest. *You* she'll kill, but Forest can do no wrong."

"We're going to have a family thing. Just need to keep it quiet." He rubbed at an aching spot between his eyes. "It was a spur-of-the-moment thing, between us, you know? Sometimes—and I love our family—but there are times when I'm sick of them being around for everything. This was just… us. Intimate. Well, crazy, but it was just ours."

"Yeah, I know how that is." His brother nodded, his smirk a flash of white teeth and mockery. "But see, out of all of us, you're the only one who she could count on to be walking down the aisle. And you took that from her. She's going to kill you so slowly. You're going to be begging for your death before she's half-done with you."

"Did you miss the part where I said we're going to do a family thing—"

"Then I'd suggest you let her plan it, because there's no going back on this, Con. This is possibly the stupidest thing you've done since you convinced Riley he could make his dick longer by shoving it in the vacuum hose and turning the damned thing on."

"God in Heaven, he was a stupid kid. We couldn't get Quinn to fall for anything. I never figured the rest of them would be so stupid."

"Riley isn't stupid. He's just not Q," Kane pointed out. "Now, what are you going to tell Mum?"

"That I'd want her to help plan the family ceremony." Connor shrugged at Kane's disbelieving snort. "It would go a long way in mending fences, and she's not that bad, really. As you said, she loves Forest. All he has to do is say *please*, and she's bending over backwards and giving him the moon. Not like you and your Miki are ever going to be exchanging rings."

"I don't know. We've never really talked about it," he replied. "Miki's not… it's hard around him. There's no framework for him. I don't know if marriage is even something he thinks about. If it's important to him. I'm guessing not. Once he loves, I don't think he needs anything else."

"What about you?" Connor asked, slowing his pace so they could talk without their lovers hearing them. "What do *you* want, Kane? Have you talked to him about any of that?"

"Con, I don't know," Kane said. "I'm not thinking about where we're going to be in five years. Maybe one day Miki will look at me and say, 'Hey, I want to get married.' Maybe I'll say it to him. I don't know, but I'm not going to worry about it. We'll do what we do. But I can tell you this, I sure as hell wouldn't let Mum plan the wedding. I'd never see Miki again."

"He *is* her white whale."

"They get on, you know? But he's prickly and so's she." Kane nodded. "Truth now. Do you really want the two of them on the same side of the fence? I'd get no fucking peace. I'd have nowhere to hide if the two of them get the same idea in their head—"

Something was off about the man crossing the street head of them. Connor couldn't put his finger on what it was, but something odd grabbed at Connor's mind and shook him like a terrier with a bone. It wasn't him cutting through traffic. There were plenty of idiots slicing through the spaces between the parade of slow-moving cars. It could have been his hunched-over shoulders and the hoodie he'd pulled down low over his eyes. The night was cold enough for a jacket for some, although the brisk cold wind on his face felt good. There was the threat of rain in the air and an electrical crackle on Connor's skin, warning him of an incoming storm.

Still, even with his attention drawn to the dark-clad man jogging up to the sidewalk, Connor almost didn't see the knife in his hand until its edge was nearly to Miki's ribs.

Then all hell broke loose.

FOREST WAS a decent guy. Oddly decent despite every shitty thing he'd come up against in life. The way Miki saw it, Forest would end up a lot like Donal, tossing out little pebbles of wisdom and understanding while the rest of them couldn't get their shit together enough to microwave a bowl of oatmeal.

Whereas *he* was going to spend the rest of his life wondering why his brain insisted on turning everything he heard into music.

It was a bad thing for the most part. Sometimes the thrum of tires on a road lulled him into crashing, but more often than not, he caught the beat of a baseline, and then his fingers and mind itched to fill in the blanks. There was a reason he loved being home. It was *quiet*. A stillness where the only voices he had to worry about were the ones he knew and the jangle of metal meant Dude was strolling by or scratching at a phantom itch somewhere in his wiry blond fur.

Except nothing was turning into music now.

Las Vegas was the kind of chaos bright and loud enough to drive Miki insane if he stayed submerged in its flashing cacophony for longer than a few hours. The drummer seemed to thrive in it, bouncing on the balls of his feet when they stopped to watch a man in brass-paint-covered clothes pretend to be a windup toy dancing to the recorded plinking of a badly played toy piano.

He kind of envied Forest's wholehearted disregard of the world around them. It was as if Connor came into his life and suddenly everything dangerous was outside a hamster ball and couldn't touch him. Miki knew better. There were things out there with mouths bigger than a hamster ball and powerful enough to crush his seemingly impenetrable world with one snapping bite.

"Man, that's some crazy shit," Forest shouted over the crashing chimes of a passing one-man band's performance. "Worse than drums, I think. You'd have to keep track of everything you're—"

"Hey, you're Miki St. John. I've got your CD, man!" A guy in a black hoodie and camo pants appeared in front of Miki, sliding out of the crowd to thrust a plastic case at Miki's stomach. "Can I get you to sign—"

"Mick!" Connor yelled down the sidewalk. "Get—"

Crowds were a curious thing. In the face of panic, some fled while others stumbled about, unsure of where to go or what to do. A few screamed, drawing the energy on the sidewalk up tight, and people broke off from the foot traffic, crashing into one another when they scattered away from the thundering rush of Morgans coming at them.

"Hey, wait—" Miki held up his hand for Kane to stop, for Connor to take away the crazed look on his face, anything to hold off the wall of rage barreling down on him. The crowd was thick and frantic, shoving at his back. Someone's hand glanced off his head, and he turned to tear into whoever hit him.

Then he saw the knife.

The blade was small enough to be hidden behind the CD case being shoved at him. The guy twisted his wrist, and the case fell away, its cheap knockoff album art from an '80s hair band flying up into the air as it flipped open. The paper flapped across Miki's left hand, a black-and-red butterfly sporting Aqua-Net coifs and spiked leather jackets on its wings. The knife dug in next, its tip burying into Miki's skin to pull up a long thread of blood along its matte silver blade.

"Motherfucking son of a bitch," Miki snapped.

Fear did odd things to him. It haunted his thoughts, shadowy reminders of pain and terrors past, and Miki found himself in the throes of anger when slammed up against a wall of panic. The slice on his arm stung, bleeding out onto the sidewalk and leaving crimson snowflake splashes on the rough concrete slab beneath his feet. He'd grown up with the smell of his own blood in his nose. Miki knew the feel of his skin being torn apart and the ache of swollen flesh and torn muscles before he could even read his own name.

He was fucking tired of tangling with the nightmares in his life shoving into his every waking moment until he couldn't take a breath without it tasting like the regurgitated shit sandwich he'd been left to eat at birth. The asshole with the knife was simply another pebble in the road, a path he'd smoothed out carefully when he'd fallen in love with Kane and reunited with Damien.

And he was really tired of people thinking they could take him down without a fight.

His fist was bloody when Miki planted it in the guy's thin lips. His knuckles took the brunt of the hit when he scraped them across the man's teeth, but the shot was enough to make his attacker stumble back and drop the knife.

Miki tried to grab at the man's zipped-up sweatshirt. He needed something to hold on to, to twist around and drive the guy down so he could hammer at his head. Punching out again, he got a glancing blow off the man's cheek, pushing the hoodie back from his face.

It was a shock of sorts to find himself staring into the face of an older Asian man, his left incisor flashing gold in the blood smeared across his lips. The sunken hollow of his cheeks was at odds with the pink, fleshy bags beneath his hard, glittering eyes. His messy crop of hair was more wiry silver than black, and as Miki tugged at the sweatshirt's hood, he pulled apart the top's zipper, exposing a patchwork quilt of mottled blue tattoos running down his crepe-like wattle and spotted neck.

Including one that looked so much like the one Miki had on his arm, it shocked him speechless to see it.

The man jerked free of Miki's numb fingers, spinning around. Kane's hand closed over Miki's shoulder, pulling him back, and the man's arms flailed about, his foot sliding off the sidewalk. One of his hands smacked Miki's cheek. Then the world went hot with Irish curses and black-haired cops pushing into Miki's space. Frightened, the man turned to flee and lost his balance, falling away from the sidewalk.

Everything moved too quickly to make sense out of but too slow to do anything but watch in horror as the man's arm flung wide. Miki felt a shove from the right, a woman still caught on the edge of the fray. Then he saw the street entertainer make a grab for the man.

Miki's attacker shoved back, but the performer was stronger, muscles thickened from time spent holding himself in impossible poses. The man in the hoodie bounced off the gold-painted performer and tumbled right into a Las Vegas tour bus.

"AND YOU'VE never seen this man before in your life?"

For the fifth or sixth time since he'd been shoved into the tiny gray room with its uncomfortable chairs and flickering yellow lights, Miki stared down the cop who'd led him into their little slice of Groundhog Day hell and shook his head. They'd been at it for more than two hours, and the questions kept circling back around to the one thing Miki couldn't answer—who the hell was the guy who stabbed him, then pancaked himself against a bus.

It was funny that cops still made Miki nervous. Especially considering he spent most of his days surrounded by people who lived, ate, and breathed badges and justice. By now Miki felt the snarl in his belly at the scent of a police officer would have gone the way of the dodo. Instead, being a ringside spectator at the Morgan show only seemed to make things worse. Probably because he judged every cop he met by one golden standard—Captain Donal Morgan and his badge-sporting brood.

The asshole spitting on him as he talked was sure as hell no Donal Morgan.

Miki slid the photo of the dead guy back across the table with a flick of his fingers. He'd studied the battered, bloodied face for nearly half an hour, trying to make some sense out of the whole thing. There were tantalizing peeks of ink, but when Miki'd asked for a good shot of the guy's neck, a thick-necked cop who'd dragged him into the station jumped on him for it, then passed Miki over to a skinny detective for questioning. He'd agreed to it at first, but as his ass grew colder and number from sitting too long on the metal seat, Miki wondered if he'd been stupid to tell Kane he'd go it alone.

"Look, for the last fucking time, I don't know him," he repeated slowly. "It's not like you guys don't have his fingerprints. Hell, you've got his damned fingers. I'd *like* to know who the hell he is, but I *don't*."

"Yet you think he's got a tattoo on his neck that matches the one on your arm?" Up close, the cop's breath smelled oddly of mint and pastrami. "Guy's got a beef with you, knows your name, and maybe has the same tattoo as you, but you don't know him?"

Ginger-haired and lean but for a pop of a belly straining two buttons of his sweat-stained blue cotton shirt, Detective Jenkins of the LVPD looked like he could only have ended up as a cop. Or maybe a high school principal. Either way, his fleshy pink lips continued to flap, spittle flying across the table's slick surface.

"Won't know for sure unless I can see it again." Clenching his fists, Miki steadied his voice. "Asshole tried to stab me, and I grabbed his hoodie. That's when I saw his neck, but I can't be sure. Look, it's all I've got for you."

A knock on the door jerked the cop up, his spine snapping straight at the sound. His gray polyester pants squeaked when he walked to the door, a faint whispering slither not unlike the sound of anoles fighting on Miki's rooftop. Jenkins's shoulders grew stiff, and he barked over a meek-voiced uniform standing in front of the now open door.

"What?" Jenkins moved, blocking Miki's view of the hall outside. "I'm in the middle of questioning a witness."

"Fucking lizard," Miki muttered to himself. The cop didn't spare him a glance, but Miki was pretty sure the guy heard him—just like he heard a familiar cock-arousing Irish baritone rolling through the crack of the open door.

"Either he's coming out, or I'm going in to get him, Jenkins." Kane's threat was a low roll of sharpness softened with a velvety burr. "Your captain's rolling through that door in about ten, and she's going to want to know from you why he's still in that room when he's told you everything he knows."

"I could use a Band-Aid." Miki raised his voice. "Back of my hand's bleeding again. Opened it up."

Another deep rumble, indistinct but definitely Connor. Then Kane said, "Con's going to find something. Just for God's sake, don't suck on it."

"I'm not." He lowered his hand before he could lick the daub of blood seeping out of the cut. The back of his hand hurt, and Miki had a tiny bit of regret at refusing the gauze and paper tape he'd been offered by an EMT. "It's, like, two drops. Sheesh."

"Worse than your dog, I swear to all the saints," he muttered. "What's it going to be, Jenkins? In or out?"

"He's all yours, Inspector." Jenkins flung the door open and waved an elaborate flourish with his arm. "Don't go anywhere just yet. I'm not done with any of you."

As welcome a sight as Kane's massive shoulders and worried, rugged face were, Miki was rounding past disgruntled and heading into pissy. He was hungry, tired, and an asshole trying to kill him ruined what he'd hoped would be a late-night walk down the Las Vegas strip with nothing to do but watch people and sneak a few kisses off Kane. They were on the rattles-end of a snaking tour, and everyone's nerves were stretched tight. He'd wanted to grab a steak, blow off some steam, and have the kind of sex where the people in the hotel room beneath their bed would call security on them. Instead he was sitting in a cold gray room with his hand dotted with blood and wondering about the only inheritance he was ever going to have—a shitty, blown-out tattoo he didn't know the meaning of.

He took Kane's kiss anyway, because it was a hell of a lot sweeter than the bile churning around in his empty stomach.

"How are you doing, Mick?" Kane pulled one of the other chairs in close, then cupped the back of Miki's head. "Do I need to kill that asshole? He kept you in here long enough."

"I don't need you to defend me against some cop, K," Miki reminded him. "I've been telling your kind to fuck off since before I could play a guitar. And I'm fine. Quit worrying. You look like your mother."

"Oh, that's a punch to the balls there, love," Kane grumbled, but his smile lightened the storm in his eyes.

"Did you really call his captain?" He didn't think Kane would pull shit on another cop, but after more than an hour with Jenkins, Miki didn't really care what Kane did—short of shooting the man—but even that was on the table. Slyly, he said, "Or did you have your dad do it?"

"You're mean when you're hungry." Kane pulled a granola bar out of his jacket pocket and put it on the table in front of Miki. "Here."

"I'm hungry, and you bring me oatmeal-flavored cardboard?" It was a green wrapper, familiar but still low on the list of things Miki considered edible. "The vending machine didn't have chocolate? Chips?"

"You know that saying about beggars not getting to be choosers?"

"Bullshit, best money I made before we got to headline a stage was from begging." The granola bar was stiff in his hands as he unwrapped it. It reeked of honey and gruel, and Miki resigned his stomach to its fate. "Don't know why I'm still here. Not like I was the one who pushed the guy into the bus."

"That's what I love about you, Miki, besides that ass and mouth of yours. You're practical down to the bone." Kane shook his head. "We're going to be stuck here for a little bit longer yet. I told Con to let the other guys sleep, because there's nothing to be done, and they'd just be walking the halls with us. Told Con to go back to the hotel and try to crash for a while, but—"

"He told you to fuck off," Miki said around a mouthful of mealy granola.

"Pretty much. But Damie and the others? If we're still here in a few hours when the sun comes up, then there's room in the hall for them. Hopefully we won't be here that long, but you never know."

"So how come they won't shake me loose? Did anyone say? Jenkins kept pushing me about the guy with the knife, but shit, I stared at that damned photo until my eyes were about to bleed, but he doesn't ring a bell." The granola bar was turning to mush, and belatedly, Miki realized he had nothing to wash the mash down with. "Why not just look up his fingerprints? Not like he's going anywhere."

"See, that's the problem, Mick." Kane grimaced. "He did go somewhere. Coroner's van got jacked on the way to the morgue. Driver's in surgery with a shot to the head. The guy's body never made it to the morgue, love, and they have no idea who took it."

THIRTEEN

*There are times when I wonder if the
life I've got wasn't stolen from
someone else. It was a shit beginning, got better, then went to shit
again.*
Then it got... it turned glorious.
It scares me. This life I have now.
*Because I've lost everything once
already.*
I won't survive losing it again.
—Notes from a black notebook hidden
under the bed

MIKI KNEW the exact moment when he broke.

There'd been times in the past when he'd felt the
jagged, rough surface of the universe's depths scrape
his soul raw—too many times to count, if he were

honest. He'd lived pain and terror for so long he'd grown accustomed to its sour taste in his mouth, tainting even the air he breathed with its brackish yellow foulness. Survived a childhood of invasion and bruises, withstanding his body being used and torn, nothing more than a piece of meat for others to play with. Then he'd curled up against the storm of losing his world, stripped back down to the bone after wrapping a family of music and brotherly love around him.

It scared Miki senseless to scrape up the walls of his soul again to house the loves he'd gathered, the unexpected, glorious feel of Kane's soul mingling with his, Damien's resurrection from the ashes of the past, then the arrival of two men who shared his love of music and the need to scream out that love from the light-drenched stage.

But he'd begun to rebuild, finding a solid foundation of a patchwork family under him and a glimmer of something bright on the horizon of his dark soul.

So it was all the more terrifying when the van's windows were suddenly filled with a semi's churning tires and rivet-studded yellow trailer.

Then he couldn't stop screaming.

The Seattle roads were wet, winding around one another until Miki couldn't tell which way was up anymore. Green dominated his senses, a smack of leaves, rain, and verdant clouding his eyes and nose with a pungent slap of color and scent. There was just too much of it around him, crowding down over the yellow-striped black ribbon curling around corners and singing beneath the van's humming tires.

Overwhelmed and tired, he'd pulled his knees up, then reached for the notebook he'd been writing in.

Rafe and Forest bickered lightly about webbed feet and swamp-surrounded gigs, pretending not to hear Damien telling them to fuck off from his sprawl across the rear seat behind Miki.

It was normal, a playfully contentious normal they'd all established after weeks of being cooped up in the van and traveling to their next beer-soaked, scream-riddled gig.

A moment of screeching brakes was all it took to shatter Miki's new normal.

There was a scab on his mind, one Miki had no idea was there. Rough and stuck firm to the flesh of his memories, the scent of smoking rubber and tearing steel grabbed the necrotic debris, then yanked it clean off, leaving Miki torn open and bleeding.

It was raining in his memories, a river of blood, whiskey, and smog-muddled water pouring into his open mouth. Someone was moaning, and Miki couldn't open his eyes. His joints were iced over, frozen in place, and no matter how hard he strained, his arms and legs refused to straighten out. Images flashed through the darkness, Johnny lying in broken-off pieces in the middle of the road while Dave's dead-empty eyes stared at him from a nearby shadow, his body twisted about so far his collarbone jutted out of his shoulder. Metal pieces were everywhere, punched through the black leather seat he'd been sitting in. Then Miki blinked, and the seat's leather softened to a dove gray.

Then came the hit, and the world began to spin.

There was shouting, but none of it came from Miki's raw throat. He could only scream, caught in another time, another rain where the wet road turned crimson under orange streetlights. Tumbling, Miki slammed into something hard, rolling about the cramped space, trying to cover his head with his arms, but they were moving too quickly or he was going too slow, because the trees played a game of Ring Around the Rosie, waiting for them all to fall down.

Miki tasted blood, a smear across his teeth. Then he hit the side of the van. It rocked, sliding and grinding over the ground, then lurching once, twice across something in the way. The whole cabin shuddered, thunderous crashing sounds shaking the windows, then another skidding jerk.

The van came to a rocking stop, and Miki was left with the blood, rain, and his scraped-open memories.

Hands were on him. In the eerie silence of his muted mind, Miki felt someone grabbing at him, touching his shoulders and poking at his ribs. His face was wet, metallic-seeped rivulets coming from his forehead to run over his cheek. He tried blinking, but his vision was too red, too swollen with the pain in his heart to see much of anything—to *feel* much of anything but the emptiness inside him.

"Damie! I have to find...." He couldn't fight off the specters of police uniforms, white coats, and sirens. Outside somewhere in the rain, Damien lay dying, and Miki couldn't let him go. Not again. Not in the messy knot of fear and echoes rushing his thoughts. The hands were on him again, forcing him back down, and he struck out, his fists finding meat and bone beneath them. "Have to find D—"

"Right here, Sin. Right here. Come on, man."

Damien's husky British-gin-and-tonic voice cut through the coppery panic in Miki's mind.

"I'm here, Sin. Right here. It's okay. We're okay."

"Cops are coming."

Miki *knew* that voice—Rafe. It was Rafe.

"Hold on. Forest's grabbing the first-aid kit from the back."

"The guitars—" More blood, watery this time and stinging, got into Miki's eyes. His tongue hurt on one side, imprinted with his teeth, and he spat, wanting his mouth clear so he could yell at someone—anyone—nearby.

"Here. Hold still, Sin."

Forest's voice became a shadowy glyph in front of him, and then a lemon-spiced wet paper dabbed at Miki's face. Things got clearer, changing from shapes to a worried-looking dirty-blond drummer with world-weary eyes and an angelic broken smile.

"There you are. Just lie there, okay?"

Miki tried to speak around the swell of his tongue, but his words came out garbled. "Damien… where?"

"I'm right here, Sin."

Damien came up behind him, wrapping something thick and warm around Miki's shoulders. A whale song echoed off in the distance, turning sharper and louder until it changed, a chorus of sirens bouncing around them and folding over the rain's *shush-shush* whisper.

"Rafe! See if you can get one of the ambulance guys here. I think he's going into—"

The blood washed from his face, a cold settling under Miki's skin as the storm began to fling its fury down on his battered body. Something—everything—hurt, but his heart was slowing from its gallop, his nerves spangled and bright from fear dulling back to a throbbing din. Sitting up was difficult, mostly because he ached, but it was necessary. He needed to see where he was. Needed to know he wasn't imagining the air in his lungs or the sounds of the others moving around him.

He'd been flung or dragged out of the van. That much was clear. It was crumpled in on its rear, spun about so it was facing the wrong direction—or at least Miki thought it was the wrong direction. A heavy delivery truck was rammed up the van's side, nearly parallel to its length. The van's tires were off the road, and it was tilted slightly, resting at an angle in a drainage ditch filled with runoff water and spinning leaves.

The others were soaked through. Both Rafe and Forest were digging out towels from their gear while Damien fought the wind to keep Miki dry in the dubious shelter of their canted van. The open doors kept most of the storm's gusts away, but a few slithered in from under the vehicle, catching the small of Miki's back. A small dark-haired man paced the side of the road, his legs carrying him nearly ten feet away before he edged back to the van. He was shouting to someone on a phone, but his words were snatched up in the wind, tossed away before they could settle down.

"Cops are here," Forest said abruptly.

Miki's stomach turned, going hard and tight. The back of his throat seized up, and his chest began to hurt, the chill kicking into his hips and knee. "Cold, D. I'm so fucking cold."

"Ambulance guys are right here, Sin."

Damien sounded far away, unconvincingly earnest, and as shattered as Miki's fragmented memories of a night not that long ago when his life turned to ash.

"You're fine. Just a bump on your head. Rafe—"

More voices, some of them ringing with authority, and another, mewling and uneasy, accusing someone of something Miki couldn't make out. None of it mattered anymore. The cold was taking him in, locking his thoughts down in its encroaching arctic wasteland. An anger lingered in him, but Miki couldn't find its beginning, only the ripples of anxiety and loss it threw out, resonating along the edges of Miki's thoughts.

"I can't do this, D," Miki said, grabbing at his brother's arm. His fingers were numb, unresponsive, and as hard as Miki tried to hold on to Damien, he couldn't seem to feel anything beneath his hand. His brother was slipping away, falling into the cold and out of Miki's reach. The shivering took him, coming up from his marrow and spreading over Miki's skin, his teeth chattering against his chewed-up tongue. "I'm *scared*, D."

There were monsters in his shadows. Miki knew his demons, nursed them on the fears he cut back every damned day of his life, but these phantoms were larger, meaner than the terrors he battled from the time he woke until the time he lay against Kane at night. These were ghosts wearing faces peeled from men he loved, vacuous and lifeless, hollowed-out voices begging him not to leave them behind, not to bury them in coffins made of the twisted remains of a broken award and unsung music.

"It's okay, Sin."

Damien's raspy plea sounded too much like the gasping, tortured cries Dave gave before his unfocused eyes went empty.

"We're going to be okay. The van'll be fine after a few—"

Miki found his anger, a lean, hungry wolf skulking around the edges of his fears, and he snapped, slapping out at the man he loved as much as he did Kane. Their shared years were iron bands around their friendship, unbroken by time, death, and tragedy, but now a spot of rust appeared, a speck of rain and blood eating into their ties and spreading. His rage turned into a corrosion, chewing up long stretches of patience and bickering, because in the midst of all of his pain, he felt alone in his grief.

The sky was white, filtering through the greenleaf shroud draped over them, and the storm carried the voices Miki tried to keep out of his thoughts whenever it rained. Miki was breaking apart, losing the when of where he was, and everything he'd used to hold himself together unraveled.

"We're not going to be okay. You don't remember. You don't fucking remember a goddamned thing about that night, but I do. I hear them, D, and I can't get to them. I can't get to you. And it hurt so fucking much, I would have given anything to die with them… with *you*," he ground out. "I can't watch us die again, Damie. Please… don't make me, D. *Please*."

THE BLACK-LASHED sapphire-blue eyes Miki woke up to were achingly familiar. As was the deep, growling Irish drawl murmuring his name in the dim light of the hotel room Damie'd booked for him. But the granite-faced cop sitting in the one-and-a-half chair next to the couch wasn't Kane.

Instead, some fickle god decided to send him Donal.

He refused to cry. Flat-out refused.

Then Donal whispered his name, and the Jericho he'd built for himself came tumbling down.

"Hey, Miki boy. I've got ye now." Hands callused from working the yard and in his garage woodshop patted at Miki's back, Donal's strong arms wrapping around Miki's slender body tight enough to drive his breath out of his chest. "It's okay, son. I'm here. It's all right, it is. Everyone's fine. Ye just smacked yer skull around a bit, but what they tell me, ye'll be right as rain after some rest."

It was safe and warm in his Donal cave, and Miki hated himself for clinging to the man, but he couldn't—wouldn't—let go. Confusion slithered out of his battered brain, mingling with words caught in his throat, and he couldn't make sense of the thoughts racing about on his tongue. The heavy plaid shirt Donal wore smelled of apple pie and vanilla, a hint of cigar smoke at the aroma's edges. Blinking, he lifted his head, pulling back a bit, intending to wipe his face when Donal pulled him right back in.

God, it felt too fucking good to be held by a man who called him son. As much as Miki's guts burned and screamed at him to jerk away, to break loose of the embrace, he forced himself to stay. It was a test of wills, fighting against the years of trusting no one, of edging away at any sign of intimacy other than a quick fuck and a sloppy kiss.

Damien might have taught him to care, but he'd never called it love. Not until he'd been knee-deep in the carnage of his life and Kane pounded through his front door. *Then* the scary, tearing emotion rose up and slapped Miki in the face hard enough to make a stone bleed, and Kane shoved his way into Miki's heart, taking no prisoners along the way.

Donal was different. Donal waited and lured, letting Miki feel him out and tossing small nibbles of affection until Miki searched for the chocolate among the empty wrappers of worn conversations. The Morgans were a loud, messy chaos, but in the center of them stood their father, a touchstone for their souls.

Who in time became a rock for Miki to hold on to when the Morgan storm grew too furious for him to stand upright.

A warm, whiskey-voiced rock Miki held on to for dear life as the memories of the day washed over him.

"You've had some sleep, but you know I'm going to be asking you this." Donal's chest rumbled when he spoke, curving around Miki's tremors to find his spine. "When's the last time ye've *had* food?"

"Depends on what time it is." He lifted his head, trying to gauge if the blanket of night outside of the bedroom window was waxing or waning. "And if it's tomorrow yet."

"It's late. I'll give ye that. Around ten." Another long pat down Miki's back, then Donal laughed. "Yer probably wondering where m' boy's at."

"No, I figure if he left SF one more time they were going to fire his ass." Miki reluctantly let his arms drop, then slid out of Donal's hug. "I'm good. Thanks."

"There's no shame in needing people, Mick. Someday ye'll be understanding that," Donal said softly. After giving Miki one last squeeze, he let go.

"And no, Kane's out getting yer things, and he's not in danger of being fired."

"'Cause they're probably scared you'll yell at them or something." Miki chuckled at Donal's derisive snort. His stomach growled, and Miki pressed a hand over his belly. "Okay, yeah. So it's been since… fuck, when did we grab breakfast? About six? And why is it every time I wake up, there's a Morgan trying to shove food into me?"

"Because it's what we do. Now, in the morn was that six?" Donal's frown was fierce and quick. "Didn't they shove something inside of ye when the doctors let ye go? And did they give ye leave to sleep, or is that something I'm going to have to be taking up with Damie when I see him next?"

"Wasn't hungry. I just wanted to…." He'd wanted to die. Curl up into a black hole and die, but Damien wouldn't let him. Instead his brother-in-music cajoled, then bullied Miki into a cab and off to a hotel with enough stars in its rating to rival a clear night sky. "They told me I just bruised my brain a bit. Nothing cracked."

"Just yer brain that's been bruised, then?" Donal took hold of Miki's shirt, tugging at the hem. "Or yer soul too?"

The scab Miki'd torn off earlier bled still, leaking out whispers of loathing and doubt. It wasn't fair for Donal to poke at the wound, even as gently as he'd done it. Miki jerked back reflexively, anticipating a deluge of pain and anxiety.

He wasn't disappointed.

Donal pressed his palm against the small of Miki's back. "Ye can talk to me, Mick. Ye know that, right?"

If it'd been anyone but Donal Morgan probing at his anguish, Miki'd have snarled and flung barbed curses at them. Instead he dug his fingers into the thick duvet and clenched his hands into tight fists.

"Yeah. I just don't know if—" A sob cut through his words, trapping them against the roof of his mouth. Miki swallowed, tasting the rain and tears he'd gulped down along with his terrors while he'd argued with Damien about going to the hospital. He'd lost, and the sulfurous fear remained, tainting even the water he'd sipped at hours later. "It's stupid, you know? Today. It was just so fucking stupid."

"That man hit yer van, Mick. Nothing stupid about that," Donal reassured him. "Rafe saw him coming out of that side street, and he wasn't planning on stopping. Yer all lucky the boy got the van to the side, or he'd have T-boned ye."

"Not the accident." Miki eyed Donal. "After it. I kind of fucking lost my shit, Dad. Just fucking *lost* my shit."

It was an odd place for firsts. He'd slid around calling Donal Dad a few times, but now the word simply tumbled out, as natural as taking his next breath, and Miki waited for the slap. There was always a slap. Presuming too much. Reaching for too much. It'd been ingrained in him for as long as he could remember that he'd not been worth the gum most people scraped off their shoes, and there he was, calling the best man he knew *Dad*.

Donal merely nodded and said, "Damien told me ye were shaken. More than when ye were stabbed or even when that arse at Vegas tried to kill ye. And ye've had a lot of arses trying to kill ye, Mick, so for a car accident to shake ye had me worried. It's why I came up. It sounded like ye needed a da."

There was a point where Miki was sure he couldn't find tears anymore, but he hadn't reached it yet. Something about the Morgans—about Brigid and Donal—seemed to fill his eyes with salt and water. Love shouldn't hurt, Kane'd told him, but with each soft word and gentle stroke Miki was pried open, and his stitched-together heart ached and wept.

"Talk, Mick. It's just ye and me here. No one else. I told Kane I'd call him when ye were ready to deal with his smothering."

Donal's smile was broader than Miki's, but the moment warmed the cold in Miki's gut.

"And yes, I know how Kane is. He's like his mother in that. I can imagine it's a bit of a pain in the arse to deal with his shite, but he loves ye. Ye know that, right?"

"Yeah, I do." Miki crossed his legs under him, nearly falling off the edge of the bed. Donal caught him up, chuckling when Miki grabbed a pillow to hug to his belly. He couldn't look at Kane's father, not straight in the eye, but Donal's presence was big enough to wrap around him even without them touching. "I didn't before. You know? Believe him, I mean. Took me a long time to figure it out. And now I don't know what I'm going to do without him. Damien... I survived Damie dying. Sort of.

"But Kane—God, it fucking scares the shit out of me some days, knowing he's out there with a damned gun and a badge. I've never been scared for anyone before, Dad. Then today I got scared all over again." Taking a deep, shuddering breath, Miki tasted the pool of stark terror he nursed in his soul, smearing its oily blackness over his words. "I'm so fucking weak. I couldn't... there were things coming up at me, stuff I don't know if it really happened or just shit my brain made up, because I don't fucking remember *knowing* this crap before. And it scared me so fucking much, I lost it."

Once the words started, they poured out, and Miki's tongue stumbled over the sharp threads gushing from his mind. He told Donal everything, recalling Dave and Johnny dead and dying on the road and his plunge into darkness when the van's back end skidded off the street. Just when he thought he'd run out of things to say, something dark and nasty snaked out, injecting its poison into his heart.

"I am so fucking angry at Damien, and I shouldn't be but I am," Miki whispered, staring at the night-filled window because looking at Donal would have been too much for him to take. He didn't want sympathy. Hell, he didn't deserve any, especially after he let go of the one thought he'd refused to ever bring to the light of day. "I'm wicked pissed, Dad, because he doesn't remember us dying. He doesn't remember any of it. But I do, and it's stupid, but I'm mad. When we got hit today, it all came back and choked the fuck out of me."

"Today wasn't Damie's fault, son," Donal said, breaking through Miki's rage. "Nor that night either."

"I know that. See? It's so fucking stupid," Miki confessed through the sob he was holding in. "And now I don't know what to do, because as much as I love D, the last thing I want is to get back onto a stage and play with him. I can't hear the music anymore, Dad. *I fucking can't hear my music.*"

FOURTEEN

I found a letter you left me
Words written when we were in love
Every pen stroke a forgotten dream
All of your promises were broken
Shattered as clean as my heart
I don't know why you hurt me
I don't know why the thought of you still
    does
If I could have one thing in the world
It would be to forget what you looked like
It would be to forget how we loved
—Letter from Nowhere

AGED BRICK and terracotta usually made for shitty acoustics, but the piano's notes were a gold pour off the tiny room's walls. He'd wanted someplace quiet to drink, and twenty bucks got him to a door where the staff rarely went. There was only one working light, a warped metal pendant lamp hanging from a thick black cord in the middle of the room, its burnished yellow glow picking out the gold specks in an old lobby couch's upholstery. Two of its three bulbs worked, but the room was barely twelve feet square, and it was enough for Damien to find his way through decades of broken chairs and stacked crates, cradling his shattered heart as tightly as he held the whiskey bottle in his hand.

At some point in its almost one-hundred-year life, the space served as a bar or at least a dumping ground for one, judging by its litter of wooden advertising signs, beer-soaked tables, and the old upright piano with worn-down keys and nicked paint set against the far wall. Gravitating toward the instrument, Damien sat down on its bench, set the bottle down, then lifted its keyboard lid. Most of the action was gone in its pedals, but enough life remained in the upright for Damien to find a melody or two. The *plink-plink* of the upper white keys was off enough to strain Damien's sanity, but he didn't imagine he'd spend much time in that range.

"Not fucking likely." Swigging down an amber mouthful, Damien let the whiskey's burn open up his throat, searing off the regret he'd refused to let out. Setting the bottle down, he studied the keys again, then found a mournful C, sliding his fingers around on the scale. "God fucking hell, things have just gone to shit."

It was three in the morning, his body ached from being thrown around the van when they'd been hit, and there was an open bottle of Jack sitting on the top of the battered piano. Tucked into a dark corner of an old luxury hotel whose walls held whispering secrets of loose women, flamboyant men, and cold, hard nights, Damien's instinct was to scrape up a few Delta Blues classics and let his soul wail about the injustice of life and death.

Instead his fingers picked out a Tempest, and Beethoven filled Damien's tiny, private hall.

He couldn't remember the last time he played any classical music.

Not since… forever.

Damien sailed through a few pieces, blending composers and years as his brain dug out memories old enough to vote and share his whiskey. He'd hit the opening notes of a Mozart concerto in C minor when he felt a piece of his soul come into the room.

Sinjun.

There was something binding them, something inexplicable and unexplainable, but it was there.

Miki reached for the bottle and edged onto the piano bench next to Damien. His brother—there really was no other word for how he felt about Miki—sipped at the whiskey while Damien continued through the piece. The music sounded like shit. Mozart wasn't written for a busted-up secondhand upright, and Damien's fingers were now more used to rock than the classics, but none of that mattered.

Especially when Miki rested his head on Damien's shoulder and quietly sighed.

He softened his playing, drifting over into something lighter and smoother. Before today, Damien would have teased Miki with hints of old bluesy tunes, remnants of a time when everyone who was anyone knew the words to "Polk Salad Annie," or even "Chopsticks," something that always made Miki smile.

But now Damien wasn't sure if Miki would ever smile again. There was no sense of time in their hole. It was a forgotten space, holding its walls in tight and tucked away in the belly of a busy hotel. They marked the time by sips of whiskey and ill-tuned notes.

Until Miki's strangled sob caught Damien up and wrapped him in misery.

"I'm fucked up, D." Miki pressed into his side, lanky and warm. His breath smelled of mint and whiskey, and his eyes were unfocused, hazel glimmers around his blown-out pupils.

"Shit, you're not supposed to be drinking," Damien cursed, easing the bottle from Miki's hand. It worried him more than he'd like to admit when Miki didn't argue with him. "You cracked your head open."

"Did you hear me?" Miki sat up, turning those damning eyes toward Damien. "Do you ever really fucking hear me?"

"I hear you all the time, Sinjun," Damien admitted softly, capping the bottle, then placing it carefully on the piano's flattop. "I just don't always know what to say. Right now I want to get us off this bench and over onto that couch, because you and I? We need to talk."

Miki seemed so small, almost the same size when Damien'd found him on the fire escape years ago. Curled up against one another on a couch covered in cigarette burns and stains, Miki was bird-bone light and fragile, a pale shadow of the cocksure singer Damien knew. Under the pendant lamp, Miki's eyes were sunken in, bruised rounds of faded green and gold. His lips bore teeth prints, chapped scrapes where he'd gnawed on his own flesh, and his nails were bitten down short, a crusted dot of blood mottling his left thumb where he'd lost part of a cuticle. Oddly enough, Miki's feet were bare, his toenails still painted with the matte black polish Forest talked them all into while they waited out a storm in a fleabag motel on the side of a Montana highway.

"How'd you find me?" Damien shifted to the right, trying to give Miki more room to lie down. His head was in Damien's lap, feet propped up against the arm of the couch, and Miki's lashes played with shadow fringes across his cheeks. A spring or something hard dug into Damien's asscheek, but a shimmy to the left took care of it, and Miki didn't seem to mind. "'Course, not like there's a lot of people wandering around the hotel this late at night."

"The luggage guy said he brought you here. Recognized you. Me too," Miki murmured. "Said you paid him fifty bucks for a bottle of Jack and some quiet."

"Yeah, Jack's expensive here."

"You overpaid for the Jack." Miki dabbed his tongue across his lower lip, leaving it damp.

"But not for the quiet," he countered. "Didn't expect to find a piano, so… I'm thinking I scored on the deal."

"That's a pretty shitty piano." He craned his head back, arching his neck to look at the piano. "And it's *green*."

"One does not look a gift piano in the keys," Damien mockingly scolded. "It might be blue. Hard to tell in this light."

"It's fucking split pea, D. There's no coming back from split pea."

He gave a whispering chuckle, one Damie joined in on.

"God, that was an ugly piece-of-shit van you bought that time."

"Held together long enough for me to win that bet with Johnny." The Chevy had been a steal at two hundred bucks but smelled of fish guts and fertilizer, despite everything the previous owner had done to air it out. "We must have spent more money on those damned air freshener pine trees than I did to buy the damned thing."

"Kane doesn't understand why I hate Pine-Sol." Miki wrinkled his nose. "You guys could have bought another kind, you know. Just because they looked like pine trees doesn't mean they had to smell like them."

"Hey, Dave was in charge of that. Not me. I just found the van." He stroked Miki's hair, tracing his eyebrows. "You were supposed to wash it."

"I never did." Miki spread his toes out. "I was too fucking short back then."

"Yeah, I remember. It was like having a lawn gnome for a lead singer." Damie tugged at Miki's chin. "'Course, without the beard. Because fuck, Sin, when are you going to grow some hair on this face of yours?"

"Screw you," Miki sniffed. "Least of my fucking problems."

It was the opening Damien was hoping for.

"Why don't you tell me the worst of them, then?" he asked. "Problems, I mean. Because unlike your

chin hairs, Sin, I think you and I have got some fucking big ones."

"SO YOU'RE pissed off at me because I don't
remember the accident?" Damien scratched his head
and stared down at him. "You know I busted my head
back then, right? I don't even fucking remember win-
ning the goddamned award."

He'd poured his heart out to Damien, going
through every sliver of foul memory he'd puked up
when they'd been struck on the road. Miki was left
trembling, a shiver under his skin even Damien's
touch couldn't soothe. He'd even shared how he felt
when he'd seen Donal in his bedroom and how twisted up inside he felt whenever he tried to think of their
dead bandmates.

Damien, of course, latched on to the one thing
Miki had no control over—his irrational ire at
Damien's memory loss.

Miki grunted. "I didn't say it made sense. I just
said I was fucking pissed off about it."

He'd have to sit up to punch Damien, and at that
moment he didn't want to do anything but lie against
his brother's thigh and stare up at the room's ugly ceiling. An ache throbbed in his belly, either hunger or
something darker, meaner than the demons he already
had inside him. Miki was hoping for hunger, but the
creeping doubts in his mind whispered otherwise.

He also wasn't ruling out the whiskey.

"No, but it doesn't have to make sense. It just is,
right?" Damien asked. "I get that."

"The worst part is that I can't hear anything like
I used to, D," he spoke to a water stain in the tiles. It

was easier to talk at the amorphous brown butterfly than to Damien's face. "Nothing sings to me anymore. No lyrics. No music. Shit, it's storming, and all I hear is the rain. Who the hell hears just the rain in a storm? I think it's why I'm angry. Inside. I'm just so... *angry*."

"Do you want to cut the tour short? We can go home—"

"No, we've got a few shows left. I can do the music. I just can't...." He puffed his cheeks out. "I can't write it. On stage, I'm good. That feels normal. You... Kane... the band are okay. It's just *me*."

The world was silent now. It was still filled with noise, but nothing knitted together anymore. Nothing sang to Miki anymore, and the chaos was growing too loud for him to ignore. The accident played over and over in his head, the crash of glass, metal, and then the taste of blood, but he got nothing from it. No resonance to capture and fold into music. Nothing to turn into a song. Even the words were gone, leaving him lifeless and mute, his tongue slack and motionless.

The darkness inside him even stole his words.

"How long?"

"How long what? Miki blinked.

"Since you've been like this? Weeks? Months?" Damien asked. "Before I came home?"

"I don't know. Maybe a few weeks. It just snuck up, you know? And I can't stop crying. Like I'm leaking out everywhere, and it won't *stop*." Miki rubbed at his nose, dismissing the ache behind his eyes. "God, it's so stupid, D, and I don't know how to fix it."

"Sin, I wish to hell I could make it better, but I can't." Damien's hand made circles on Miki's belly, warming his skin through the SFPD shirt he'd stolen from Kane's duffel bag. "Maybe it's time you talked to someone, you know?"

"Like that's going to work?"

"Has anything you've done worked so far?"

While Damien made a good point, Miki scowled up at him.

"Don't make that face at me. You're mad at me for something I can't change, and I can't fix something inside you that's broken. Maybe we're just too close to it, Sin. But today you scared the shit out of me, dude. Not going to lie. Scared the living shit out of me. I think you need to go in and talk to someone. Someone who can work this crap out for you."

"It's all bullshit, D. Like the assholes at juvie. It's like I'm a checkbox, and they get a handful of cash." He'd been through offices with diplomas on the wall and sweater-wearing, creepy men and women sneering at him from behind their desks. "They want you to play these stupid mind-fuck games, but it's smoke and mirrors. You can see right through them—"

"That's your biggest problem. You're too damned suspicious. Too fricking smart." Damien snorted. "You think that most of the shrinks at Skywood were there for anything other than money?"

"They thought you were some guy hung up on a dead guitarist," Miki pointed out. "Can't blame them for thinking you were crazy. Not like anything's changed there."

"Yeah, fuck you, Sinjun." Pinching Miki's nose, Damien twisted at the tip. "Point is, there were a couple of guys there who really thought they could help me out. There just wasn't anything they could do to fix me because there wasn't anything wrong—"

"There's plenty wrong with you." Shoving away Damien's hovering hand, Miki grumbled on. "Maybe I'm mad at you because this shit today wouldn't have happened if we'd been in a bus."

"Shit would have happened no matter what," he replied. "Thing is, we can't run away from life, dude. You did enough of that after we lost the guys. You holed up in your place and hid from the world. That's not something I ever thought I'd see you do. You're not like that. You've never run from anything in your damned life—not even yourself.

"So don't run now, Sinjun. You're scared deep down inside, and I fucking get that. God, I so fucking get that, but you're not alone, and you sure as hell aren't weak. You're the strongest person I know, but sometimes, no matter how strong you are, shit's going to take you down." Damien bent over, tenderly leaving a brief kiss on Miki's forehead. "We're here with you—me, Kane, and everyone else—but you need to see someone. To get some help for all of the goddamned shit you've been through, because you're dying inside, Sinjun. Just as sure as if you took Kane's gun and blew your head off."

IT WAS still dark when Miki slipped into their suite. With his head buzzing from the ill-advised whiskey sips he'd taken and Damien's raw scraping of his abraded emotions, Miki didn't see the man sitting on the couch in the living area until he was nearly to the bedroom door.

"You've got to be leaving me a note, Mick." Kane broke through the dark silence. "Especially after something like today."

"I didn't think you'd wake up." A note would have been a good idea, and it was nice of Kane not to bring up Las Vegas or Boston, but they hung over the conversation, ghostly harbingers of Miki's twisted life. "Sorry. You're right."

There was very little light, a sliver of dawn sneaking past the heavy curtains across the windows, so Kane sat in silhouette, his profile strong and firm. Miki's heart grabbed at a swell of prickly warmth growing inside his chest. Love was still so very new, and despite months of Kane's presence in his life—in his heart—Miki could only wonder when it would all end.

Miki slid onto Kane's lap, facing him with his legs straddling his thighs. His chest was bare, warm beneath Miki's fingers, and as he settled in, Kane's cock thickened beneath his ass, shifting under his thin cotton pants. Pushing his fingers into Kane's hair, he tilted his lover's head back, finally seeing the blue in his eyes when Kane's face moved into the band of light cutting across the room.

Tugging at the ends of Kane's thick hair, Miki cocked his head and asked, "How do you know I love you, K?"

"We've been together a bit long to be asking that, Mick. I know you love me as much as I love you. Not a question about it." Kane's eyes narrowed. "Why? What happened? Where'd you go?"

"I found Damie." He tsked at Kane's snort. "Don't be a dick. I had to talk to him."

"At three in the morning? You two are insane. You both were in a car crash. You're supposed to be resting. Did you wake him and Sionn up?"

"Nah, he found some storeroom with an old piano in it. One of the front desk guys pointed me in the right direction. Found him playing some funky classical shit."

"And you just knew that he was awake?"

"Kind of how we work." It was exactly how they worked. Had been since the beginning. The thread binding them tugged and pulled at their consciousness. There'd never been any doubt in Miki's mind about Damien being out and wandering. He'd snuck out of the suite knowing in his gut Damie was waiting for him somewhere. He just had to look. And the rush of guilt swamping him reminded Miki of when he'd given up. "It's probably why I had such a fucking hard time after the accident. I couldn't… let him go, K. Shit, I fucking asked Edie to help me get a statue for Dave and Johnny, but nothing for D because I wasn't… I just fucking didn't believe he was gone. I knew he wouldn't leave me like that."

"But you still believe I *will*?"

Kane's words were a hot knife to Miki's soul.

"Because don't think I worry about that for you. You challenge everything, *a ghra*. Including me. You worry I'm going to leave—"

"No," Miki corrected. "I don't worry you're going to leave. I'm scared you're going to be taken from me. Look at the shit in my life, Kane. As soon as I get my feet under me, everything gets yanked right out again. So it's a totally fucking different thing, K. Totally fucking—"

"That's not going to happen, love." Kane's wide hands cupped Miki's face, pushing his hands out of

Kane's hair. "You and I are in this for the long run, Mick."

Kane's mouth was on his before Miki could take his next breath. With the air stolen from him and Kane's hands moving down over his body, Miki let his lover turn him over and press him into the couch. He ached where he'd hit the van's inner walls, but Kane took all of that away. The room's slightly cold air was a shock against his lust-heated skin, and Miki slipped out of Kane's kiss, finally needing air.

"I don't know what to do to make you understand this, love," Kane growled. "I wanted to spend my life buried in you, wrapped around you. Any way I can have you, I will, Mick. Any damned way. Do you know that?"

"I do." He was tired and sick to his soul, but Miki's body throbbed with awareness of Kane's closeness. There'd never been a question in his mind of wanting Kane. Even when he'd first seen the angry Irish cop on his doorstep, some primal instinct urged him to claim Kane, to bite into his strong neck and leave him gasping for more. "Like you gave me a fucking choice."

"So then what did you need to tell Damien that you couldn't tell me?"

The jealousy was soft, more an undercurrent of hurt in Kane's deep, rumbling voice, and Miki winced at hearing it thread through Kane's words.

"Telling you I was mad at Damie wasn't going to do him and me any good," Miki pointed out. "We needed to talk about the band and shit. About how I was feeling, which you and I already talked about. He told me what you told me. What your dad told me.

That I should go talk to someone about the shit in my head. That maybe it's time."

"So if three out of three men who love you say get the fuck to the doctor, are you going to one?" Even in the shadowy confines of a blackout-curtained room, Kane's eyebrow was a skeptical shelf on his forehead. "Because, babe, maybe it's time."

"Yeah, and not just because Damie said so." He sucked at Kane's lower lip, shuffling his legs so he could cant his knees between Kane's legs. "Because I'm fucked up, K. So fucked up I can't even think straight anymore, and I just want to be... happy. I want to *trust* happy. And I don't. Not really. So yeah, I think... I've got to get some help with this. It just feels weird. Saying that out loud. That I can't deal with my own shit."

"Sometimes we can't. Nothing to be ashamed about, but you can't go through life waiting for the other shoe to drop, Mick," Kane murmured, brushing the back of his hand over Miki's cheek. "Although with you, there's always shoes dropping... just not us doing the dropping. I'm not going to lie to you and tell you I was happy you all continued the tour, especially after Vegas. I'd feel better if you had security around you. As much as I know you live, eat, and breathe music, I'd sacrifice *anything* so you and I can grow old and grumpy together."

"I'm already grumpy. Shit, even my dog's grumpy."

"True. Very true. Just me, then. I'll grow grumpy. You'll stay your sunny, positive self and steal my shirts." Kane's smile flashed white. "The asshole in Vegas still worries me."

"The inked guy?" Miki nodded. "Yeah, me too. I'm just not… sure if that's what I saw. Hell, not like I even look at the thing anymore. I don't even *see* it. For all I know, it's *nothing* like what I've got on my arm."

"Someone hijacked the coroner and took the body. That tells me there's shit attached to someone's shoe." He sighed. "So now we're going to talk about what you should have done back in Vegas. You're still going to need some muscle with you."

"A security guy? I don't know. We got into a car accident, not—"

"Well, you're getting Sionn for the rest of the tour. He and I decided on that. The family'll feel better knowing you've got someone along for the ride."

"Huh, that kind of shit is worse than me not leaving a note, dude. And don't go saying shit like the *family'll* feel better when I know damned well it's you and Con."

"I'll apologize for your hurt feelings later. But you're on the road for another three weeks?" Kane's tone gentled. "I need you safe, Mick. You're killing me here with the worry. And yes, it is the family. You think I'm the only one who loves you? I need to know you've got someone with their head on straight around you, and as much as I love the guys you're with, you've got to be able to see that."

"Yeah, I can," he agreed. "How's that go? Closing the barn after the cows go out? We're almost at the end of our gigs."

"Horses. It's horses." This time it was Kane who did the biting, and Miki's neck was left wet and stinging from teeth and a suckling kiss. "We fought about it in Vegas, remember?"

"You lost, remember?"

"I'm not losing this time. And since the only one of us who can break away for that long is Sionn, he'll be the one riding with you until you guys come home." Kane sighed into Miki's ear before he could protest. "Just... trust me. Okay? Have faith in me. Let me take care of you for a change."

"Faith in you, I've got," Miki replied. "What I don't have is a stinking tour bus and a driver, because I'm not fucking riding in a goddamned ice cream truck anymore."

"The tour bus I can work on with Edie." Kane carefully sat up, moving off the couch to sit on the coffee table. "Now how about if we also be talking about the whiskey I taste in that sweet mouth of yours? Or had you forgotten you rattled your head?"

FIFTEEN

*You sure you're okay with letting them
run around the country, K?*

*Like we've got a choice, brother? What
would you have me do, Con? Tie
him up?*

*Hell, I'd help you do it. You're cranky
when he's not around.*

*Yeah, the thought's occurred to me, but
there's nowhere on Earth I'd be safe
once Miki got loose.*

*Come on over to our house. I'll protect
you.*

*Gonna be hard you doing that, Con,
considering you'd probably be next
on his list.*

—Repairing the roof, Monday afternoon

"FREEEEBIRD!" SOME asshole behind Con screamed. "Play some Skynyrrrd!"

A lighter flamed in the air next to Connor's head, dangerously close to his eyebrows. He had a split-second argument with himself about whether or not to blow it out before the skunkweed-perfumed guy holding the lighter immolated everyone around him, but gravity and physics took their natural course. The constant surge of fire overheated the stoner's thumb, and he dropped the lighter a few seconds after holding it aloft, its plastic case bouncing and skittering on the cement floor.

But it only bounced once, then was lost in the crowd. Anticipating the stoner's flailing, Connor grabbed at the guy's elbow before its pointy bend caught him in the nuts. Fighting against the surge of noise from the packed crowd, Con shouted, "Be watching where you put that thing, or I'll be having to break it off."

"You're such a fucking cop!" Sionn appeared behind him, then yelled into his ear, "Let him go, and I'll take you round the back! I've got an in with the band!"

"Just keep to the one you've got, cousin," Con warned him off with a wolfish smile. "And we'll be doing just fine, you and I."

Klamath Falls was an itch and a scratch place to find in Oregon, and Connor'd been on the road from Medford for nearly two hours after his plane hop from San Francisco. Coming off a five-day warrant spree, he'd tossed his house keys at Kane and told his baby brother to water his plants and feed the fish. He was scruffy, a bit ripe, and worn nearly down to the bone, but he'd made it in time to hear the band play.

And play they did.

It was as if he'd fallen through a looking glass, with nothing and no one appearing as they should be.

He'd heard the band play before, hit a few of the shows along the tour, but something'd changed in the weeks since he'd seen them in Texas. They'd been good before—damned good—playing a tight show with hard, driving music, but *this* was different.

The venue was packed, but they'd all been stuffed nearly to the fire marshal's limit each time Con'd caught a show. A swell of singing followed along with the chorus of a song Connor could now recite in his sleep. The voices were a blend of off-key enthusiasm and worship, nearly loud enough to drown out Miki's smooth, growling rasp coming through the banks of speakers running along the stage and the club's walls. Then Damien's guitar swooped in, and the band flung out everything they had.

It was a wall of sound, words, and attitude cemented together by Miki's fierce snarls and blues-shot voice. Connor could see glimmers of the men he knew in the iridescent gods playing on stage a few feet away, but the fire they built up between them nearly burned it all off. Kane's Miki—sullen, proud, and aloof—challenged the crowd to keep up with him, yanking at their hearts and souls with carefully sharpened words from his brilliant origami mind. He and Damie glided around the lyrics and melody, slowing its pace down, then ramping back up the energy before it stalled. Then Miki was off, sensual and slithering, while Damien strutted across the stage, cockerel proud and loose hipped, his nimble fingers flying across his guitar's buzzing strings.

Sionn grinned when Damie tossed a wink into the shadows backstage. The guitarist didn't miss a beat, egging the crowd on while flirting with his lover. Rafe was lost in his own world, bathing in the lights and the adulation. His childhood friend looked *good*, healthy and happy while singing boisterously into his mic, then laughing when Miki bumped their hips.

But Connor was drawn mostly to the tall dirty blond playing the massive drum kit set up at the back of the stage—to Forest, who he'd fallen for nearly since the first time he'd seen him, smudged with soot and grieving his adopted father's death. Something switched on in Con's heart that day, a miniscule flicker of what-if catching the edges of his awareness, smoldering slowly until he was fully engulfed and in love.

With another man.

A man who was pounding the fuck out of a set of drums and living a dream he never knew he had.

Seeing Forest's wickedly beautiful smile was worth every second they'd spent apart. It was like watching his lover nip at dark chocolate while having sex during a thunderstorm, and Connor loved seeing Forest's soul light up his face.

Con would have bet money Forest couldn't have gotten any brighter, glowed any more than he was in the middle of a song with his bandmates, but he'd have been wrong. A flash of lights drenched the edges of the stage, pulling Connor and Sionn out of the shadows. In that slice of time, Connor knew when Forest saw him just by the deepening of his dimples and the scarlet blush ghosting across his cheeks.

And he fell in love with his guileless, open-souled blond drummer all over again.

"CON... THE bus. Dude—" Connor's mouth was on his before Forest could get another whisper out.

Firm, strong fingers knotted his hair, Con's not-so-gentle tugs pulling his head back, exposing his throat. Teeth dug into his skin, and Forest gasped at the sharp, brief pain. A touch of damp on his stinging skin, and Forest's stiffening cock rubbed against his jeans' thick inner seam. When he'd gotten dressed before the show, underwear hadn't been an option. The hotel misplaced his and Miki's laundry, and the other two were too thick in the waist to borrow any of theirs. Going commando after his post-show shower seemed easier than stopping someplace earlier just for a pair of BVDs, but as his cock left a damp trail between his pants and his skin, Forest was rethinking his no-underwear decision.

"Or I could just take the pants off," he muttered to himself.

"You're having a conversation with yourself again, aren't you?" Connor chuckled against Forest's collarbone, then blew a soft, flaccid raspberry on his neck. "But if your inside voice is telling you to strip, then I'm voting yes as well. I've got lube sleeves in my pocket and a hell of a lot of need for you."

The ground fell away from his feet, his sneakers squeaking across the laminate floor when Connor lifted him up and shoved him against the wall. The barrier between the lounge and the bunks shook, and something heavy hit the ground, thumping loudly, then rolling somewhere beneath the bolted-down table

in the middle of the space. A knob or handle dug into
Forest's side, and he tried to shift himself, but Connor's hold was too strong, too tight.

Then Connor's mouth returned to his, and Forest
lost all sense of reason and time.

His husband—God, his husband—tasted of chocolate stout and Irish whiskey. Scents clung to Connor's hair and clothes, the heavy musk of a man's skin
and the fresh rush of the rain they'd been caught in
between the club and the bus. The press of metal on
Forest's cheek was a reminder of the slender weight
he wore on his hand, a warm band firm enough to be
one of Connor's kisses and just as snug around his
soul.

He wanted more. Needed more, and Connor
seemed willing to give it to him. He groaned when
Connor hitched him up, then worked a thick thigh in
between Forest's legs, easily supporting his weight.
Straddling his husband's leg, Forest canted forward
and wrapped his arms around Con's neck. Their
tongues flicked and danced, their kisses going from
gentle to fierce. Forest was running out of breath,
catching sips of air amid Connor's lingering assault,
but his chest began to burn. Sliding both his hands
under Forest's T-shirt and up his back, Connor broke
their kiss, then grinned, probably at the bemused expression on Forest's face.

"God, you are so fecking gorgeous, love."

Connor's low whisper was hot, tickling Forest's
balls with its promise.

"I can't wait to get inside of you—"

The windows were tinted, nearly as black as
Connor's hair, but transparent enough to let a flash of

headlights span through the interior, catching Forest in the face. For a brief second, Forest got a good look at the long space he'd been traveling in since Seattle. For a last-minute swap, the tour bus was a solid vehicle with wide, comfortable chairs arranged in circles around tables and a wide-screen television. It'd come with a bus driver named Stan, a hefty black man from Kentucky who'd spent a few hours teaching Miki how to play a harmonica and bragging to his grandson on the phone about the rock band he was dragging down the coast. He was decent, and Forest was fond of him.

Stan also had *one* hard, fast rule—no sex on the bus.

He'd agreed to it, thinking he was safe. With his shirt shoved halfway up to his shoulder blades and one of his husband's hands down the back of his jeans, Forest wished he hadn't nodded as quickly as he did.

"We can't do this here," he whispered as the car turned away from the bus, leaving them in the shadows again. "Not on the bus. Shit! Did we even close the door? Fuck. Put me down—"

"I'm not putting you down, *a ghra*." Connor shook his head. "Not unless it's someplace flat and I've got your jeans down around your ankles. I've missed you, and this is one of the few times in my life where I'm going to be saying *fuck* the rules."

Forest's ass hit one of the chairs, and its back tilted, giving under his weight. He scrambled to reach the lever to push the seat flat, but he couldn't find the button and lift up his hips for Connor at the same time. Connor seemed to be everywhere, his fingers undoing Forest's pants, then tugging at his shirt. He couldn't hear anything over their breathing, and Forest grabbed at Connor's wrist to slow him down.

"Is the damned door closed?" He panted, sucking in the air he'd lost when Connor tumbled them to the seat. "I don't want—"

"Live dangerously, love." Connor grunted, tugging Forest's pants from his ankles. "Fuck the door. I'm not even going to look. Right now you're *all* I see. *All* I want. Anyone coming through that door best just turn back around, because I haven't seen my husband in much too long."

The air was cold on Forest's bare skin, pulling up goose bumps by the yard, but the chill taking him over fled under the heat of Connor's naked body. His husband stood between Forest's parted knees and stripped. It wasn't a seductive dance. No teasing, longing looks or peek-a-boo reveals of skin. Connor undid his clothes like he took apart his guns, with a deadly precision and focus.

But his eyes never left Forest's face.

Curled up into the curve of the broad reclined chair, Forest propped himself up on his elbows and stared up at his husband.

His *husband*.

Those words were *never* something he thought he'd ever say, and the deep, soul-quenching love he had for the blue-eyed, black-haired Irish *cop* he'd married was nothing like Forest imagined he'd ever feel. When he'd been taken in by Frank, he'd thought he'd gone as far as his luck would hold. Finding the beat within music and having it resonate inside him had blown his mind, and Forest truly believed he'd reached for the one star he had a chance of holding.

But Connor Morgan—his *husband*—was life pouring him a glass of the universe's glimmer and telling him to drink his fill.

Forest would never stop being thirsty for the Irish man who'd stolen his heart. He loved folding his life into Con's. Even the stupid little things they did together were so damned magical. His heart ached when he thought he couldn't take any more in. From the Saturday-morning farmers' market crawls to the late-night video games with Con's brothers and friends, Forest *felt* married—joined to the man who made his skin itch with want and drew his mouth dry with longing for a kiss.

And he was never more sure of Connor's love than when his naked husband leaned over him, kissed him, and whispered delicious, sweet Gaelic nothings.

Connor's arousal was impossible to miss. His cock jutted up, its thick base cupped in a nest of ebony curls, and its sensitive head broadened, slicking Con's foreskin from its spreading ridge. Con's thighs and chest were lightly dusted with hair, thinning out to a line down his belly and to his crotch. The light coming from the dimmed spots near the front of the bus was too faint to see the blue in Connor's eyes, but it was enough to pick up the strength of his jaw and high cheekbones, his chin shadowed with a few days' scruff.

"I'm glad you came up," he whispered at Connor, arching into his husband's grasp when Connor rested his knee on the chair's seat. "And if we get yelled at, I'm telling everyone you made me do it. 'Cause you're a cop, and you've always gotta listen to what a cop tells you to do."

"Right." Connor snorted. "Like you've ever listened to me in your life."

"Maybe this once," Forest suggested, trying on his best leer.

It was an ultimate failure as a seduction tool, but it wiped the serious off Connor's face.

"Well, then," he murmured in between peppering kisses across Forest's chest. "Why don't you lean back and do everything the nice officer here tells you?"

"How long have you been wanting to say that?" Forest bit back a groan.

"Forever and a day," Connor confessed sheepishly. "But to be fair, love, you're the only one I've ever wanted to say it to."

THEY WERE always a tight fit, snug and perfect into the valleys and dips of their bodies. Forest gasped at the touch of hot lube, the slick liquid warmed from its time in Connor's pocket. Their need for one another simmered, slowing down to long strokes and tender kisses. There was a sense of languor despite the very real risk of their discovery, but for the moment Forest simply let go of his worries, aches, and frets and held on tight.

He loved the burn of Connor entering him, the stretch of his hole giving way to the pressure of Connor's cock, then the sighing release as the head slid in. Connor always stopped at that moment, giving Forest a chance to catch his breath, but this time Forest wanted more of his husband, not time.

"Go in, babe."

Trapped against the back of the chair, Forest couldn't maneuver his hips enough to push up on

Connor, something his husband found amusing if his smirk was anything to go by. Definitely hilarious for Connor, because he shifted, rocking his hips to roll his head around Forest's tight entrance. It was a tantalizing, overwhelming tease, and Forest hissed with alarm when it felt like Con was about to pull out.

"Swear to God, if you don't do this, I'm going to fucking kill—"

Connor slid in, nesting his balls up against Forest's ass, and Forest forgot how to speak.

Their lovemaking would carry his soul into eternity. Forest was sure of that. As familiar as Connor's body was, he loved exploring Con. The way his SFPD tattoo rode his skin when Forest dug his fingers into Con's upper arm to the soft brush of Connor's silken chest hair on his nipples, every inch of Connor's body on his was a unique kiss. Connor's cock pushing into him, resting there and moving while he shifted his knees on the chair, stretched and pulled at Forest's core, his hole aching with want and his balls roiling in anticipation. The familiar prickle of an orgasm tightened Forest's sac, and he bit down on his lower lip, hoping to hold himself together long enough for Connor to reach his own peak.

"You are so tight, Fore," Connor murmured. "And you feel so *damned* right around me."

"You've got to move or…."

Gasping, Forest felt Connor's cock edge in deeper when his husband pushed his shoulders back and rested his hands on either side of Forest's head, depressing the chair's cushions. He couldn't get his legs up high enough, catching his calves on Connor's hips.

"Just hold on, love." Connor rocked into him. "And let me do all the work."

Forest held on.

His body was hyperaware of the heavy cock pushing and pulling him open. The sensations at his center dominated his thoughts, and Forest forced his mind away from the delicious sear of Con's intrusion, focusing on Connor's sweat-damp skin sliding under his hands or the flicking touch of Connor's belly on his cock when they moved.

Headlights tucked away the space's shadows, flashing long beams slicing a brightness across Con's arms and shoulders. Forest didn't need the light to know he was clutching at Connor's tattoo. He intimately knew where the phoenix flamed under Connor's skin. It was a symbol of who Connor Morgan was, a cop down to his marrow, living by the standard inked on his arm. *Oro en paz, Fierro en guerra*—gold in peace, iron in war—a gentle man who raised a gun to protect and shielded the world from its own violence.

The words were Connor, but the mythical bird belonged to them both. If anything stood for Forest, it was the reborn streak of fire and power clutching Connor's soul. He held on to Con's tattoo because he'd risen from the ashes of his own tragedies and found the man beneath the ink to love him.

The same man who was now slowing his strokes and drawing out every little bit of pleasure from Forest's body.

Crouched over Forest, Connor was drawn in tight, their shoulders touching and arms tangled in close enough to keep most of the light out of their embrace, but Forest could still see the wistful smile on Connor's generous mouth and the crinkle of crow's-feet beginning to crease his long-lashed eyes.

"I love you," Forest murmured, hugging Connor as tightly as he could, considering he was wrapped around his husband's body.

"No threats?" Connor stilled, then gave another teasing twitch of his hips. "Well, I love you too, *a ghra.*"

Forest clenched Connor's hands, squeezing tight when Connor began to pump harder. The gentleness slithered away beneath the aggressive push of Connor's powerful body. His shoulders bunched up, and his legs strained as he fought to keep his balance. Anchored against the edge of the chair and the floor, Connor drove into Forest, slamming their hips together over and over, tearing Forest's attention away from everything but the shaft powering through his defenses.

The prickle in Forest's balls and belly exploded into a firestorm of tingles. His sac was tight, rubbed and caressed by Connor's undulating hips. His dick wasn't far behind. The buildup was immense. The slow ride of Connor's body on his skin resonated through Forest, curling his toes. Connor's short nails dug half-moons of light pain into his hands, and then a small nip on Forest's neck from Con's sharp teeth drove him over the edge.

He fell—or burst—Forest never could describe the feeling of Connor's body breaking his control, but it rushed over him, a tide of stars and pleasure so intense he was blinded by the flashes across his skin and mind. His belly clenched, gripping in much like his ass held on to Connor's length, refusing to let go of its prize even as his own cock was releasing his coiled-up energy. His cum broke through the space between their pressed-in bodies, seeping hot liquid finding every crevice available to it. Unable to slow his orgasm, Forest could only ride its rapids, clutching Connor while his nerves sparked and his balls churned.

Between Forest's gasping realization he'd found his release and a flickering beam cutting across them, Connor came, a simmering wave cresting through Forest's body and stealing his breath away.

The aftershocks were nearly as tender and cataclysmic as his first gush of seed. Overwhelmed at the press of Connor's weight against him and the stretch of Con's cock plunging and diving into his ass, Forest struggled to surface from the swirling uproar drowning him.

He drew in a mouthful of cold air, then peppered Connor's face and throat with kisses, murmuring for his husband to finish, to fill him again if he could. Connor's hands were in his hair. Then a thumb ghosted over Forest's cheek while he slowly—and, from the tortured groans Con made deep in his throat, reluctantly—spent the rest of himself into Forest's clench.

"God—just—fucking God," Forest whispered between shuddering breaths. His body ached from being stretched apart and open, splayed and sacrificed to the Irish man he'd come to love more than music and life itself. "Makes me wish I'd never left."

"Don't say that, love," Connor admonished gently. "That's not something I'd want to ever hear from you. I miss you, but you… hold on."

Brushing his lips over Forest's sweaty brow, he gathered Forest up, sliding free of Forest's ass. A few slithering moves, and Forest found himself sitting nearly side by side with Connor on the broad chair. His ass hurt, and at some point in the past hour he'd scraped his knee on something, but Connor's hand stroking at his spine soothed most of his discomfort.

"I love you, Forest Morgan Ackerman," Connor murmured, then kissed what felt like a spreading burn on Forest's cheek. "And ah, how I've gotten you with my beard. You look like you've fallen face-first into a hedgehog's ass there."

"Yeah. Next time you molest me in our tour bus, shave first." Rubbing at the spot, he felt the prickly bumps of his abraded skin, then said, "I meant what I said. I missed you so fucking much, Con. I hurt thinking about you, and that sounds stupid, but it's like I can taste you on things and my guts ache. Right now—this—us—makes me wonder why I went out on the road when you're there at home."

"Because tonight—before you saw me—you were the happiest I'd ever seen you." Con's Irish thickened, his emotions deepening his words. "You love playing. You love being with these guys, and your heart opens up its wings and soars when you've got your sticks in your hand and you're driving the music. Home? That's in our souls… in our rings… in our hearts. Your music is as much a part of you as my being a cop is a part of me. I'd no sooner ask you to stop playing than you'd ask me to lay down my badge."

"There might be some rough shit ahead of us… the band… not you and me," Forest cautioned. "We're still fitting into each other, and the others—"

"They have their problems. Just like you have yours." Their lips met for another kiss, a skipping tease between them. "But you'll all overcome anything tossed in your way. It's what you do, Forest. You look at the mountains put in front of us and remind us all of what we've already climbed. I can't take that away from the band. I can't take your music away from you. I'd sooner die than try. So stay on the road for however long you have to. Bring your sounds and words to anyone who'll listen, because no matter how far you roam, I will always be there for you to come home to."

EPILOGUE

Rain on the glass, reminds me of you
A sip of hot chocolate, a song played
    in blue
Lyrics written on a postcard
Melody slick, deep, and charred
Anyone not loving you
Ain't trying that hard
Shout at the moon, dance in the rain
Give me your heart, I'll keep back the pain
—Rain and the Blues

IT WAS damned good to be home.

San Francisco welcomed them like it took back all its children, spitting out rain and coyly hiding behind a fan made of fog and seagulls. The streets were slippery and packed with tourists looking to be scammed by the eternally going-out-of-business jewelry stores dotting Chinatown, while street performers set up tiny fiefdoms along the piers, charming hapless pedestrians out of bits of cash and coin.

The band scattered nearly as soon as the tour bus came to a stop, going their own separate ways, away from the Crossroads where they'd meet to play and sing. It would take them all a few hours to reconcile themselves to the road not moving beneath their feet and the bed smelling like home.

Miki wasn't sure Kane was ever going to get the smell of Dude's pee out of his sneakers after the dog got so excited at seeing Miki, he'd pissed all over Kane's feet. It'd been hard to leave the terrier behind, but the band had one last gig to play before calling the tour done.

Finnegan's.

A blackboard sign under the covered patio announced the pub was closed for a private evening event, but the doors were open, and from the cluster of off-duty cops gathered around the entrance, Miki guessed no one was waiting for the band to show up before they started partying.

The foot traffic on the pier was light, not odd considering the erratic rain slicing over the shoreline, but the pub was definitely packed with loud voices and clinking glasses, both Irish in one way or another. The air held a splash of the ocean, a tint of fish and salt with the peculiar seafoam whiff of water birds. The bridge's beams strung lights through the mist, speckles of flares and dots cutting through as the nearby buildings began their evening business. Somewhere close by, someone spun cotton candy, threads of vanilla and berry sweet peeking out from between the waves of sardine and sourdough.

Chatter ebbed and flowed, a tide of sound from the meandering groups of people along the walk. Every once in a while a burst of laughter erupted from Finnegan's, as hearty and rich as the stew Donal made on cold nights when the family showed up to be fed. One of the women standing in the crowd turned out to be Kiki, and she flicked a wave at them with her beer bottle and continued on with her spirited conversation with the two blond men standing next to her.

"So, Finnegan's. It's like *your* Moby Dick, isn't it? Like you're Mum's?" Kane said, rocking back on his heels and watching Miki drink in the sight of the pub they'd always been forbidden to play in front of.

"Damie got here first," he reminded his lover, shifting his knee to better balance the weight of the electric guitar he'd brought with him. "Without me too." He took a breath, then spat, "Fucker."

There were already too many Morgans to keep track of, but there seemed to be more of them, or at least more Irish than Miki ever knew San Francisco had, much less under one roof. A taller, younger version of Brigid appeared to be holding court by the bar, her accent as thick as the Guinness Connor was carefully pulling into a glass. To her right, Braedon leaned on the rail, his glower nearly as fierce as Connor's, but the girl paid him no mind. A few feet away, Donal stood with a black and tan in one hand and his other arm around his wife's shoulder, a faint blush coloring Brigid's round cheeks when he bent down to whisper something in her ear.

"Hey, that's my cousin Cassie." Kane nodded at the young woman. "On my mum's side. She's a Finnegan, of sorts. You'll have to come meet her."

"Later, K." Miki had to shout slightly over a chorus of hellos when a group of detectives spotted them. "Got to get my gear set up. I'm here for a gig, remember?"

"Fucking musicians," Kane muttered playfully. "Fine, but after the show, Sinjun, you're mine."

"Always am." They brushed fingertips, a discreet kiss of skin. Then Miki headed to the makeshift stage. "Tell Kel I said hey."

Forest was already behind the drums, tightening one of the skins or maybe replacing it, Miki wasn't sure, but the drummer gave him a nod, then dove back down behind his kit. Rafe was busy uncoiling a cord but flashed Miki a broad smile. It was going to be a casual gig, worn jeans, old T-shirts, and a two-foot stage held up by blocks of wood and risers. The amps were small, and their gig pretty much depended on the pub's sound system, but the black-painted stage felt good beneath Miki's boots, even if it creaked a bit to the left.

Miki ignored the wolf whistle coming from somewhere in the crowd behind him as he unzipped his jacket and slithered out of the black leather. Quinn came up to the stage to grab the cord end Rafe held out for him, and Miki glanced around for his guitar relay but couldn't see the equipment box.

"Where are the relays?" It dawned on him what Rafe was doing, and Miki groaned. "Why aren't we doing this wireless?"

"Pub's old. It's got a lot of steel beams and shit. Ceiling's low, and there's interference bouncing all through our amps. So...." Rafe held up a cord. "We're old-schooling it today."

"Shit." Miki looked around at the stage floor. It was a tight space already, but having cords underfoot was going to be a bitch. "Well, not like we're going to be jumping around up here anyway."

"Not unless you want to look like you've been in a fight when we're done. One wrong step, and you're over the edge of the stage." Forest popped up from behind the drum kit. "Okay, I'm good. Skin came loose coming over here. And I needed to get something underneath one of the pedals. Stage's wonky."

"I got this. You hook up the mic. Q's already strung that out and taped it off in the back." Rafe unlatched Miki's guitar case. "And where's your evil twin, Sinjun? He come with you guys?"

"They left before we did." A phosphorus coil of panic flared up along the base of Miki's skull. "*Fuck.*"

He took a quick breath, shoving in a huff of air to cool the rising electric heat building up in his chest. They were supposed to play in less than half an hour, hadn't done a sound check because up until that afternoon there hadn't been a stage, and now their lead guitarist was missing.

"Nothing's happened to them, Sin," Forest reassured him, crossing to the front of the stage with a few long strides. "They'll be here."

"Then we can kick his ass for not helping set up." Rafe grimaced. "You're excused, Mick. That knee of yours—"

"It's doing okay. Better than a sharp knife to the gut." He rubbed at his side where he'd taken the hit in Boston.

"Hey, still don't know if it was a knife," Forest reminded him. "Well, in Boston."

"Right," Rafe scoffed. "Because the riser tore itself open and attacked him. And what about that guy in Vegas? *Anything?*"

"Don't know, and that kind of pisses me off," Miki confessed.

"He's probably not too happy about it either. Being dead and everything." Tapping Miki's leg to move him aside, Forest began to set the mic stand in place. "There's D."

"Hey," Damien grunted as he mounted the short stage. His black cowboy hat tumbled from his head when he slung off down the cases he'd brought with him. Scrubbing his wet hair back, he reached for the hat. "Sorry. Ran a bit late."

"You left the house an hour before we did. You guys were supposed to head straight here." Miki sniffed at Damien's shoulder. "And you took a shower after breakfast. How'd you get your hair wet?"

"Raining hard just out front, maybe?" Rafe leaned forward and looked out of the pub's pier-side windows. "'Cause you're soaking wet, and it's only drizzling back here."

"It's wet *under* his hat." Forest took one of Damien's guitars. "Hat's dry."

"Huh." Rafe craned his neck. "And Murphy's got a huge fresh hickey on his neck."

"Shit. Stan's still in town." Miki narrowed his eyes. "You guys went and fucked on the tour bus. Jesus, you... dude, really?"

"Yeah. Kinda. Really. Don't like stupid rules, Sinjun, so... challenge accepted, and Stan gets to spend the weekend with his family in a nice hotel." Damien smirked and slid his Phenix's strap over his neck and around his shoulder. "Now, where the fuck are the relays? We've got a pub to bring to its knees."

THE GIG was more walk down memory lane than anything else, a mishmash of classic rock and Sinner's Gin songs, and they began to take requests when Riley set a bucket with TIPS scribbled in Sharpie on the edge of the stage. Their set list ran the gamut, delving deep into the archives of their minds for old standards about Texas floods to a silly tune about chicken dances. By ten Miki was dead tired, but his nerves were thrumming, high on the music they'd played for nearly four hours. After an hour break with the tip jar overflowing, they'd returned to the stage and played a rollick of blues until last call at 2:00 a.m.

Ears still ringing and his voice turned to broken glass from the hours he'd spent slinging out vocals, Miki was grateful for the cold beer Kane pressed into his hand. He was even more thankful for the soft-armed couch Sionn'd placed up by the pub's wood stove and the upside-down milk crates he could use to rest his feet on. The others eventually joined him, shoved away from brooms and damp towels with a fierce admonishment to go sit down, have a beer, and just enjoy themselves.

"We've been enjoying ourselves since we plugged in our shit," Damien grumbled as he sat next to Miki, a thick weariness in his voice. "God, this beer is good."

"Anything cold's good right now, but yeah, Sionn's got a good lager going." Rafe stretched out on a tapestry-upholstered love seat to the right of Miki. Then Forest shoved at his feet. Lifting his legs, he groused playfully, "Fuck, goddamned drummers. Always wanting in my space."

"That's 'cause you leave so much of it empty," Forest countered, sitting down on the love seat only to have Rafe put his bare feet in his lap. "Really?"

"Hey, they don't smell." Rafe wiggled his toes. "Much. Not like your playing."

"I'd say fuck you, but everyone already has," the drummer retorted, reaching for the open beer Damien offered him. "Thanks."

"Hey, good show." Damien hefted his beer bottle at the band, then leaned against Miki, resting his head on Miki's shoulder. "You fucking killed it, Sin."

"Feels like I swallowed rocks. We went too long." The beer soothed his throat and settled in his stomach with a happy glurp. Yawning, Miki stared off toward the bar, where their lovers stood talking to Donal. Kane lifted his eyes from whatever Connor was showing them on a scribbled napkin, and Miki's heart sped up its beat. "Shit. Look at them. Gotta be dangerous to have that much hot in one corner of a building. Place is going to catch fire, and we're all going to burn to death."

"Nah, Braeden's outside. He'll save us." Forest yawned, and it spread to Rafe, who slapped him once they were done. "Hey! *Dick.*"

There was a noise at the door, gleeful but cautious, and then Kane's face dimpled with a gigantic smile. Miki was too tired to turn around and look. Resting his head back on the couch and closing his eyes, he let out a sigh and felt his muscles slowly unknot.

A pair of heels crossing the pub's hard floor normally would have gotten his back up, but it'd been a month since he and Brigid rubbed each other raw. The gait was wrong—the music of the walk was off. His eyes flew open, chasing the tantalizing whisper of a rhythm ghosting through his mind. The flavor of the beat was less… expressive, gentler, as if coaxing something or someone out of a tight space.

Blinking, Miki stared up at Edie's hawkish, pale face and yelped.

"Shit, Edie! A fucking warning!"

Miki sat up, nearly losing his beer. The others stood up around him, going in for a hug or, in Rafe's case, dipping Edie back and kissing her on the cheek.

Slender to the point of gaunt, their manager, Edie, was all sharp angles, her suit tailored in tight and her mouth glazed with a bright coral lipstick. She'd done something with her hair, lightening it to a caramel brown, and softened the severity of the bob cut along the line of her strong jaw. Yet her hands were still soft and slightly cold when she cupped his face and her laugh as husky as ever when he bent down to kiss her faintly wrinkled cheek.

She'd been the only person in the world who'd given a shit about him when Miki'd thought he'd lost his entire life. It'd been Edie who cajoled him to eat and railed at him to get out of the house. She'd also been the first one to ever order him to fall in love, and

she'd celebrated like a mad woman when Kane finally moved in to the warehouse. She was Dude's fairy
godmother and the one woman in Miki's life who he'd
allowed to boss him around.

In so many ways, Edie was as much a mother to
him as Brigid, and his eyes stung with a fierce regret
when he realized he'd never ever told her how much
he'd needed her when he'd been drowning.

"Hey, it's good to see you." He meant it, and
as he wrapped his arms around Edie's slender body,
her breath hitched, and she patted his back. "Shit, we
didn't know you were coming up or we'd have waited
for you."

"I was going to surprise you, but I had to miss
my first flight. Someone… a woman… came into the
office, and well, I had to speak with her." Edie's pack-
a-day voice turned reedy with emotion. "I don't know
how to tell you this, so I'm just going to say it. Sinjun honey, this woman says—and we've got to take
this with a grain of salt—but she says she knows your
mother."

SEE HOW THE STORY CONTINUES IN

BOOK SIX OF THE SINNERS SERIES
RHYS FORD

SIN AND TONIC

"The perfect ending to a spectacularly touching series that meshes mystery, romance, and family." — Mary Calmes

Sequel to *Absinthe of Malice*
Sinners Series: Book Six

Miki St. John believed happy endings only existed in fairy tales until his life took a few unexpected turns… and now he's found his own.

His best friend, Damien, is back from the dead, and their new band, Crossroads Gin, is soaring up the charts. Miki's got a solid, loving partner named Kane Morgan—an inspector with the SFPD whose enormous Irish family has embraced him as one of their own—and his dog, Dude, at his side.

It's a pity someone's trying to kill him.

Old loyalties and even older grudges emerge from Chinatown's murky, mysterious past, and Miki struggles to deal with his dead mother's abandonment, her secrets, and her brutal murder while he's hunted by an enigmatic killer who may have ties to her.

The case lands in Kane's lap, and he and Miki are caught in a deadly game of cat-and-mouse. When Miki is forced to face his personal demons and the horrors of his childhood, only one thing is certain: the rock star and his cop are determined to fight for their future and survive the evils lurking in Miki's past.

www.dreamspinnerpress.com

ONE

Locking down my heart
After I'm done with you
I've run the course of our love
There's nothing left to do
Can't listen to your lies
Won't let you into my life
Gave you everything I had
Your love's like a knife
—Lock and Stab

DEATH SLIPPED in over life in many ways, from stealing the breath from a slumbering child with a feathery touch to a shockwave of anguish of a man striking the Bay's hard, cold water from a fall off the bridge. Miki St. John always believed Death was the most insidious, volatile, and unpredictable thief a man ever had to face in his life, an unyielding brutal force even nature could not cow or hold back.

That is, up until a few seconds ago when Miki discovered, to his amazement, pain was a greater monster than any death ever could be.

Today, pain came in the form of a forty-year-old Vietnamese woman with long, silver-streaked black hair and a face life gouged out with a hard awl. The lines on her face so deeply etched into her skin, a heavy rain would pour rivers from her jowls. Her pallor was stark, the slate gray of the sky over an icy Bay, but her cheeks ran florid with angry lesions, red constellations of flaking skin and puckering scabs. Her tongue darted across her lips, a gecko-quick daub over cracked fissures. One corner of her mouth was puffed up, or at least it appeared to be. It was difficult to tell from where Miki and Kane were standing, their view filtered through a curtain of palm fronds and mist from a nearby sprinkler. The green-yellow fans couldn't obscure her bright clothing, a too tight, too short wrap of spandex and large eye-bleeding flowers on a sea of pink.

Miki knew Kane well enough to know that his cop was assessing the woman, judging her appearance, and every once in a while sneaking a glance in Miki's direction as if to check to see if he was holding up. His cop was a massive block of Celtic warrior, a slab of granite carved from a mountain who taught Kane how to be a man. He didn't know how the woman could miss the blue-eyed, black-haired Celtic warrior barely hidden behind a row of ornamental foliage, but then, Miki supposed, it could've just been him. His eyes always searched the shadows for Kane—hell, he searched the light for him too—there was something about his Irish cop that both calmed him down and fired him up.

Miki ached for Kane like he ached for music.

Unfortunately, he'd stopped aching for music, but his desire for Kane stayed steady and strong.

"How good are you at reading lips?" Miki strained to see around the cement planter, disliking the hitch in his hip when he shifted his weight from one foot to another. "I can't... I can see her talking but I can't figure out what she's saying. We should have had Edie open her phone line or something so I could listen in."

Kane's midnight gaze flicked over Miki's face, an amused grin teasing at the corner of his mouth. As he turned his attention back to the women standing near one of the garden's tall cement signs, his sexy, whiskey-amber voice purred with hints of rolling emerald hills and ancient myths, "And here you say you don't think like a cop. That was a very cop thing to say, Mick. If it weren't against the law."

"Well, if I've picked up anything cop-like, I got it from your father." Miki sneered. "Considering he's the only real cop I know."

"I'll be reminding you of those very words later on tonight when I have you in bed and I've got a pair of handcuffs nearby."

"Is that supposed to scare me?" Miki jabbed Kane in the ribs. "For some of us, we just call it Tuesday."

The words were out of his mouth before Miki could stop them—before he could actually *hear* them—and the stab of pain in Kane's expression dug out what little guilt he had in his soul. Joking about sex was something the band did on the road, something the group fell into, a sideshow banter about the hard life they lived slogging music and their equipment across the blacktop and the stage. It said something about how far he'd come—the teasing of Kane—and how little he picked at the scabs in his psyche or contemplated the scars on his soul.

"I didn't mean—" Kane started to say but closed his mouth when Miki shook his head. "I didn't think. I just—"

Everyone close to Miki knew his body had been a plaything for men with little regard for him other than to be their toy. But Kane—his righteous, slightly off-white knight—had seen Miki at his lowest, at his least human. Kane had not only seen Miki's nightmares captured by a flash of the camera and a spot of film, but still dealt with the aftermath of those memories.

"You don't have to watch your words with me, K," Miki reassured his lover. "Damie says shit all the time and I don't jump down his throat. It's just words. And if ever you actually wanted to use a pair of handcuffs, you'd tell me so I'd have a chance to tell you *fuck off and die* or *sure, just don't lose the key*. Because if there's one thing that I am *not* ever going to live through, it's calling up one of your sibs to unlock my wrist from our bed."

"The siblings I can handle," Kane growled. "It's the parents—Brigid—that I'm scared of. She'd skin me alive."

And just because he knew Kane would shudder at the thought, Miki said softly, "Dude, you don't think your dad's used his cuffs on your mom? She's got eight kids. Probably wants to change things up every once in a while, you know?"

"Thank you for that. There isn't enough bleach in San Francisco to get that thought out of my head." Kane made a noise that sounded like Miki's dog swallowing a fly, and Miki smirked with satisfaction when Kane's shoulders actually shook. "Now, if ever I do lose a handcuff key and you're involved, I'm just going to leave you there. And no, I can't tell what they're saying. Next time we do something like this, I want to make Edie wear a wire. As illegal as it is, I'm wishing we'd done *something*."

Miki snorted. "How the fuck many women do you think are going to come out of the gutter and say they knew my mother? Only reason I'm giving this one the time of day is because Edie said she sounded legit."

If Crossroads Gin was Miki's salvation, then Edie, their manager, was the mother of all things. She was a sharp-faced woman with a cutting manner only softened by her affection for the young men she herded and cared for. He'd not liked her when he first met Edie across a long conference table in a room at their record studio's main building. She'd been aggressive, brash, and stood toe-to-toe with Damien, arguing about percentages and copyrights until the lead guitarist's British accent was so thick with fury, Miki expected the fog to roll in and the coffee in his mug to turn to tea. Just as Damien was about to walk out the door, Edie's manner gentled and her tone shifted.

"Now do you understand why you need me?" she'd said to the shocked band members. "You just lost an argument with the person who is willing to go to the mat for you. Imagine how far you'll get when you go head-to-head with somebody who wants to bleed you dry? Now, sit your ass down on the chair, Mitchell, and we can get down to making sure you hold on to every penny the four of you earn, and I am only going to charge you five percent to do it."

Through Sinner's Gin's rise and then death, Edie was Miki's rock. She'd been with him as he struggled to walk and battled every lawyer Damien's family threw at him, bloodsucking leeches hoping to turn a quick buck on Damien's corpse. When Damien returned, alive despite a lie his family concocted to bilk his estate, Edie donned her armor once again, ensuring their assets—and lives—were secure. It had been a no-brainer to ask her to manage the new band, but when she came to the final show of its Resurrection Tour, she'd brought with her a revelation—news of a ghost Miki never knew haunted him—and a woman who said she knew Miki's mother.

When they agreed to meet the woman at the Yerba Buena Gardens, Edie cautioned him to remain at home. Her arguments were sound, but Miki needed to see the face of the one person who'd come forward about the woman who'd carried him but hadn't kept him.

"Hey, look." His cop jerked his chin toward the women. "She's handing Edie something."

From what Miki could see, it was one of those padded envelopes he often got ordering things online, its oddly unique but familiar brown-yellow surface wrinkled and grimy. It looked old, beat-up around the edges, and torn at the top instead of cut open, but Edie handled it as if it were treasure, carefully taking it from the woman's hands and glancing into its depths.

Kane was moving before Miki realized his cop was no longer next to him. His lover's hands were on him, moving him. Miki's shoulders were turned, then the sky tilted, slivers of blue dotted with clouds turning into a kaleidoscope through the leaves above them. The pops were loud, echoing booms Miki knew all too well. The screaming began nearly the moment Miki's knee gave and he struck the ground, Kane's heavy body stretched out over him.

It was a hellish agony when Miki struggled to get out from under his lover's prostrate body. Kane's forearms were up, covering Miki's face, smearing dirt and debris into his mouth, but Miki couldn't see, couldn't tell if Kane had been hit. His world became a single moment, turning only when he felt Kane's chest rise against his belly, and then the voice that murmured sweet, filthy things into his ears during sex told him to stay down.

Everything happened so fast—the gunfire, the shouting, and then the squeal of brakes coming from the road. Miki heard sobbing, but he was too concerned about running his hands over Kane's sides, feeling for any bit of wetness or, worse, injury he couldn't heal with a kiss. His panic must have shown on his face because Kane brushed his mouth over Miki's lips, then rolled off him.

"Are you hit?" Kane barked, startling the shock from Miki's belly. "Tell me you're okay."

"I'm fine. Edie—" But Kane stood before Miki could say another word.

"Stay here," Kane ordered as he scrambled toward where the women met. "*Call 911.*"

And then he was gone, taking his warmth and comfort with him.

Kane's long legs easily ate up the distance between the planter and where Edie lay on the ground. Her pristine, sunflower-bright power suit now bore bloodied poppies across her side and arms. A few feet away, the woman he'd watched through the palms was sprawled against the cement monolith with its maps and directions splattered with her blood. Her eyes were open, her jaw slack, and the bullet wounds on her stomach made a polka-dot mess of her clothing, but it was the shattered remains of her forehead that shocked Miki into moving.

Kane was two hundred pounds of muscle and bone, but he moved like a shark through still water, cutting through the stream of people running away from the road and into the surrounding buildings.

"*Edie!*" Miki wasn't as fast as Kane, but he was going to be damned if he didn't get to Edie's side.

There were already sirens in the air, drowning out the crowd's murmuring shock and startled cries. Miki caught his foot on the pylon or maybe one of the stones used to decorate the mulch surrounding the trees and the palms, but he ignored the hit of pain in his hip, scaling the wide staircase to do what he could.

It was hard to kneel, but it was even harder to hold Edie's hand as her life poured out of her. Something dug into his knee, finding the one too-tender spot he never seemed to be able to heal. He shoved the envelope aside, jerking his head up when Kane hissed at him.

"Don't touch that. It's evidence." His lover's eyes were hard, stony bits of blue marbled with an arrogant authority with no tolerance for argument. "If you're going to be here, press down on her wounds.

Ambulances are going to be here soon. Stay with her. I've got to see if anybody else was hurt. There's a couple people down by the sidewalk."

"This is *Edie*," Miki spat. He didn't know where the rage came from or, rather, maybe he did. She was a connection to his past, a life he built with her and then cobbled back together when it fell apart. "Don't you fucking walk away from her. I *need* you. *She* needs you."

The smile he got from Kane was resigned and bittersweet, and Miki had to blink away his tears to see it. Kane's fingers brushed Miki's jaw, then ran through his wind-tangled hair, pulling away before Miki could lean into his lover's touch.

"I know you'll take care of her, babe." Kane's whisper dug down deep into Miki's love for him, hooking into every thread of every moment they'd shared. "She'll be all right, but I have to go. This is what I do. I'm a cop, Mick, I *have* to go."

It WAS never a good thing when Captain Book called one of his inspectors into his office. Even worse when Casey, their lieutenant, was waiting with him. Book was a congenial man, someone who worked to be approachable, the kind of captain a police officer felt comfortable talking to, even when washing their hands and standing side by side in the bathroom. Kane liked and respected the man nearly as much as he respected his own father, so when his partner, Kel, tapped Kane on the shoulder and jerked his head toward the captain's office, Kane would never have thought in a million years he would be standing in the middle of the greatest ass-chewing in his life as soon as he walked through the door.

"What were you thinking, Morgan?" The beefy man's snarl was ferocious, years of riding a desk hardly putting a dent in the street-tough cop who'd been dragged up from one of the worst neighborhoods in Los Angeles. "The DA tells me he thinks you were there for a sting of some kind and that rock star you sleep with is ass-deep in it. Tell me you weren't there doing something sketchy."

"No hard feelings, Morgan," Casey assured him, patting him on the shoulder. "Internal Affairs isn't looking at you, and I sure as hell don't want you at a desk, but the DA is pushing it. I might not have a choice if they go up the chain of command."

"I *am* the damned chain of command." Book slapped at his desk, nearly upending a wire basket of pens. He caught it before it spilled, righting it with a scowl on his face. "If the DA wants a fight, I'll be more than happy to give it to that bastard. He's not going to take one of my cops off the streets because he needs to show he's tough on anyone wearing a badge. Just explain to me, Kane, what you were doing there, and make sure that none of it includes an undercover operation I knew nothing about."

"It wasn't a sting or anything undercover," Kane replied. "Do you think I would take St. John with me on something like that? His manager was meeting with a woman, one who said she had information about St. John's mother. She'd been in contact with his management company, and they'd arranged to meet at the gardens. St. John wanted to be there, but his manager cautioned him to remain behind until she had more information."

"So why didn't he stay home? If she told him she didn't want him there, why was he there?" Casey asked. "He was setting himself up for a confrontation, or worse, her attacking him."

"Because the surefire way to get Miki St. John to do something is to tell him he shouldn't," he informed his superior officers, unable to keep a grin off his face, but he sobered up quickly when Book shot him a hard look. "It was supposed to be a simple meet. She was coming with the packet that was recovered on the scene and anecdotal evidence of her connection to St. John's mother. At the most, we expected her to shake down the manager for money, precisely the reason St. John shouldn't have been there."

"Stop calling him St. John. We all know who he is. It's one thing to be formal when you're giving a report, but it's another thing entirely when you're talking about the guy you go home to every night," his captain interjected. "The manager? That's the survivor, right?"

"Yes, sir. She took a shot to the ribs, which deflected into her abdomen. She's in surgery right now, but I was assured by the hospital she will be okay. I'm hoping that once she regains consciousness, I'll be able to question her about—"

"You're not going anywhere near her, Morgan," Casey cut him off. "One, you're too close to the case. Two, we still haven't decided if you are going to be placed on administrative leave."

"I've decided." Book leaned back in his chair, nestling his shoulders into its padded leather cushion. "Morgan isn't going to ride a desk, not if I have anything to say about it. We are already overloaded and down three inspectors this week. There's a dead woman in the morgue with sketchy identification and nothing on her but a manila envelope of photos and a couple of letters. You were on the scene—tell me what happened. Was the shooter random and they were caught in the cross-fire spray, or was the manager targeted? Did it look like the woman signaled to someone?"

"No, she was fully engaged with Edie, the manager. The victim wasn't looking at the road; her left side was facing the street and I could see her face." Kane distanced himself from the turbulent emotions he'd been suppressing since he first heard the gunfire and shoved Miki to the ground, praying nothing struck the man he loved. Thinking back on what he saw, he parsed out the woman's expressions and body language. "She was aggressive, a little pushy, and if I had to guess, she was trying to get something out of Edie, either money or maybe she wanted to talk to Miki. I didn't get a chance to talk to either of them and, well, listening in on the conversation could have potentially been sticky. The meet happened quickly. I only got notification about it about half an hour before it happened."

"Did St. John know?" Book asked. "Does he know the woman's name?"

"He might. I don't know if Edie shared it with him. Up until she knocked on our front door, he was adamant about not having a damned thing to do with getting into contact with the woman. I think Edie pressed it because she said she had things to give to him, things from his mother." Kane looked down at his hands, surprised to see speckles of blood along his knuckles. "They might've talked before, but he didn't want—no, he refused—to even consider meeting with her."

"Then why did he?" Casey straightened, getting up from his perch on the credenza against the office's long wall. "Why did he change his mind? And why did you go with him?"

"Because Edie said please. And after everything he's been through with her, Miki will do anything if it is something she feels strongly about. He was found in the middle of the street—on St. John—covered in bruises, wearing a dirty diaper, and some asshole had put a tattoo on his arm. He wasn't even three years old and someone tossed him out like he was trash." Kane squared his shoulders, looked his lieutenant straight in the eye. "To answer your question, I went because I love him, and I'm never going to send him out to face his monsters without me standing right next to him. As long as I have breath in my body, I'm going to be there."

RHYS FORD is an award-winning author with several long-running LGBT+ mystery, thriller, paranormal, and urban fantasy series and is a two-time LAMBDA finalist with her *Murder and Mayhem* novels. She is also a 2017 Gold and Silver Medal winner in the Florida Authors and Publishers President's Book Awards for her novels *Ink and Shadows* and *Hanging the Stars*. She is published by Dreamspinner Press and DSP Publications.

She shares the house with Harley, a gray tuxedo with a flower on her face, Badger, a disgruntled alley cat who isn't sure living inside is a step up the social ladder, as well as a ginger cairn terrorist named Gus. Rhys is also enslaved to the upkeep of a 1979 Pontiac Firebird and enjoys murdering make-believe people.

Rhys can be found at the following locations:

Blog: www.rhysford.com

Facebook: www.facebook.com/rhys.ford.author

Twitter: @Rhys_Ford

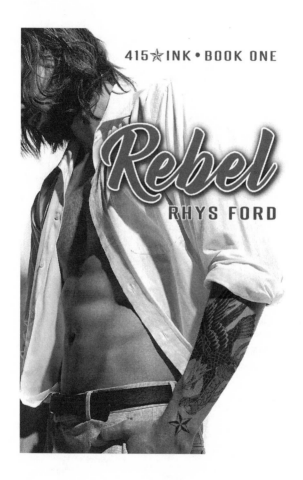

415 ☆ INK • BOOK ONE

Rebel

RHYS FORD

415 Ink: Book One

The hardest thing a rebel can do isn't standing up for something—it's standing up for himself.

Life takes delight in stabbing Gus Scott in the back when he least expects it. After Gus spends years running from his past, present, and the dismal future every social worker predicted for him, karma delivers the one thing Gus could never—would never—turn his back on: a son from a one-night stand he'd had after a devastating breakup a few years ago.

Returning to San Francisco and to 415 Ink, his family's tattoo shop, gave him the perfect shelter to battle his personal demons and get himself together… until the firefighter who'd broken him walked back into Gus's life.

For Rey Montenegro, tattoo artist Gus Scott was an elusive brass ring, a glittering prize he hadn't the strength or flexibility to hold on to. Severing his relationship with the mercurial tattoo artist hurt, but Gus hadn't wanted the kind of domestic life Rey craved, leaving Rey with an aching chasm in his soul.

When Gus's life and world starts to unravel, Rey helps him pick up the pieces, and Gus wonders if that forever Rey wants is more than just a dream.

www.dreamspinnerpress.com